MURDER BY MISTAKE

Further Titles by Veronica Heley from Severn House

The Ellie Quicke Mysteries

MURDER AT THE ALTAR
MURDER BY SUICIDE
MURDER OF INNOCENCE
MURDER BY ACCIDENT
MURDER IN THE GARDEN
MURDER BY COMMITTEE
MURDER BY BICYCLE
MURDER OF IDENTITY
MURDER IN HOUSE
MURDER BY MISTAKE

The Bea Abbot Agency mystery series

FALSE CHARITY
FALSE PICTURE
FALSE STEP
FALSE PRETENCES

MURDER BY MISTAKE

Veronica Heley

This first world edition published 2010
in Great Britain and in the USA by
SEVERN HOUSE PUBLISHERS LTD of
9–15 High Street, Sutton, Surrey, England, SM1 1DF.
Trade paperback edition published
in Great Britain and the USA 2010 by
SEVERN HOUSE PUBLISHERS LTD

British Library Cataloguing in Publication Data

Heley, Veronica.
  Murder by Mistake. – (An Ellie Quicke mystery)
  1. Quicke, Ellie (Fictitious character) – Fiction. 2. Rape
  victims – Fiction. 3. Detective and mystery stories.
  I. Title II. Series
  823.9'14-dc22

ISBN-13: 978-0-7278-6911-1   (cased)
ISBN-13: 978-1-84751-249-9   (trade paper)

All Severn House titles are printed on acid-free paper.

Severn House Publishers support The Forest Stewardship Council [FSC],
the leading international forest certification organisation. All our titles that
are printed on Greenpeace-approved FSC-certified paper carry the FSC logo.

Mixed Sources
Product group from well-managed
forests and other controlled sources
www.fsc.org Cert no. SA-COC-1565
© 1996 Forest Stewardship Council

Typeset by Palimpsest Book Production Ltd.,
Grangemouth, Stirlingshire, Scotland.
Printed and bound in Great Britain by
MPG Books Ltd., Bodmin, Cornwall.

ONE

Ellie Quicke, once a tearful widow, is now comfortably remarried to her best friend Thomas. However, having been on her own for so long, she is inclined to act hastily, not always consulting him on matters which affect them both. When she took in a young rape victim she guessed that the commitment might become a burden, but she didn't expect it to be an invitation to murder.

Monday morning

They weren't expecting trouble. The recent interview at the solicitor's office was the only thing on their minds as they walked along the pavement. They took no notice of the passing traffic until . . .

Woosh!

A roar from a powerful car engine, a squeal from mistreated tyres. A woman's scream. A man's hoarse shout.

Ellie staggered, cannoned into from behind. She fell. A heavy weight pressed her down, squeezing all the breath out of her.

Someone screamed.

The weight upon her was removed and she managed to lift herself enough to see a car speed off and turn left into the traffic on the main road ahead.

Mia! Where was the girl? Was she all right?

Ellie looked around, pushing herself up on to hands and knees with an effort.

Oh, thank the Lord. Mia was all right. At first glance, anyway. The girl had been thrown against the wall, was crouched there but was looking around. Bewildered. Frightened.

Ellie tested her arms and legs. Everything seemed to work, after a fashion. She tried to stand and didn't make it. Went down on her knees again, with both hands on the pavement. Her pretty blue dress was no longer pretty. She'd scraped the skin down both forearms. A pity it had been a hot day, because she hadn't worn a coat. If she had, she might have saved herself grazed arms. She was trembling, but she was all right. She told herself.

Someone was screaming. Well, it wasn't her, and no, it wasn't Mia, who'd been walking on the inside of Ellie, nearer the wall. 'Mia, are you all right?'

Mia nodded, over and over. Like a puppet. Speechless. In shock. Someone was still screaming. A child was crying, thinly, hopelessly.

A big black man towered over Ellie, offering a helping hand to get her to her feet. She made it, somehow. Gave him a reassuring smile. He had blood on his T-shirt and jeans.

A youngish woman clad in Lycra cycled up. She got off her bike and looked beyond Ellie and the man to where . . . Don't look, Ellie. Don't even think about it for the moment. Concentrate on getting yourself to stand unaided.

A car came by, slowly. Drew to a halt. Another car came up behind the first car, tooted its horn. Why the hold-up?

The man who'd saved her from being run over asked, 'Are you hurt?' A deep voice, reassuring. Rough clothes. Torn jeans. A workman? Big hands.

'Did you get their number?' The cyclist had a high, thin voice. She hauled her bike off the road and on to the pavement.

A man, a businessman, got out of his car. 'What . . .? Are you all right, missus?'

Ellie nodded. She was, sort of. More or less. Blood was dripping off her chin on to her dress. She checked that she still had her handbag – which she'd worn across her body to deter muggers – and scrabbled inside for some paper tissues. Used them.

The child was crying, hopelessly. Ellie wished it would stop.

The businessman got his mobile phone out. The car behind him tooted again, then swung out into the road and went round him. The driver of the second car then saw what had happened and slowed right down. Traffic began to pile up behind them.

The cyclist leant her bike against the wall and bent over, making retching noises. Ellie didn't want to look.

Mia had her eyes closed. Just as well.

Two large women in their forties panted up. Dyed blonde hair strained back into unbecoming pony tails. Both were overweight, bursting out of tight sleeveless tops and even tighter jeans. 'OhmiGawd!'

That was a prayer, not an obscenity. Please, God, don't take it the wrong way. The women might or might not go to church, but they knew when God was needed in the aftermath of a tragedy.

They bent over the toddler, who was lying on the pavement. Flat on his back, arms and legs stretched out. Like a starfish.

A muddle of voices. A child wailing. Ellie lunged for the wall, needing to be propped up, telling herself it would do no good to faint. There was blood running down her arms and from her knee, where she'd scraped herself. It dripped from her chin again, too.

The businessman used his phone, calling for the police, an ambulance. Ellie turned her head away from the toddler. He didn't seem to be crying now, but she could still hear another child's voice. Shock, no doubt. An echo.

Ellie's rescuer had fresh, shiny blood on his hand. His jeans were ripped, and there was blood on them, too.

Ellie didn't want to look, but had to know. 'Is she . . .?'

'Yes. Are you hurt?'

'No. Yes. Not to worry. Only in bits. Mia . . .?'

'Come on, girlie,' he said, turning his attention to the girl who still crouched by the wall. 'Let's have a look at you, eh? Does it hurt anywhere?'

Mia screamed. She curled into a ball, ducking away from his hand.

Ellie said, 'Don't touch her.'

He was bewildered. 'I just wanted to help.'

'She was frightened by some men in the past. Leave her be.'

Now he wasn't sure what to do. 'Well, I suppose if she's broken something, maybe she oughtn't to move.'

They were talking to avoid thinking about the bloodied mess on the pavement. Or about the child, who was being cradled by one of the large women who'd arrived, heaven sent, in the nick of time. Large, and efficient, those women. One was tearing up her cotton top to staunch the flow of blood from the child's arm. His legs trembled. He was still alive.

'Is the mother really . . .?' said Ellie.

The cyclist stopped retching, wiped her mouth. 'The n–number of the c–car? D–did you . . .?' She stuttered. She was shaking.

The businessman clicked his phone shut. 'I didn't see anything, and I'm late for an appointment. Is there anything I can do here, because if not . . .?'

Ellie shook her head. Mia turned her face to the wall.

The black man held on to his thigh. Suddenly aware of pain? 'I left my van in the car park. Was just going to cross the road, saw the car coming. Too fast, I thought. Out of control. I looked and saw you were in the direct line. He was bound to hit you. I only just got to you before . . . but I couldn't . . . couldn't . . . The car went straight for them. Oh God!' He staggered to the wall, leaned against it, curled both hands over his head. Tried deep breathing. He, too, was in shock.

The two fat women were by now practically naked, tearing up their tops in their effort to stop the little boy from bleeding to death.

Ellie thought, *Dear Lord above. Dear Lord . . . dear God. Help us! And the woman who died.*

A tiny baby raised its voice, puzzled and anxious. Hungry. A very new baby.

Not the toddler. The toddler had been walking alongside the woman, holding on to the buggy. Was there a baby still in the wreck of the buggy? Still alive, by some sort of miracle?

More people were arriving by the second, gaping. Shocked. Anxious. Asking who was hurt, but not wanting to hear that someone was dead. The businessman got into his car and drove off. Traffic moved slowly along. Very slowly.

The baby went on crying.

An ambulance came charging along, bell ringing.

Ellie thought, I've got to stop men from touching Mia.

Her saviour pushed himself upright, wiping his forearms across his face. Ellie saw he was trying to hide tears and handed over one of her tissues. Blood was staining her dress from her own injuries. She said to him, 'You saved my life. Were you hurt, too?'

He shook his head. Sniffed. Used the tissue. Put weight on his right leg and winced. 'Got me right here. I'll have a bruise tomorrow, shouldn't wonder.'

More than that, Ellie thought. But at least he's standing upright, so he can't have broken his leg. Hopefully.

Don't think about the woman who'd been killed.

The police arrived, sirens wailing. One of them went to sort out the traffic. Another asked questions to which there were no clear answers. No, no one had the number of the car. Ellie's rescuer said his name was Leontes Spearman – at least that's what it sounded like to Ellie – and he'd hardly had time to notice anything about the car before . . . he stopped, throat working. He said he must have tripped as he fell and he hadn't been able . . . hadn't been able to . . . he shook his head. He was on the verge of breaking down.

The ambulance men – man and woman – worked on the toddler, taking over from the two big blowsy wonderful women. More bystanders arrived. To Ellie's horror, many of them got out their mobile phones and photographed the scene.

Ellie coaxed Mia to her feet and told her not to look. Mia looked. Of course.

There was nothing to be done for the woman on the pavement.

One of the big women plucked a crying, teething baby from the buggy, while the other sought through the wreckage in a hunt for a bottle. Found one. Thrust it in the new baby's mouth. 'There, there, my sweetling. There, there.' She rocked backwards and forwards, her bra straps slipping, her hands red with someone else's blood.

Another ambulance was summoned. More police.

Ellie gave her name and address.

'Come again?' the policeman said.

She repeated it in a louder voice. Was the policeman stone deaf? Gave Mia's name, said no, Mia wasn't her daughter, just a friend who was staying with her.

Leontes – was that really his name? – gave his name and address all over again. 'I was on my way to pay my council tax. Sorry. Got to sit down.' And did. His voice was pure Thames Estuary. Like the two big women. Wonderful women, wonderful man. Britain does know how to produce them, doesn't she?

The cyclist was thin, thirties, blondish. 'The car was a Volvo, not new. It had a "Baby on Board" sticker on the back window.'

Ellie heard this and believed the girl. The police didn't.

And it didn't sound all that likely, did it? A Volvo was a family car. Not the sort for a boy racer who might have pinched a car for a joy ride and then failed to control it. Boy racers didn't 'borrow' family cars, did they? The girl insisted that that was what she'd seen. Her father had a Volvo just like that. Ten years old, maybe? But no, she hadn't caught the number.

Ambulance doors were opened. The toddler was carried in. He was still alive, then. Leontes was helped in. His leg had been caught by the car's bumper. It might be broken, they'd have to X-ray it. Ellie and Mia were ushered into another ambulance, and the doors shut on the outside world.

Mia trembled within Ellie's arm. 'It was meant for me.'

'No, no,' said Ellie. 'It was an accident. The driver lost control of the car.'

Mia shook her head, disagreeing.

The ambulances arrived one after the other. The hospital was bright and efficient. The toddler was rushed through to a cubicle. Leontes, also. The nurses wanted Ellie to let go of Mia, so that they could both be examined. A male doctor hovered, clicking his fingers, impatient to get on with the job.

Mia clung to Ellie, closing her eyes, desperate not to be separated from her.

Ellie stroked Mia's head. Ellie was feeling poorly herself. Her scrapes and bruises hurt. Mia's body didn't seem to have suffered much damage, but her mind was another matter.

'If you'll fetch a woman doctor?' said Ellie. 'I can explain.'

After some time a woman doctor arrived. Pakistani? Sikh? No head scarf, so not a Muslim. Dark-haired and capable.

Ellie trusted her on sight. 'Mia was subjected to a period of sexual abuse some months ago. She can't bear to be touched by a man. I don't think she's badly hurt, but she was flung up against the wall. May I accompany you while you examine her?'

Sharp eyes took in the problem. 'She will come with you, while I look at you first, yes? Then she will know it's all right for me to examine her. Come this way.'

Curtains round a bed. Her handbag removed and given to Mia to hold.

'Can you move your fingers, your elbows? Your legs now? Any pain here . . . or here? You will have some bad bruises,

I think. A nick here on your chin, yes, but not bad enough to be stitched. First we clean you up, and then . . . Have you had a tetanus injection recently? No? Well, we'll see to that, too. Someone will come to take you home in a little while, yes?'

'Oh.' Ellie struggled upright. 'I must let my husband know. He'll be wondering what's happened. My mobile's in my bag. Mia, could you . . .?'

Mia located Ellie's mobile and handed it over.

Ellie tried to gather her wits together. If Thomas were out – and quite likely he would be at that time of day because he usually took a break at lunchtime and went for a walk after- wards – then she must leave a message which would not alarm him too much.

Yes, he was out. The phone rang and rang. Perhaps their housekeeper might answer it? No, apparently not. Of course, Rose would be having her afternoon nap.

A message must be left. 'Thomas dear, we're not badly hurt or anything, but we got involved in an accident, a runaway car. Cuts and bruises. Can you fetch us in about an hour's time? What's the time now? About one. Shall we say about two? Or maybe half past? Outside the main entrance. Oh, it's Ealing Hospital, by the way. At least, I think it is.'

'Yes, it is,' said the doctor, smiling. 'You're doing very well. Now while you're being cleaned up, will Mia let me have a look at her in another cubicle?'

Ellie tried to rouse herself. 'What of the toddler who was caught up in the accident? And the black man? He saved our lives. Is he all right?'

'I will find out.'

Mia went with the doctor and Ellie, suddenly exhausted, lay back and tried not to think. Her mind flashed back to the accident . . . No! Don't think about it. She tried to switch her mind to something pleasant.

The wedding. She was so looking forward to the wedding on Saturday. She had the greatest respect – bordering on love – for Mia's friend Ursula, who had rescued the girl from a fate truly worse than death. Ursula had found a man worthy of her and they were to be married in five days' time. Think about that.

Think hard. Think about the pleasure of having Thomas marry the pair in church. Think about the arrangements that

had been made to hold the reception at Ellie's house . . . all
the delightful details.

Think of the pretty mist-grey dress and hat, with shoes to
match, that she'd bought for the occasion.

A mental picture of the dead woman slid into Ellie's mind.
And the blood. The smell of it. Leontes holding on to his
leg.

She couldn't push these thoughts away entirely. She concentrated on thinking about a nice hot cup of tea instead. She
could murder for a cup of tea.

*Dear Lord, I ought to be thanking You that my life was
spared, and Mia's, too, instead of worrying about . . . No,
stop that thought. I'm sure Mia's wrong in thinking this was
an attempt on her life. At least, I hope so. Hasn't everyone
been locked up who wanted to harm her? Admitted, they'd
like her to change her testimony before the case comes to
trial, but . . . No, ridiculous!*

*Oh, I can't cope if it really is those horrible people trying
to kill her, but at least she's not badly injured, like Leontes –
silly name, isn't it from Shakespeare? I must have heard it
wrong – anyway, many thanks. Praise the Lord and all that.
Will You go on keeping an eye on us, please?*

At half past two Ellie and Mia were free to go. Ellie enquired
again about the toddler, to be told he was in surgery. The man
who'd saved their lives was still there, being X-rayed at that
moment. Ellie hoped he hadn't broken his leg, but . . . no, she
mustn't let herself dwell on what had happened or she'd get
the horrors again.

They walked slowly out of the hospital, hoping Thomas
would be there in his car, waiting to pick them up. He wasn't.

Ellie hurt in so many places she didn't know what to do
with herself.

'Take some painkillers,' they'd said, and had shoved some
at her. She'd refused them because she needed to be on top
of things when Mia needed so much care. Taking painkillers
slowed her reactions.

Mia hadn't much to show for their brush with death, except
a graze on one shoulder and bruises down her left side. She
wasn't complaining. That wasn't her style. When in pain,
Mia held her tongue. Now she was shrinking behind Ellie,

who wasn't really tall enough to shelter her from harm.

Ellie tried her home phone number again. The sun was hot on her head outside the hospital so she moved herself and Mia back into the shade of the entrance hall. The phone rang and rang. Finally, Ellie's housekeeper picked it up.

'Rose? Ellie here. Is Thomas around?'

Rose yawned. She'd probably just woken up from her afternoon nap. 'Don't you remember, he's gone up somewhere north, I think he said it was Leeds, but it might have been Durham. A conference of some sort. He won't be back till late tonight. Did you have a nice lunch?'

Ellie could have kicked herself, except that it would have hurt too much. How ever could she have forgotten that Thomas was going away? She'd ordered a cab to take her and Mia to the solicitor's office and they'd intended to go on to have lunch somewhere after their appointment. Ellie still didn't know what the solicitor had said to Mia, but whatever it was, it had knocked the girl sideways.

Don't think about being knocked sideways. That was just a figure of speech. What she meant was, that Mia had been upset when she came out of the solicitor's room and hadn't got round to telling Ellie why before . . . before being knocked down. Well, don't think about that now. Ellie's stomach rumbled, which reminded her they'd missed lunch.

'Sorry, Rose. Silly of me. I quite forgot. We got delayed by a traffic accident in Ealing Broadway. I'll get a cab home.'

She'd never learned to drive but, having inherited some money, kept an account with a local cab firm. She got through to the minicab office, who said they'd pick her up as soon as, if not sooner.

As the cab turned into her own drive – it had turned up quickly as promised – Ellie spotted a well-known car parked by the front door. She sighed. She found it hard enough to deal with her daughter Diana when she was feeling strong, and at that moment she felt as weak as a newborn kitten. Or baby.

Don't think about the baby. Or the toddler, or the mother. She signed the chit for the cab firm and sought for house keys in her handbag.

Would the two children remember their mother when they

grew up? Would Social Services find a good foster mother for them, or put them up for adoption? Would the two big women get their husbands or partners to give them a cuddle and maybe a beer or two that night, to take the edge off what they'd seen and done that day? Would Leontes – really, that was a ridiculous name – be all right?

Mia shivered, her eyes on Diana's car. 'A visitor? I'm not sure I feel up to . . .'

'Let's go in through the kitchen door. We can grab a bite to eat and then you can slip upstairs to your own room, have a little lie-down.'

'What about you?' Mia's manners were, as always, perfect.

'I'll manage,' said Ellie, telling herself that over the years she had sometimes won battles with her ambitious daughter Diana; but not when she'd just been knocked over. Ouch. Maybe she could faint or something? Get Diana to show some sympathy for her mother's plight?

Well, probably not, knowing Diana. Best get it over with. 'This way, Mia.'

Monday afternoon

She should have died, the witch, the bitch. When his mobile had rung, he hadn't expected to receive a picture of her, back in Ealing! She ought to have died. No ordinary person could have survived. But she wasn't ordinary, was she? She was a witch and ought to be burned at the stake. And so she would be. He'd see to it if no one else did.

TWO

Monday afternoon

Ellie slipped through the back door, towing Mia after her. The kitchen smelt fresh and every surface sparkled, so the cleaners must have been in today. Rose was bustling around while their ginger cat Midge watched from a nearby chair, waiting for titbits.

Rose had been Ellie's friend since the days when they'd worked together in the local charity shop. Later she'd become housekeeper to Ellie's elderly aunt, Miss Quicke, and after the old lady died had decided to carry on doing the same job for Ellie and Thomas.

Rose was a little mouse of a woman who'd struck a bad patch last winter, but had bobbed up again with the warmer weather. She had, however, developed an eccentricity, in that she believed her previous employer to be still around the house, observing and commenting on everything that went on. It wasn't spooky. It was, said Thomas, just Rose's way of showing that she missed the old lady. Ellie had almost got used to it by now.

Rose squeaked when she saw Ellie. She threw up her hands, one of which held a rolling pin. 'What's happened to you? I thought you were going to see a solicitor. I don't know, I turn my back for five minutes, and look at you!'

'Don't fuss, Rose. We got involved in a traffic accident, that's all. It looks worse than it is. We'll be all right when we've changed and had a bite to eat. Can you magic something up for us?' She bent down to stroke Midge, who was winding round her legs hoping for a treat . . . which he was not going to get until teatime.

'What would you like?' Rose darted to the fridge to investigate. 'Soup and a boiled egg with toast fingers? I'll bring it up to your bedroom for you won't get much peace with *her* around. You know what she's like. How did she get in, you'll want to know? Well, it was the electricity man, come to read the meter. I was showing him where it was and the next thing I know she steps inside after him, bold as brass and twice as sharp, telling me to be off back to the kitchen. So I did. And there'll be a nice batch of scones for tea, but none for her, not if I have anything to do with it.'

'Agreed,' said Ellie, with a smile. 'Don't let's offer her tea. Before that, soup and an egg would be wonderful. We missed lunch, and I'm sure we'll feel better for having something inside us.'

Rose whirled round, throwing food from the fridge on to the kitchen table. 'Is that blood on your clothes? What have you been up to, for goodness' sake?'

'It's worse than it looks. We got in the path of a runaway

car, but someone pushed us out of harm's way. Mia, would you like to take the back stairs up to your room, have a wash and brush up, and then a nice quiet lay-down?'

'Yes, but I was only supposed to be staying with you the one night, and I ought to be moving to a hotel so—'

'Rubbish. You stay here as long as you like. Now go and get some rest, there's a good girl.'

Mia produced a tiny, anxious smile. 'What about you?'

'I'll get rid of Diana and be up in a minute.'

'Humph!' said Rose, rattling saucepans. 'Easier said than done.'

Mia disappeared like a shadow up the stairs, Midge the cat gave up on Ellie and went back to watching Rose, while Ellie braced herself for an encounter with her daughter.

Diana was in the hall, dark-haired, dressed all in black as usual. Almost, she blended with the dark panelling. She was scratching notes on a pad, measuring tape in hand. A ring glittered on her left hand.

A ring. What on earth? A horrendous idea shot across Ellie's mind. What was the worst that could happen? Oh, no. Please, no!

'Hi!' Diana rewound her tape, making more notes. She looked preoccupied, but not guilty. 'Where have you been? Not that it matters, don't bother to make excuses, I really don't need to know. Out nursemaiding that stupid little girl that there's been so much fuss about, I suppose. I wonder she dare show her face around here again. But there, you're a sucker for punishment, aren't you?'

'Am I?' The ring was on the third finger of Diana's left hand. She'd got engaged again? Not to Dubious Denis, pray not to him! Diana and her estate agency partner Denis had been an item for some time, but Ellie had never liked or trusted him.

Diana looked up long enough from taking notes to observe that her mother was not looking her usual trim self. 'You look like somebody's dragged you under a bus.' Distaste in her voice. 'Someone tried to mug you?' Diana had a hard, clear voice, which expressed her personality rather well.

'A traffic accident. A man kindly pushed me out of the way. I'm all right but I need to rest, so if you don't mind, perhaps we can talk tomorrow.'

Diana was eyeing the space between the wide uncarpeted stairs and the heavy Victorian front door. 'I'm wondering where to have the photographs. If we have a really large stand of lilies here . . . that might be best. Or in the garden, if it's fine?'

'I don't think I want to know what you're talking about,' said Ellie, beginning to climb the stairs, pulling herself up by the banisters.

'I expect you've guessed. Denis has asked me to marry him, I've agreed and we're doing the deed this Saturday because it's the Bank Holiday weekend. Registry office, of course. The reception will be here.'

'No,' said Ellie, reaching the top of the stairs. 'Out of the question.' She stifled a laugh because she had a perfect excuse for refusing to do what Diana asked. 'As it happens, I'm hosting another celebration here that day.'

'Don't be ridiculous. What can possibly be more important than my wedding?'

'Your second wedding, actually. You got rid of one perfectly good husband some years ago; remember? By the way, has Denis managed to shed his own wife and four children already?'

'Yes, of course. I know it's all a bit of a rush, but it's a quiet time in the office, and we've tickets to fly to Barbados next day for a honeymoon, so that fixes the date.'

Ellie leaned on the newel post at the top of the stairs. She was looking forward to putting a spanner in Diana's plans. 'You should have consulted me before making your arrangements. I'm hosting a wedding party here that day for someone else. It's been arranged for months.'

Diana took a step back. 'You can't be!'

Someone pressed the doorbell and didn't let up. 'You answer it,' said Ellie. 'I'm not coming down.'

Diana pocketed her tape measure and opened the door, only to have a huge bouquet of Madonna lilies thrust into her face. Someone said 'Sign here,' and disappeared, pulling the door to behind him.

Ellie leaned over the banister. 'Who are they for?'

'Dunno.' Diana found an envelope with a card inside it. 'All it says is, "You should have died."'

Ellie shuddered. 'Are they meant for Mia? That's horrible.'

Diana shrugged. 'I suppose so. She's ruined so many people's lives, it's not surprising.'

'They ruined hers first, and they've only got what's coming to them. We mustn't let Mia see them. Put them in the kitchen sink and I'll think what to do with them later. Hide the card. We don't need to show it to Mia.'

'First we must get the details for the reception settled.'

'No. First I go to the bathroom, get changed, and eat something. Then I must have a little nap.'

'All right. I'll come back at, say, six this evening. We can have it out then. But it's too late to change anything, as the invitations went out last week.' Diana left, slamming the front door behind her and leaving the flowers on the hall table. Ellie stared after her daughter. Had she really meant . . .? No, impossible.

Rose appeared in the doorway to the kitchen, carrying a tray laden with food for an invalid: soup and tiny sandwiches. 'Good riddance. Where did those flowers come from?'

'She's coming back. The flowers are . . . I think they've been sent to us by mistake.' Yes, that must be it. She hoped. 'As for Diana, I'll tell you later.' Ellie was wearily conscious of all the battles she'd had with her only daughter over the years. Most of which Ellie had lost.

'What does she want now?' Rose climbed the stairs with the tray in her hands.

'To hold her wedding reception here, on the same day as the one for Mia's friend.'

'Diana's never stupid enough to marry that Denis, is she? Miss Quicke will have something to say about that.' Rose preceded Ellie into the big master bedroom at the back of the house and put the tray down on a table near the middle window. 'Tell her she can't.'

'She says the wedding invitations have all gone out.' Ellie shed her bag, slipped out of her ruined shoes, and made for her bathroom.

'Or so she says.'

Ellie grinned. 'You're right. She may well be bluffing.'

Ellie cleaned herself up and ate what she could, then slid under the duvet for a rest. The moment she closed her eyes, the picture of the carnage on the pavement leapt into her mind. She banished it. Turned over. Tried again. Heard the baby crying, hopelessly, hungrily. Saw those two wonderful women trying to staunch the child's bleeding arm . . . Saw the big man curl up, hands over his head. No, no. Go away. I must try to rest.

A whisper of sound. Was that Mia, sobbing?

The house was quiet around her, except for a blackbird singing in a tree outside and the murmur of a car along the road on the other side of the house. She'd not let this get to her. Of course not.

Praise the Lord for looking after her. That was the first thing. The second was . . . I'm too tired to cope with Diana. Yet she knew she must.

Monday evening

Diana arrived at six o'clock on the dot as Ellie returned from dumping the lilies on the compost heap in the garden. Out of sight, out of mind. Probably.

Strictly speaking, of course, they were not lilies, but Zantedeschias. Only, who was going to remember that? They were Madonna or Arum lilies to most people, and that was how they'd remain.

Thomas had rung from the train on his way back and would be with them for supper. He'd sounded tired, but had said the conference had gone well and Ellie should congratulate him because he hadn't lost his temper once. He'd been concerned that his paper was going to be rubbished by an old adversary of his, but in the end all had been well. Perhaps, said Thomas, his old mate was going down with a virus.

Ellie hadn't told him about the accident, or that she'd asked Mia to stay on. Mia had originally been asked to stay for just the one night while she went to see her solicitor. That was the night that Thomas was away, so he wasn't supposed to have been inconvenienced by her visit in any way.

Mia's friend Ursula had promised to find somewhere else for her to stay tonight, and no doubt would do so. Only, the girl really wasn't fit to be turned out like an orphan into the storm, was she? Not that she was an orphan, precisely, and it was midsummer and they hadn't had any storms lately.

What was it that the solicitor had had to say to Mia, to make her look so shocked? Ellie told herself that curiosity killed the cat, but she was very fond of cats and after all there was plenty of room for Mia in this big house, wasn't there?

Ellie told herself firmly to calm down and think clearly. It really would be best all round if Mia stayed on with them for a while. At least till after the wedding. Ellie was sure Thomas wouldn't object, but she did have just the slightest of twinges in the conscience area because she hadn't discussed the matter with him beforehand. True, the big house had been left to her by Miss Quicke before Thomas joined hands with her in matrimony, so in theory she had the right to invite whomsoever she liked to stay. Hadn't she? But . . . Oh, well. She'd work it out in due course.

To deal with Diana, Ellie had changed – with many a wince – into a china blue jersey dress which didn't press on her cuts and bruises. Diana had also changed, into something clingy and a trifle too skimpy for her thin figure. Mauve and black. In Victorian times that would have signified she was leaving off her widow's weeds to wear garments of dark purple, working through lilac and shades of grey as she gradually returned to society. Not to white. Ellie couldn't remember her daughter ever wearing white. It wouldn't have suited her, anyway.

'Where's the problem child?' asked Diana, running her finger across the mantelpiece to check for dust; not that there ever was any, since Ellie employed a firm to clean and do all the heavy jobs in the house. The cleaning firm was most efficiently run by Diana's discarded first husband's new wife – but we don't mention that nowadays, do we?

'Mia's in the kitchen, helping Rose with supper. Now listen, Diana—'

'No, you listen to me for once. This is my chance of happiness with Denis, and I'm not going to let you spoil it. We've been together now for long enough to know we can make a go of it as a couple, and we want to make it official in every way.'

'I didn't think estate agents were doing all that well in the present economic conditions. Do you really think it's wise to—'

'You don't have to think. You just have to behave like a mother for once.'

That was a blow below the belt, wasn't it? Ellie told herself not to lose her temper. She counted to five, slowly. 'All right. You are both adults and can be presumed to know what you're doing. You want to get married again. Can he afford another wife? What about his first wife and their children?'

'She keeps their house and he gives her what he can spare. He's renting a big house for us with six bedrooms, two en suite, plus two more bathrooms. We'll let out rooms to students in term time and have all the children to stay with us in the holidays.'

'What, all of them?' Ellie sank down on to the big winged chair by the fireplace. 'Are you including your own son? You know very well that Frank doesn't get on with Denis's children, and he's perfectly content living with his father and stepmother. He likes the odd day with you, of course, but—'

'Mother, don't interfere. It's nothing to do with you what arrangements I make for my son.'

'You're happy for me to look after Frank whenever you're too busy to cope.'

'Leave it out!'

Ellie left it. Let Diana's first husband fight that battle.

'Now –' Diana seated herself opposite Ellie – 'the wedding. We can't change the date. So whatever arrangements you've made—'

'Can't be undone. It's been fixed up for ages. The cleaning firm I use is going to help by clearing the reception rooms. Mia's friend Ursula is getting married that morning and we're having a buffet lunch for them here before they fly off to their new life together. Mia will be the only bridesmaid. It will be difficult for her as she doesn't like being in crowds any more.'

'Why can't they have the reception somewhere else?'

'Ursula's mother doesn't earn much. She's long-time divorced and lives in a tiny flat on the Avenue. Her father is American. He's flying in with his second family for the occasion and will stay in a hotel, but he can't afford a big splash, either. The bridegroom's family are all professional men, long on lineage and short on cash, but they've offered to pay half the cost. The couple want Thomas to marry them at a local church, and I offered this house for the reception afterwards. Ursula's a girl in a million. She was the only one who believed something terrible had happened to Mia when she disappeared. If it hadn't been for her, Mia would probably be dead by now. I wish them both well.'

'But you don't wish me well?' Colour rose in Diana's cheeks. 'Don't answer that. I know what you think of Denis. You're quite wrong, of course. He's the perfect mate for me.'

Ellie grimaced. Sexually, she had no doubt that Diana was right, but there were other things that should count in a marriage, weren't there? Such as honesty, and integrity, and trustworthiness. She didn't think Denis scored highly on any of those.

'Well,' said Diana, frowning, 'I don't see that there's much of a problem. We're booked into the registry office at two in the afternoon, so we can have our reception here at five. That will give you plenty of time to clear away from the luncheon party and prepare for a sit-down meal for fifty at six. Then there'll be a disco in the evening, to which we've invited just over a hundred people.'

Ellie gaped. What? Impossible!

Diana stood, smoothing her dress down over her hips, pleased with herself. 'I'll let you have all the paperwork; I've got the top man on the job as Party Planner, and he'll coordinate everything with you: the caterer, florist, photographer and wine merchant. No bridesmaids, but little Frank will be my ring bearer. I've had the sweetest little outfit made for him, and he's going to wear it or I'll know the reason why! All the bills will be sent to you, of course. And –' as she left the room – 'do please, find yourself a good outfit for the occasion. I'd like to think I can be proud of you for once.'

Ellie didn't know whether to laugh or cry. She heard the front door open and voices in the hall. Thomas had returned. With an effort she got herself together, wondering how much and in what order she was going to have to explain things to him. She heard him exchange greetings with Diana, and then she heard the front door shut.

Slowly, she got to her feet. Diana had left the door to the hall open, and she could hear Thomas check the phone in the hall for messages.

Too late she realized she hadn't erased the call for help she'd made at the hospital. She heard her own voice, high and clear, breaking the bad news.

She got to the door and spoke his name. He turned and saw

her, his face reflecting anxiety and relief. He had dumped his overnight bag and briefcase, and was halfway out of his old jacket, but he almost fell over himself to get his arms round her and give her a big hug. His beard tickled her neck, as always. And, as always, she felt deep gratitude that this wonderful man had chosen to make her his wife. She could hear her own voice on the telephone, going on and on. Finally, the call ended.

'Sorry,' she said. 'Ought to have erased it. Storm in a teacup. All over now.'

He held her at arm's-length. 'I turn my back for five minutes.'

'That's what Rose said.' She tried to laugh, tried to smile, buried her face in his shoulder, held on to him. He was big enough to take it, luckily. He was a large, bearded man who looked like a sailor, but was a respected academic. Once the minister of her parish church, he was now editing a national Christian magazine and being invited more and more often to speak at high-level conferences.

'Should I check that you've still got both your arms and legs?'

'How about my fingers and toes? I'm all right. Hungry, though.' She picked one of her silvery hairs from his shirt. 'I'm afraid quite a lot's been happening. I should have rung you.'

'Now what?' He tucked her within his arm. Midge the cat arrived from nowhere to wind around his legs. Midge – a misnomer if ever there was one – approved of Thomas because he had a frontage large and comfortable enough to sit on.

The door to the kitchen quarters opened, and Mia crept out into the hall. Thomas checked for a moment, taking in the fact that they had a visitor, and then – blessed man that he was – held out his free arm to Mia. 'Lovely to see you, my dear. How are you doing?'

Mia wasn't afraid of him, much. She didn't take his hand, but she didn't run away, either. 'Fine, thanks. And thank you for having me to stay. You've heard what happened?'

He swept them both into the sitting room. 'Sort of. Tell me all.'

He sat with his arm around Ellie on the big old settee, while Mia perched a little way off on a stool. Six months ago she had been 'a little cracker', as one of her admirers had put it; a stunningly beautiful girl with long dark curls, peach-like skin and eyes which were at once soft and intelligent. She'd been studying modern languages at Thames Valley University while living at home with her mother, her wealthy stepfather and two stepbrothers.

She and her best friend Ursula had been part of a bright, party-going set until, at a party on New Year's Eve, Mia had been drugged and offered to a local councillor in an attempt by her family to influence the outcome of a controversial planning permission. If it had stopped there, it would have been bad enough, but a young man who'd tried to come to Mia's rescue had been thrown from the top of the building and killed. Worse; still drugged out of her senses, the girl had been taken home and locked in her bedroom for further abuse by her family and their friends. After all, as one of her stepbrothers had said, she was second-hand goods by then, so what did it matter?

She'd survived after a fashion, but it was only Ursula's insistence that something terrible had happened to her friend which had brought Ellie into the picture. It had taken a lot of hard work to find Mia, and then more hard work to mend the broken doll. For she had been broken and, despite a long stay in a clinic and a lot of therapy, she would never be the same bright, carefree girl again.

Nowadays she crept around with her eyes down, cringing if a man came anywhere near her. She'd chopped off her long hair after her ordeal, but though it had grown again, it was now pulled back untidily into a band. Her skin looked unhealthy, and she no longer cared how she dressed. Today she wore a long-sleeved black T-shirt over jeans, but had lost too much weight to look good in them.

Ellie watched as Thomas's large heart filled with pity for the girl. 'Tell me,' he said, using his gentlest voice rather than the lion's roar which he could employ on occasion.

Mia twisted her hands together between her knees. 'They tried to kill me again today.'

MONDAY EARLY EVENING...

She'd escaped! Grinding his teeth, he wondered what it took to kill one woman. He had her in his sights, and then — that big black man had leaped up from nowhere and shoved her out of the way. Infuriating!

Worse. Catastrophic.

If she didn't die soon, he was going to be totally up the pole without a safety net.

Well, if at first you don't succeed . . .

THREE

Monday evening

Thomas's eyebrows shot up. 'Someone tried to kill you today?'

Ellie said, 'Well, I don't really think so, Mia. It was the most awful accident, and I'm sure it wasn't aimed at you.' She explained what had happened.

Thomas gave her another of his bear-like hugs and said again, 'I turn my back on you for five minutes!' Then to Mia, 'And you, my dear? Not hurt?'

Mia shook her head. 'A bit bruised. Not that that matters. I know I'm on borrowed time. I don't really expect to live long enough to give evidence.'

Thomas rubbed his eyes. He'd had a tiring journey and didn't really need to cope with this at the end of the day. 'Well, my dear, as far as I know, all the men who hurt you are now locked up in jail.'

'Yes, but they have friends who could act for them, don't they? That's why I was so glad to leave London for a while, with only the police and Ursula knowing where I was.'

'Where were you? Can you tell us?'

'I have an aunt whom I hadn't seen for ages, though we'd always kept in touch with birthday and Christmas cards. When I was convalescing I realized I'd missed her birthday, so I wrote and told her what had happened. She invited me to stay if I'd help with the housework. I needed to be somewhere quiet away from London. It seemed a perfect solution to the problem of what to do with myself until the trial. So I went.

'She lives in a big house in Cambridgeshire, the nearest village nearly a mile away. She's very frail. At first I was so grateful to her for taking me in that I couldn't do enough for her. I took on the shopping and cooking, and kept the house going as best I could. I wasn't strong enough to do the garden as well, but she had a couple of lads come over now and then to mow the lawn. They heard what had happened to me and assumed that I would like them to . . . Oh, it was horrid.'

'Didn't your aunt stop them?'

'She is of the old school. She means well, I suppose, but . . . when we went to church that first Sunday, she told everyone what had happened to me. Gossip like that spreads. She really believes I'm ruined. Maybe I am.

'I'd written to tell Ursula where I was. She replied, asking me to keep in touch, but though I wrote back, she didn't reply. I tried phoning her mobile, but the number was no longer obtainable. I thought she probably didn't want to be friends with me any more. My aunt had a landline phone which she kept for emergencies only. She was always on about the cost of everything, and I didn't like to ask if I could use it just to keep in touch with my friends. I tried my best to please her, but she became more and more demanding. I hardly had any time to myself, and then I was so tired in the evenings I just went to bed and slept. I didn't notice how the weeks had gone by until one day I realized I hadn't heard from Ursula for ages.

'I asked my aunt if I might use her phone for one call. She didn't like it, but eventually she agreed. I rang Ursula's mother, who gave me a new mobile number, and when I got through to Ursula, well, did I get an earful! She'd been writing to me and ringing me and why hadn't I replied? Was I or was I not going to be her bridesmaid when she got married? I didn't even know she'd got herself engaged!

'My aunt had been intercepting my mail and phone calls. I understood why. I'd been her unpaid carer for twenty-four hours a day, seven days a week, which had made it possible for her to stay on in that big house. The next day Ursula arrived and there was the most almighty row.'

Ellie smoothed out a smile, and Thomas guffawed. 'I can imagine. If you're going to get into a fight, you need someone like Ursula by your side.'

'Yes.' A tiny smile. 'She is rather wonderful, isn't she? She tore into my aunt, who had an attack of hiccups and swore she was going to die. She didn't, of course. Ursula told me to pack up and return to London with her. She said I could sleep

on the settee at her mother's for the night, and she'd find somewhere else for me to stay next day. She demanded the letters
which my aunt had intercepted. There were six from Ursula
and two from a solicitor here in Ealing.'

Mia stirred, uneasy. 'The solicitor is the one my stepfather
used. I didn't want to open those letters and I didn't want to
come back to Ealing, but Ursula isn't afraid of anything, is
she? She opened the letters and made me read them. The
solicitor wanted to see me because one of the men who . . .'
She gulped. 'I used to call him Uncle Bob. When he went
abroad, he used to bring me back little presents. He didn't
have any children of his own, you see. He always took an
interest in me, encouraged me, praised me. Which was more
than my stepfather ever did. I used to like my Uncle Bob
more than I liked my stepfather.

'Anyway, he was one of those who . . . after . . . when I was
kept prisoner at home, he came in and . . .'

'Yes,' said Thomas. 'Give that bit a miss.'

She shuddered. 'I can't think about what happened even
now without getting into a state. I know they're all locked up
and can't get at me. None of them got bail except Uncle Bob
and my mother, who swore she knew nothing about my being
kept in my room . . . though how anyone can believe that, I
don't know. But then, they don't know what she's like, do
they? Uncle Bob got bail because he was diagnosed with
cancer of the liver. He died six months ago. The solicitor
asked me to see him, as he had a letter for me from Uncle
Bob and I was mentioned in his will. I thought Uncle Bob
wanted to say sorry for what he'd done to me; perhaps he'd
left me a keepsake? I didn't want it. I didn't want to hear that
he was sorry, either. But Ursula . . .' She sighed.

'Of course you didn't want to,' said Thomas, 'but Ursula
was right. You had to find out what he said.'

'I suppose so. Anyway, I stayed at Ursula's that first night,
but you know, her mother isn't exactly . . . Well, it is a tiny flat,
and I suppose I was in the way. So Ursula asked Ellie if I might
come and stay here last night, to make sure I got to see the
solicitor today. Ursula would have looked after me herself, but
she had job interviews to go to. Ursula thought – and she's
probably right – that I'd duck out of going to the solicitor if
someone didn't make me go. Ellie said, "Yes, of course."'

'Of course,' said Ellie. 'Stay for as long as you like.'

Mia gave Ellie a smile so sweet and genuine that both Ellie and Thomas caught a glimpse of the charm that had once been hers. Ellie could feel Thomas turn to look at her, and knew that sooner or later she was going to have to apologize to him for arranging to take the girl in without asking him.

'Ellie was lovely. She collected me from Mrs Belton's and brought me here and showed me her beautiful guest room and we ate with Rose in the kitchen, and although everything was very strange, I did manage to sleep for a couple of hours last night. Ursula rang this morning, before we went to the solicitor's, and said she was on the track of a nice B & B for me, and she'd ring later to confirm. Which she did a little while ago, but if you really mean I can stay on here for a bit, I'd really like to.'

Ellie saw Thomas take this in, but to his credit he showed no dismay at the news.

'Then this morning Ellie delivered me on time to the solicitor's and stayed in the waiting room while I went in to see him. He gave me a letter from Uncle Bob, asking for my forgiveness. I read it through and couldn't feel anything. Not a thing. Then I got angry. How dared he! Did he really think I could forgive what he'd done to me?'

She was trembling, on the verge of tears. 'I didn't know what to say to the solicitor. I wanted to tear the letter up, but it was on very good thick paper and I didn't know if I had the strength to do it. The solicitor said something about the will. He wanted to read it out to me, but I couldn't concentrate. I said I needed to go, that Ellie was waiting for me. He gave me a copy of the will to take away.'

She started to cry. 'I trusted Uncle Bob! When he came into my bedroom, I thought he'd come to rescue me and I ran to him, only . . . he . . .' She broke off and covered her face with her hands.

Ellie got herself off the settee and put her arms round the girl. 'There, there.'

'I trusted him. How can I forgive him?'

More silence. There was a stir in the corner of the room. Rose had come in and seated herself near the door. 'Supper? Things will look better when you've all got some food inside you.'

'Yes, indeed,' said Thomas. 'I don't know about you, but I'm famished, haven't eaten a decent meal since I left. Mia, you're welcome to stay as long as it takes. As to forgiving the people who've hurt you, well, that's easy to say and almost impossible to do.'

Mia said, 'What I'd like to do is to destroy the will without reading it, but I suppose that's being childish, isn't it?' She began to laugh. Ellie identified a note of hysteria. 'Do you think he's left me his cat? But it's all academic, isn't it, since it doesn't look as if I'm going to live long enough to collect. I wonder which of my family tried to kill me today? And will they try again tomorrow?'

Ellie tried to be cheerful over supper, but was aware that Thomas was quieter than usual. Rose made up for it, of course, clucking over Mia. Rose was a born mother hen without any scope for her talents since her own daughter showed no desire to produce babies.

Thomas chose to sit on the opposite side of the table to Mia, which was tactful of him. Some people might have thought this big, bearded man an unlikely candidate for the ministry. If they'd seen Thomas on a motorbike – which, by the way, he did not have – they might have put him down as a Hell's Angel, tearing up and down motorways, dressed in black leather.

Instead, he'd been in ministry all his adult life, serving in many different capacities. He was harder on himself than on others, and gentle with life's victims. Even Mia, with her phobia about being touched by a man, was able to let him near her without shrinking.

Ellie was dreading the moment when she and Thomas would be alone together, for she'd read in his eyes that he was . . . not exactly disappointed in her, but withholding judgment. It made her miserable. She knew he loved her, yes. He really did love her to bits, and he'd forgive her sins of omission when she'd stated her case. But she had yet to break the news to him that she'd agreed to host not just Ursula's wedding reception – which he already knew about – but Diana's as well.

She knew that if he'd been in her shoes, he'd have contacted her yesterday to ask her opinion and advice about taking Mia

in, and he wouldn't have agreed either to Ursula's plea or
Diana's plans without consulting him.

After supper Mia said she'd help Rose clear away the dishes
while Ellie and Thomas took their coffees into the big sitting
room at the back of the house. It was getting late and the
room was gathering shadows, but the garden outside the big
windows was still bright with colour and the sky cloudless.
Ellie fussed around, putting on side lamps and checking that
Thomas had taken sugar for his coffee.

'Sit down,' he said, taking her hand and leading her to the
settee. He retained hold of her hand, patting it, smiling. 'I
don't mind about Mia staying, really I don't. Of course it was
right to ask her to stay. I seem to remember that Ursula's
mother is a – well, a difficult woman, to put it mildly – and
of course she wouldn't want to be inconvenienced by having
someone sleeping in her sitting room.'

'I ought to have asked you first.'

He shook his head. 'You knew what I'd say if you did ask.'

'Oh, you . . .' She touched his cheek. 'Thank you, Thomas.
But I still ought to have asked you first.'

He rolled his eyes. 'I, too, have had difficulty adjusting to
marriage the second time around. Especially when I find
myself living in a mansion with a millionairess.'

She laughed, as he intended she should. Looking around at
the big Victorian sitting room, with its velvet curtains and
polished antique furniture, she, too, gave thanks. 'Some
millionairess, with everything tied up in a trust so we can't
spend it . . . for which thank the Lord. I do thank Him, you
know, for it's very pleasant to live in a big house with plenty
of room for guests and know we can afford it. But Mia may
need extra care.'

'Have you the time to give it to her?'

'You'll say I may need to call on more professional help
for her, and I think you're right. She seems convinced that she
was the target for the car today, but of course that's nonsense.'

Silence.

She turned her head to look up at him. 'You don't really
think someone might be trying to kill her?'

'I think you might check with the police tomorrow, see
who's her liaison officer, speak to them. It's highly unlikely
that anyone would have had time to arrange an attempt on

her life when she only came back to Ealing two days ago. On the other hand, her testimony could send a number of important people to prison for a long time – if she ever gets to trial. As she says, although the key members of the group are locked up, they do have friends. I don't know, Ellie. Does it seem to you that she was targeted?'

'No. Well . . . no, I don't think so. I was on the outside nearest the traffic. We were both sent flying by that remarkable young man, Leontes. Remind me to check up on his progress tomorrow. The car was travelling so fast it couldn't stop and then it crashed into . . . not that I actually saw the impact, but . . . I think it must have been some young man who'd taken the car for a joyride and couldn't handle it. I hope that was it.'

She closed her eyes momentarily and again saw the havoc on the pavement, the sprawling bodies, the wheel of the pushchair spinning, spinning . . .

He put his arm around her. 'I'm glad you're still alive. The thought of what might have happened, that I might now be coming into an empty house . . . that would be unbearable.'

'Yes. Me, too.' She flicked tears from her eyes as the door opened, and Rose pushed Mia into the room.

Rose closed the door firmly behind her. 'I thought we'd better have the reading of the will in here, before witnesses.'

Mia was half laughing, half crying. 'I wanted to put it on the fire and burn it, but Rose wouldn't let me.'

'I should think not,' said Thomas, sitting upright. 'Let's do this right, with all pomp and ceremony. Wills ought to be read after a roll of drums and a flourish of trumpets, don't you think?'

Mia managed a full laugh that time. She thrust the stiff folded paper at Thomas. 'Then you'd be the right person to read it out to us. Will you?'

Thomas stood up, hooked a thumb into his jacket, and said, 'Ahem. Ahem. Ladies and gentlemen, are you seated comfortably? Then I'll begin. Where's my reading glasses?' He sought for them in his pockets and found them.

Mia tapped her forehead. 'I can't remember the name of his cat. Was it Mog? I think I could bear to have his cat.'

Rose patted Mia's arm. 'My dear, what a lovely thought.'

Maybe, thought Ellie, but what would their own marauding

ginger tom, Midge, feel about another cat entering his domain? He wouldn't tolerate an incomer for one second. She shuddered. She told herself that it would be very good for Mia to have something small and helpless to look after. Then she sighed, because Mia had been out of circulation for six months, and the small cat that she remembered might have grown into a monster, or even perhaps be dead by now. Best not think about 'dead'. Sprawling bodies, a wheel spinning . . .

'A codicil about a cat, you think?' said Thomas, starting from the back of the will and moving forwards. 'You don't want the gobbledegook, do you? There is a codicil, but there's nothing about a cat in it.' He stared at that page, frowned, turned back to the beginning. 'I think we'd better start on the first page and work forward. My poor brain dislikes jumping around.'

A lie. His brain was razor sharp. What was going on?

Mia was anxious. 'Perhaps he didn't leave me anything, then. Oh, but I suppose he must have, if the solicitor needed to give me a copy of the will.'

'Yes,' said Thomas. 'Let me just . . . There's a paragraph about why he's changing his will and downsizing bequests that he'd made in earlier wills. No immediate family, I gather. He's left bequests to various charities, yes, yes . . . What you'd expect, roughly. Then a bequest to the live-in couple who . . .' He turned back to the end. 'He cancelled that in a codicil because they left him in the lurch when the scandal hit the papers. Mia, give me a moment or two, will you? There's a whole lot of business talk here.'

'I'd really like his cat.'

Rose said, 'It's been some time, dearie. I expect that by now they've found someone else to look after his cat.'

Mia sniffed and brushed her hand across her cheek. Fighting off tears?

Thomas rubbed the back of his neck. 'Mia, as far as I can make out, you are his residuary legatee.'

'What?' Puzzled. She looked around at each one of them. 'Well, I don't suppose there's much, after all the bequests. I think he meant to give me a keepsake. Or, maybe, his cat.'

'His solicitor was appointed executor. There may be debts, of course. They'll all have to be cleared, and taxes paid. Was he a wealthy man?'

'I don't know, do I? I mean, he used to go abroad a lot.

I used to know what he did. A family business? Printing? Yes, I seem to remember as a child going round his works to see the machinery. My mother used to hold on to his arm and squeak, pretending to be frightened of the noise, though she wasn't in the least bit frightened really, of course.' She bit her lip. 'If I'd have thought about it, I'd have said he'd have left the lot to her. Because, if you see what I mean, she and he . . . Well, on her side, at any rate.'

'Ouch,' Ellie said, quietly, to herself.

Thomas folded up the papers and held them out to Mia. 'My dear, he may have left you an estate of five thousand pounds, or fifty thousand. Probate takes time, and only after the will has been proved, and taxes paid, will you know exactly how you stand. I think you'd better go back to the solicitor tomorrow and find out.'

Mia stared at the papers, didn't take them. 'I don't want any money from him.' Her skin had turned ashen. 'His cat, yes. Perhaps.'

Something to love, yes. Blood money, no.

Rose was soothing. 'You can go out and buy a cat for yourself.'

Mia stood up. 'I don't think so. If you don't mind, I think I'll go to bed now. It's been a long day.'

Rose bustled out after her and Thomas stood, fingering the will, looking at nothing in particular.

Ellie sighed. 'You think he left her a lot of money?'

'A house in Madely Road – those big houses fetch up to a million, don't they? Then there's the business, stocks and shares, insurance policies. Deduct any debts, taxes, other bequests. Yes, I think it may be a sizeable estate.'

Blood money. 'She won't want to take it.'

'Now; no. One half of me applauds. But the other, more practical, half says that she's no money of her own, is not fit to earn her own living at the moment, and in fact may never be. That part of my mind says that she could do with a reasonable amount of compensation for what she's gone through.'

'Her family had money.'

'Her stepfather's empire took a headlong dive when he was arrested. He was deep in debt before, which is why he used Mia in an attempt to lever himself out of trouble. Would there be any of his wealth left now? And if there were, wouldn't his wife and his two boys get there first?'

'Couldn't she get compensation through the law courts?'

'Only after the trial, but that isn't scheduled for months yet, is it? What is she to live on till then? Social security? And who will pay for any further therapy that she may need? Are we to fill in the gap? Not,' he added, 'that I'd be against that. But I'm not sure that in this case it would be right for you to give her money from your charitable trust – money which might instead go to other deserving cases who haven't got any alternative – if she has money of her own. I don't know.'

She looked at the clock. It was late. She yawned. 'I'll think about it tomorrow.' If she went to bed and closed her eyes now, she'd see sprawling bodies, a wheel spinning. Let's put it off. 'Tell me about the conference. How did it go?'

'All right.' He brought his mind back from Mia with difficulty, and then grinned. 'All theory and no common sense, as usual. One of these days I must play you a tape of a typical debate. You'll be horrified how much gas the gaiters produce. Most of the subject matter is ten years out of date by the time it comes up for discussion, and the rest is too contentious to touch and so isn't mentioned.' He yawned. He must be tired. He needed sleep, even if she was afraid of closing her eyes tonight.

'Do you want to back into parish work?' She began to turn out the lights.

'The nitty gritty as opposed to the airy fairy? Did I get anything right when I worked in a parish? Do I do any good as the editor of a magazine? Are poets more important than leader writers?'

She smiled. 'Come to bed. You're overworking your brain and mine. I'll just pop in on Mia, see she's all right.'

'Quantify "all right",' said Thomas, following her up the stairs. 'An unquiet soul, landed in our lap for healing. Dear Lord above, give us wisdom to do and say the right thing.'

'Agreed. But clean towels and a hot shower help.'

MONDAY NIGHT. . .

Well, he could always try again. As soon as he could work out when and where. She had to leave the house every now and then, didn't she? What he really needed was for her to go out alone on a dark night. Not much hope of that in mid July. How about a thunderstorm, with lightning flashes and a heavy downpour of rain? People do slip and hurt themselves on wet pavements, don't they? They hit their heads on kerbs. And die. Nothing but death would do.

FOUR

Monday evening

Mia was not in her bedroom. Nor in the en suite beyond. Had she flown the coop? Surely not. Ellie nearly panicked, and then faintly from below she heard Rose's television blaring away. She hurried along the landing and peeped into the bedroom Rose had used before her illness last winter. Rose's old bedroom was empty, too.

Down the back stairs Ellie went and into the big room which had been converted into a bed-sitter for Rose next to the kitchen. There was Mia, curled up in the big armchair beside Rose's bed. Both Mia and Rose were fast asleep, with the television on. Mia was fully dressed, with a blanket thrown over her.

Ellie fetched another duvet from upstairs and tucked it around Mia. Let her sleep in peace. She withdrew as quietly as she could and went up again to tell Thomas what had happened, nerving herself at the same time to break the news about Diana's wedding plans . . . only to find him asleep, too, glasses on his nose, prayer book in hand. She removed glasses and book, whereupon he snuggled down, muttering something unintelligible.

As she slid in beside him she prayed, *Thank you, Lord, for bringing us safely through another day. Please, grant me sleep without nightmares?*

She lay with her eyes open, not daring to close them for a long time. Finally, she slept, and did not dream till the night was nearly done.

Tuesday morning

Two obstinate faces greeted Ellie when she went down to breakfast.

Rose clattered dishes. 'Before you start, Ellie, it's no good. I know what you're going to say, but it's like when you're a child in the dark, and there's nothing really to be frightened of, although perhaps in this case there is, but if Mia wants to sleep in my room, she's welcome. Besides, when I woke in the night and wanted to go to the loo, she was there to help me in and out of bed. I've said it before, and I'll say it again, that bed's a trifle on the high side for someone who's vertically challenged – which is what they say nowadays, although I've always called a spade a spade, if you know what I mean—'

'I *like* looking after Rose,' said Mia, who was wearing yesterday's clothes.

'And I like looking after Mia,' said Rose. 'And now there's a perfectly good shower room and loo down here, there's no reason on earth why we shouldn't please ourselves.'

Ellie threw up her hands. 'I understand how it happened that Mia slept in your room last night, but Mia –' playing the joker – 'I don't think your friend Ursula will think it a good idea. Sleeping in an armchair will give you a bad back, and that won't help either of you. I realize you want to be near Rose, and Rose wants you near her. May I suggest that Mia sleeps in what was Rose's old room upstairs, which is directly above her bed-sitter and which has a bathroom next door to it. If one of you needs the other, you're within hailing distance.'

Silence while the two conspirators considered this offer. Finally Rose said, 'Mia could always come down in the middle of the night for a little while, if she wanted to, and she could sleep with the door to the stairs open and a light on her room.'

Mia wriggled, but gave way. 'We could try it, I suppose.'

Having won a temporary victory, Ellie tried not to show relief or pleasure. She helped herself to cereal. 'Good. Now we have to plan what we do today. Ursula's coming round some time, isn't she? Will she go to the solicitor's with you, or shall I? Also, don't you have some kind of police liaison officer? Don't you have to tell them that you've left your country retreat?'

'I don't think I want to go out today.'

'I can understand that, but if Ursula went with you? Or I did?'

'I feel a bit tired.'

'So do I. If you give me the liaison officer's details, I'll get her to call here.'

Silence. 'They did pass me on to someone when I left London, and she did call. My aunt told her I didn't want to see her, that I wanted to get on with life without being bothered about all that, and I agreed. Honestly, I couldn't see the point.'

'I don't think your aunt had your best interests at heart, do you? Give me the name of whoever it was, and I'll see who it should be here in London.'

'I've decided,' said Mia, 'that there is no way I can touch anything that man left me.'

Ellie used Thomas's reasoning. 'You'd sooner go on Social Security and live in a hostel somewhere, waiting for a place in a council flat?'

Rose clattered a plate of scrambled egg down in front of Ellie. 'That she won't do, not while I've a penny left in the bank.'

Mia reddened. 'That's silly. As if I would take money from you, Rose.'

'Exactly,' said Ellie. 'We have to balance this and that, compensation against false pride, etcetera. By the way, Mia, I suspect your wardrobe needs replenishing. Shall we ask Ursula to buy you some new clothes, or shall Rose and I get something on approval for you?'

Rose eyed Mia's fragile figure. 'Size eight, I should think. We must make out a list. Marks & Spencer will let us have things to try on here and, if they don't fit, we can take them back. Also, she needs a good haircut and a facial. Who do we know who could come to the house to do it for her?'

Mia went white. 'You won't leave me alone in the house, will you? Please?'

'No, of course not!' said Rose, who had clearly been thinking of doing just that. 'No, no. Of course not,' she repeated, meaning it.

'If I go out, they'll get me!'

Ellie's mouth was full of scrambled egg and toast, but she knew panic when she heard it. 'We'll do our best,' she said, indistinctly. 'But you must help us, as well.'

Mia twisted a tendril of hair round a finger. 'I know I'm being silly, but yesterday . . . If I'm to live my life as if every

day might be my last . . . I tell myself to be brave, that it
doesn't matter if I die today . . . but how can I forget? I do
feel safe here. At least, I think I do. But I wouldn't want to
be left in this big house all by myself.' She brushed her hand
across her cheeks. 'Now tell me I'm being unreasonable.'

'I don't think you're in any danger, honestly, but I'll check
with the police, ask their advice.'

'Don't make me leave, will you?'

'Of course not, but you need to talk to that solicitor.'

A shadow of a smile. 'Get him to wait on me here. Why
not? He'll come if he thinks I'll let him handle everything for
him . . . which I will, right up to the point that I dump the
whole lot in the nearest cats home.'

'I suppose I could try to get him here, but you can't stay
indoors for ever. May I suggest you talk to—'

'Social services? I agree with my aunt about that. A lot of
half-trained, overworked do-gooders. I need one of them like
I need a hole in my head.'

'I'm sure they're not all like that, but . . . well, will you talk
to Thomas about it? And before you start on about not being
alone in a room with a man, think what you're saying. Do
you really imagine Thomas would take advantage of you?'

The girl put on a stone face, because her Uncle Bob had
done just that. The girl couldn't trust any man at the moment.

'All right,' said Ellie. 'When Thomas blunders in for his
breakfast – give him another five minutes because he had a
long day yesterday – ask him if you can talk here in the
kitchen, with Rose standing guard over you.'

Mia tried to smile, but her lips trembled. She nodded.
'I'll try.'

'Fear is like a virus once it gets into your head,' said Ellie,
who should know. The horrors of yesterday were still hanging
around, waiting for her to relax so that they could slip through
into her conscious mind.

A sudden thought struck Mia. She grinned. 'What I want
to do today is to make some filo pastry. My aunt taught me
how and stood over me till I got it right. My aunt was a
wonderful cook. She gave me her book of recipes because
her eyes aren't good enough for her to see them any more. I
suppose she'll have to go into care now, won't she? Not that
I mind, really. Rose, may I make some filo pastry here today?'

Ellie understood that the girl was in denial. Denial was a nice country to live in, provided nothing broke through its boundaries to threaten you with reality. So let her make filo pastry. Let her make herself useful in the kitchen. It might help to settle her, make her feel safe.

Meanwhile . . . Ellie began to make a list. Phone the hospital about that brave man, Leontes, see if they had an address for him. Phone the police to see if she could find a liaison officer for Mia. Get her some clothes. 'What clothes do you need, Mia?'

A shrug. 'I'm all right as I am.'

No, she wasn't. Ellie jotted down, 'T-shirts, jeans. Underclothing.' Also, Thomas must be told about Diana. Ouch.

Thomas arrived later than usual for breakfast, ate it on the run and departed, saying he'd lost a couple of days' work and must catch up. He didn't speak to Mia except to say, 'Hi! All right?' Ellie didn't try to stop him leaving. Rose and Mia looked pleased that he'd not interfered with whatever they'd planned for that day.

Ellie went along the corridor to her office in the old morning room. There she found her assistant Pat, dealing with mail.

Ellie averted her gaze from the pile of post. 'Small problem, Pat. Can I leave everything to you for a bit?' Pat only worked part-time and expected Ellie's full attention when she was around, but Pat wasn't going to get it today, was she? Pat would probably sulk. Well, let her.

Pat rolled her eyes as Ellie reached for the phone and dialled the number of Ealing Hospital. She enquired about Leontes, who turned out not to have been named after a Shakespearian character, but to be a man called Leon T Spearman. He'd been discharged late last night, and no, the hospital couldn't give out his home number. She wasn't a relative, was she?

'One more call, Pat,' Ellie said, dialling again. She must speak to Maria urgently, not only because she was happily married to Diana's first husband, Stewart, and was doing a great job bringing up little Frank, but also because she ran the cleaning service which Ellie used – and Ellie was going to need more help from them on Saturday. It was possible, of course, that Maria might already know about Diana's second wedding and her plans to involve Frank, but it was best to make sure.

The line was engaged. Ellie left a message for Maria to ring her back.

What next? Ellie pushed today's post away from her and turned to Pat, who was concentrating on her computer.

'Pat, give me a minute. Change of plan, or rather extension of plan, for Saturday. Diana is getting married again and has arranged for us to hold her wedding reception here on Saturday afternoon – yes, truly! I had nothing to do with it, but the invitations have gone out. If Maria rings back when I'm out, would you fill her in and say I'll ring her later?

'Oh, and yesterday a man pushed Mia and me out of the way of a speeding car which went on to kill a young woman and leave her two children motherless. The man's leg was caught by the car and there was a lot of blood. He's been discharged from hospital. How do I find him? He saved my life, and Mia's.'

'Police, I suppose.' Pat liked a good gossip, but she was evidently not pleased at Ellie's refusal to attend to the morning's post.

'I suppose so,' said Ellie, hating the thought of it. 'Oh well, I'd better see if anyone's available to talk to me.' She picked up the phone, sighing.

Tuesday morning

Mobile phones are helpful, very. Sometimes the images on the camera part aren't that good, but this one was clear enough, good enough to print off. The slut, the witch, the bitch, getting to her feet, unharmed. She ought to have been killed. Or burned at the stake. Or put in a coffin with a stake through her heart. Maybe she'd have a delayed reaction, though, and die in the night.

He hoped the lilies would give her unpleasant dreams.

Ellie asked for Detective Inspector Willis and was put on hold. She'd had various brushes with the DI in the past, and had learned to respect the woman's professionalism, while aware that the compliment was not returned. Ellie deplored the woman's abrupt manner and the variety of red dyes she used on her hair, while DI Willis clearly thought Ellie was a silly housewife who had nothing better to do than waste police time.

Well, if Ellie had wasted police time on occasion, she'd also helped to sort out one or two neighbourhood crimes, including those involving Mia's family. DI Willis owed her the courtesy of a five minutes' call, didn't she?

Pat shoved some mail in front of Ellie, who tried to concentrate on it; with indifferent results. When Miss Drusilla Quicke, Ellie's difficult but endearing aunt, had died, Ellie had inherited a fortune and a number of houses and apartments which were rented out. Ellie had put everything into a charity which was run by her with a board of trustees.

The housing stock was efficiently managed by Stewart, Diana's ex-husband. And hadn't Diana been furious about his being given the job! How Stewart had managed to survive marriage to Diana so well was something of a mystery, but he had done so almost unscathed; Ellie was very fond of him.

Stewart held as low an opinion of Denis the Menace – the Dirty Den of the Estate Agency world – as Ellie did. Which reminded her that she still hadn't told Thomas about Diana's latest plan to upset the course of their domestic happiness.

Ah, a policeman had come back to her on the phone with a message. The DI could spare Ellie a few minutes face-to-face at ten, if she put her skates on. She glanced at the clock, yelped, grabbed her handbag, said, 'Must go!' to Pat, and fled.

It wasn't far to walk to the police station, and the exercise would do her good. A happy second marriage and a love of good food hadn't done anything to reduce her waistline. Or Thomas's. They really ought to go on a diet; but not perhaps until after the wedding. Weddings.

She was kept waiting at the station. Of course. She found an old envelope and started to make a list of things to do. Ring the solicitor. Ask Ursula's opinion about Mia's clothes. What sort of bridesmaid's dress was the girl supposed to wear to the ceremony? And then . . . what next?

Ellie had her charge cards with her for major shopping, but could do with popping into the bank to get some cash. She couldn't for the moment remember what they were supposed to be having for supper. Would the leftover cold chicken stretch to four people, especially when Thomas was one of the four? She rather thought not.

'Mrs Quicke. Would you care to come through?'

Gracious me. Good manners for once? However, this wasn't

the DI speaking. It was WDC Milburn, a pleasant, robust young officer, whom Ellie had met before. Ellie was ushered into an interview room.

'Mrs Quicke.' DI Willis looked at her watch, impatience in every gesture. She'd tried a ginger hair dye this time. Oh well.

In her haste Ellie let her pen and the list she'd been making tumble to the table, and the DI picked it up. Prominent at the top of the list was the large figure eight which was, of course, Mia's dress size.

Seeing this, the DI's eyebrows went up. She glanced at Ellie's waistline – which was nearer a size eighteen than an eight – before handing the paper back.

'Important shopping to do today?' said the DI, noting that Ellie had been concerning herself with such trivial matters as underwear and nightdresses.

Ellie put the list into her handbag and snapped it shut. Then realized the WDC was handing her the pen which she'd also dropped. Ellie's colour rose. How incompetent they were making her feel! Well, someone had to look after waifs and strays like Mia, and that seemed to be Ellie's job at the moment. The police's job was to look after them, too. If necessary she would remind the DI of that.

'Mia Prior,' she said, plunging straight in. 'Can you give me the name of her support officer?'

'The Prior girl?' The DI's hard eyes glittered. 'May I ask why?'

'She was convalescing with an aunt in the country. She did receive a visit from someone in social services, but Mia's aunt sent the woman away. Mia is now back in this district and staying with me, so I'd like to link her up with a professional who can help her adjust to daily life. Come to think of it, you probably haven't heard that she was nearly run over yesterday in that road by the Town Hall.'

'What!'

Ellie nodded, considered she'd made a sufficiently sharp impression on the DI for due process to begin, and sat back in her chair. She frowned. She really ought to have inspected the contents of the small suitcase Mia had brought with her before she'd set out on a shopping expedition. Did the girl need bras? Shoes? Toiletries?

The DI accessed data on her computer and stared at it for a long moment before swivelling round to Ellie. 'Tell me.'

Ellie considered asking the woman to add the magic word 'please' to that request, but decided to overlook the omission in view of the seriousness of the situation. She told the DI what had happened the previous day, pointing to her scrapes and bruises as she did so. 'I honestly don't know whether Mia was the target or not. She's convinced she was. She's afraid that those who abused her, or possibly their friends, are going to kill her before the case comes to trial.'

The DI raised both hands. 'Her death wouldn't stop the trial. The police have her evidence on videotape, taken while she was still in the nursing home. We have the doctor's evidence, too. Even if she died tomorrow – of natural causes or otherwise – the police would still go ahead with the trial.'

'That's a comfort. I'll tell her that.'

'Of course –' the DI rubbed her chin – 'the defendants should have been told this. I'm sure they must know, but human nature being what it is, people often believe what they want to believe. They might believe that getting rid of her would improve their chances of acquittal, no matter how often they are told otherwise.'

'Ouch.'

'But –' tapping at her keyboard to access more data – 'they're all still locked up . . . the two stepbrothers, and the stepfather . . . yes, and the councillor who . . . and the man who supplied them with drugs. There were a couple of lowly lads who carried out some of the strong-arm stuff but . . . No, two of those are . . . One got bail, but he's not considered a threat to the girl in any way. Ah, one of the other abusers got bail, but he was on his last legs.'

'The one she calls "Uncle Bob"? Yes, he died.'

'And the mother . . .' More tapping. 'The mother got bail. The police objected, but she made a good impression in court.'

'Oh dear.' Ellie remembered the woman well: a monumental blonde, flashing diamonds. A deep voice threatening destruction to anyone who crossed her husband in his plans for ever bigger developments. A woman who would refuse to acknowledge defeat and would bounce back fighting.

Ellie clasped her handbag tightly. 'In my opinion, she was her husband's enforcer, if that's the right word. Her husband used his influence to get planning permission for his various enterprises, the sons assisted him in various ways – such as procuring young people to act as arm candy – and worse. If anything went wrong, the mother directed the sons to dispose of the problem. Mrs Prior gave me the shudders.'

'She said she knew nothing of the girl's treatment after she was raped and brought back to their house. She said she was told the girl was ill, didn't want to see anyone.'

'If you believe that . . .'

'Agreed. What mother never bothers to check on her only child? But others did believe it. She got bail but is not allowed to approach her daughter in any way, or to live within so many miles of her. Since Mia left London to live in the country, Mrs Prior is currently residing in the family home, Prior Place. Not half a mile from here. How long will the girl be staying with you?'

'Indefinitely. I know it's rare for a mother to side with her new husband rather than her child, but—'

'It happens, yes. By the terms of her bail, if the girl returns to Ealing, the mother must remove. I'll see she's informed immediately.'

'Could you check to see if she knows about the events of yesterday? Because someone sent Mia some lilies late yesterday afternoon. Here's the card that came with them.' She handed it over. 'As you can see, it says, "You should have died."'

A frown. 'How could she have learned that Mia had been involved in an accident so quickly?'

'I've been thinking about that. You know how everyone seems to have those mobile phones which are also cameras, nowadays? There were several people taking shots of the scene. I remember wondering how they could, but I believe some people earn money by sending camera shots to the newspapers, don't they?'

'Yes, but how would anyone know where to find her?'

'The police took statements, wanting to know who everyone was and where they lived. I had to tell the police officer my name, and Mia's. I had to tell him twice that she wasn't my daughter, but that she was staying with me. I had to give him my address. The policeman asked me to speak up because of the traffic. Anyone who was standing nearby could have heard, sent a picture to Mrs Prior, and told her where Mia was staying.'

The DI took her eyes off the screen. 'I follow your reasoning. I wonder if the newspaper will have been given that information, along with the pictures? I'll check, see if we can stop them printing her address.'

'Oh dear. What a mess. And the man who saved our lives? Leon Spearman? I'd like to thank him in person.'

'If you're right, then his name and address will be in the paper on Friday, too. You didn't know the woman who died?'

'Never seen her before, didn't really catch more than a glimpse, after . . . after. Horrible business. It keeps replaying in my mind. No one had the wits to catch the number of the car.'

'Hang on a minute. I'll see if I can get an update.' The DI wasn't long away, returning to say, 'The Volvo. A family car. It was found abandoned by Ealing Common tube station late last night. It's being examined now. It had been stolen the night before from outside someone's house. The owner's shattered, has two little boys of his own. And before you ask, they managed to save the toddler's arm, but he'll be in hospital for a while yet. The baby's been taken by social services and they're looking for other members of the family as we speak.'

'I would like to think it was a hit and run by a joyrider, but I can't quite convince myself that that was the case.'

The DI attempted a smile. 'You have an instinct for crime, Mrs Quicke. It would make my life a lot easier if you hadn't. I must admit you are more often right than wrong.'

Saying which, the DI actually held out her hand for Ellie to shake, before ushering her out of her office.

Wonders will never cease, thought Ellie. Did that woman actually admit I belong to the human race?

She looked at her watch and frowned. Everything always takes so much longer than you think it should. What was next on her list? She sought in her handbag for the envelope on which she'd been jotting down notes and found it eventually. She must go to the solicitor's first, and then – it was getting late – a sandwich somewhere? And after that she'd go on to Marks & Spencer by bus, to get a whole load of stuff for Mia to try on. After that she'd better organize herself a taxi back home.

A horrible worm of suspicion was lurking at the back of her mind. Diana had said Denis had found them a large house to rent, one with six bedrooms and two bathrooms. Of course there was no reason to suppose that he was after one of the houses which Ellie's trust owned. Of course not. Ridiculous.

Or was it? She thought she'd better check as soon as she got back.

Tuesday afternoon

He'd never wanted to kill anyone before. He hadn't thought he was capable of it. How surprised everyone would be, if they knew what he was thinking. It would be like killing a spider, or a rat. He must take care that he wasn't caught. It would be best to use psychological tactics at first. Scare her to death. If that didn't work, he was perfectly prepared to go further.

FIVE

Tuesday afternoon

Ellie tried not to dislike people at first sight, or even second. She gave herself five seconds during which she suspended judgment on Mia's solicitor, and then allowed herself to wonder if he'd had a personality transplant. Or might that be an asset in his line of business?

It was clear that he had all the facts and figures, the law and the prophets, at his fingertips – which, by the way, he was forever rubbing together in a manner which meant either that his skin was so dry it needed attention, or that he had an annoying mannerism which his parents should have checked. Provided, that was, that he had actually had parents, and had not been spawned out of textbooks by law reports.

He had arrived at the house just as Ellie was decanted from her cab, exhausted and hung around with bags from Marks & Spencers. Since Mia refused to leave the kitchen when the man arrived, he had seated himself at one end of the long table, laid out his papers, and proceeded to inform her of her duties with regard to himself and her inheritance. In a tone of reproach he pointed out that he'd been put to considerable inconvenience by her absence. He'd spent both time and money – remembering that time was money – trying to trace her whereabouts, all of which he would be forced to recoup from the estate. Now she had made up her mind to surface from wherever she'd been hiding, she should pay attention to what he had to say and, naturally and of course, follow his advice.

Mia said, 'What happened to his cat?'

He smoothed out a piece of paper. 'I have no idea. I assume it was taken by the Cats Protection League when the house was cleared. Now, as sole executor for my client, I've carried out his instructions, obtained probate, and am now ready to hand over to you, subject to deduction of any fees accruing. Do you understand?'

Ellie and Rose exchanged glances. Mia had insisted they stay in the room, and they'd been curious enough to do so. Mia didn't seem to have any curiosity at all. She had put her head in her hands and was idly twirling a tress of dark hair round a finger like a schoolgirl, showing by her body language that she didn't care what was being said to her.

The solicitor cleared his throat. Ellie was amazed that he didn't shoot his cuffs as he picked a paper up off the pile in front of him. He shot his cuffs. She tried not to meet Rose's eye, tried not to giggle, told herself that this was serious, grown up stuff and that she should pay attention. Wished Thomas were there to appreciate their visitor's eccentricities.

It didn't look as if Mia were listening as he started to read out a statement of her financial position. Ellie tried to follow, but got lost in the detail. Rose's eyes glazed over.

'That's enough,' said Mia, lifting her head. 'If I've understood what you've been saying, he left his house to me with instructions that you should clear it, bank the proceeds, and put it up for sale. Has it been sold?'

'As I was trying to—'

'Yes or no.'

He sniffed, indicating annoyance. 'We have had a reasonable offer, which awaits your approval.'

'Well, I wouldn't want to live there, would I? Close the sale. What about the business?'

'In this day and age, the recession . . . There is a manager, of course, but he lacks, if I may say so, some of the flair which my client—'

'Going down the tubes?'

Ellie was surprised how sharp Mia could be. But then, she'd been an intelligent, lively-minded university student once, hadn't she?

He sniffed again. It seemed to be his way of expressing frustration. 'I wouldn't say that, exactly. It has some orders from old clients to keep them going, but yes, there have been some redundancies. It is still a nice little business, but perhaps—'

'No longer a "nice little earner"? Hasn't moved with the times, invested in new machinery, addressed new markets?'

'I really don't—'

'Is there a buyer for it, at a reasonable price?'

'Well, not as such, no. Early days, and in this present time it is a little too much to expect . . . but of course, given time, that is the route I would advise you to take.'

'Sell everything and invest according to your advice? I don't think so.'

He excavated a pristine handkerchief from his pocket and sniffed into it. His eyelids fluttered. 'I'm not sure—'

'Good,' said Mia, getting to her feet. 'That's better. You may or may not have heard what I've been through this last year. I don't care whether you have or not. But let me tell you this; I can't afford to waste what time I have left. They may get me tomorrow or next week, and in a way I would welcome it. End the uncertainty. As for the inheritance, if I live long enough you should dump the lot in my bank account. If I still have one. Maybe I haven't? I suppose I can check it out online. Whatever. Just don't waste my time. Understood?'

Pushing papers together, eyelids fluttering, he reminded Ellie of a startled horse. Perhaps he was really a shy soul, and not just a dry one? 'Understood, understood. But have you considered, have you yourself made a will? It would be wise, don't you think? Be happy to oblige, give me your instructions, are you able to do so now?'

'No.' Mia hadn't had much colour in her face before, now she had even less. Perhaps she hadn't really believed in her lack of future until he'd taken her at her word?

'Of course, of course. Will be in touch, any time, you have only to mention. You can be contacted here, of course? Naturally. But, er, what about the business?'

'Sell it.' Mia walked out of the kitchen. Just like that.

'Oh, but – Mia?' Rose went after her.

Ellie held the door open for the solicitor. 'I'll see you out.' And did so, with him still fluttering his eyelids. Irritating man.

Returning to the kitchen, Ellie found Rose there, shaking her head. 'Burst into tears, she did. Ran upstairs and bolted the door against me. Overwrought.'

'I thought she was coping surprisingly well.'

'Mm. That friend of hers, Ursula, came by this morning while you were out. What a strong personality, a breath of fresh air, made me feel quite tired the way she swept everything along before her. But she did Mia good, at least for the time being, jollied her along, put some backbone into her, told her not to put up with anything she didn't want to put up with, which was probably good advice though I didn't expect her to be rude to that solicitor, even though he could do with a dose of Epsom salts, as my mother would have said.'

'Agreed. Should I go up to Mia?' It was odd, but Rose now seemed to have taken over responsibility for Mia. 'I brought back a load of clothes for her to try on, and oh, some stuff for supper.'

'Leave her be for the time being. She feels safe here with me. Cooking for us seems to calm her down, and I'm not going to stop her, am I, if it makes her feel useful, though as you know highly spiced foods don't agree with me. But if it helps her then I'll eat and take some Bisodol afterwards.'

'Agreed,' said Ellie.

'Oh, and Ursula left a folder of stuff for you to look at. She went through it with Mia and me, and I must say I think she's thought of everything from our point of view, but she wanted to make sure you had someone coming in to move the furniture about and clear up afterwards, which I said you were paying for because you'll be using your usual cleaning company that you always have, and that they'd been round to give us a special extra clean on Monday, which was when you were out, and they're looking forward to the wedding, too. Only, Ursula looked serious and said she ought to be paying for that, though I'm sure I don't know how she thinks she's going to do it, but she says she's put a little bit by now and then and her father's giving her something, which her mother doesn't like at all, but you know what Mrs Belton is, you couldn't please her if you gave her a thousand pounds because she'd want it to be five. Thousand, I mean.'

She took a deep breath, and Ellie nodded. 'And Maria rang and Pat didn't know what to say to her, so she called me and I went through to your study and had a word with her about the extra that'll need doing around the house and she said to leave it with her, and knowing her I could do that, though it wouldn't be many people you could trust in such matters, would there? So I told her – Ursula, that is – that we were all looking forward to her wedding enormously, and not to worry about the cleaning and moving furniture because it was giving us something lovely to think about, and it's going to be no trouble at all to us to have her wedding reception here, with the photos in the conservatory, she says, because she knows I love my flowers, though I think perhaps a trip to the garden centre first wouldn't be a bad idea, would it? We're not looking at our best in that direction at the moment, are we?'

'Garden centre. Agreed,' said Ellie, her mind whirling.

'And that Pat's been in looking for you three times now, lots for you to sign and look at, she says, and oh yes, there's a letter come for you, by hand. On the hall table.'

A hand-delivered letter? Ellie didn't often get those. Something for Thomas? She went to look. No, it wasn't for Thomas. It was addressed to Ellie in an angular script, hand-written and not typed. Very black ink on a heavy, cream paper. Ellie's first instinct was to throw it in the bin, because she guessed who it was from.

She didn't throw it away, of course. She was trained to open post and deal with it as soon as possible. Sometimes, naturally, she passed awkward correspondence on to Pat, but in this case she knew she'd have to deal with it herself.

There was an embossed address on the letterhead, that of Prior Place. Mia's old home. The tower block which Mr Prior had built on the North Circular bore the same name. Mia's ordeal had begun in the penthouse suite of the tower block, and had continued back home.

So Mrs Prior was still living at home, was she?

A square script, written with an expensive pen.

Dear Mrs Quicke,

I am desperate for news of my poor daughter. Someone sent me a picture of her taken after an incident in the Broadway. I hardly recognized her, but I am assured that it was her, and that she is staying with you, posing as your daughter.

I understand that I am most unfairly banned from meeting her, but if it is true that you have hidden her away, may I at least ask for reassurance that she is well and receiving appropriate treatment for what she suffered at the hands of her stepfather and stepbrothers? As you may know, they are now in jail awaiting trial, and I myself – another innocent victim – have in consequence suffered greatly. All that would be as nothing if I can only be assured that my only child is being well cared for.

Would it be possible for us to meet before I leave Ealing, as I understand that I must? I have been informed that I must not even shop in the Avenue if Mia is staying with you.

Yours sincerely,

Adelina Rossi, ex-Prior, née Parham.

How dare she make herself out to be 'another' innocent victim, she who had entered into all her husband's schemes and had been quick to arrange punishment for anyone who dared defy him!

So her name was Adelina, was it? Appropriate. And she was now calling herself 'Rossi'. Was that her first husband's name? It occurred to Ellie to wonder in what manner Adelina had got rid of her first husband, in order to marry the wealthy Mr Prior.

Yuk! And to pretend that her sole concern was for Mia's well-being after all that had happened! Ellie felt that she would very much like to strangle the woman . . . except – she had to laugh – that the boot would probably be on the other foot, since Ellie was neither very tall nor very muscular, whereas Adelina Rossi, ex-Prior, née Parham, was both. In fact, she was monumental. The only time Ellie had seen the woman, she'd towered over most people, including her husband.

Ellie took the letter through to Thomas, expecting him to

join with her in condemning Adelina Rossi, but he was in no
mood to listen to her, jabbing at his keyboard and growling
into the telephone. Not wanting to interrupt him, Ellie kissed
the top of his head, patted his shoulder and left.

Now what? Her mind was awhirl with jobs to do.

That letter from Mrs Prior. Ex-Prior. Ellie had been brought
up to believe that there were always two sides to an argu-.
ment. She tried to make herself believe that Adelina Rossi,
ex-Prior, might not be as black as she'd been painted. That,
appearances to the contrary, she really was concerned about
her daughter.

Ellie snorted. Unlikely.

She remembered something else that had been bothering
her earlier and went through to her study. Pat had gone for
the day, but Ellie knew her way around the filing cabinet
and the computer records. Well, most of the time she knew
her way around the computer. Enough to find out what she
wanted now.

She pulled up last week's rental returns. Stewart sent through
the latest figures to her computer every Monday, and once a
week he would come in and they would go over what needed
to be done to the housing stock: repairs, renovations, lettings,
problems and so on.

Mm, mm. Diana had said that Denis was going to rent a
big house with six bedrooms, two en suite plus two bathrooms,
presumably somewhere local. Of course it might not be one
of hers. Most unlikely.

There were only a few such large properties on their books;
four were already let out on long-term leases, one was under-
going a major refit, new bathrooms and kitchen, etc. There
was just one ready to go back on to the market; six bedrooms,
two en suite plus two more bathrooms. Newly fitted kitchen.
Conservatory. Eighty-foot garden, mostly lawn, surrounded
by shrubs. Easy maintenance.

Ellie reached for the phone and got through to Stewart.
'Sorry to trouble you. I know we weren't supposed to be
meeting this week because you're off on holiday – when?
Wednesday, isn't it?'

'Maria wants to make sure everything goes smoothly for
you on Saturday, so we've decided to put it off till after the
weddings.' An even tone, hiding emotion?

'Ah, you've heard?'

'Frank came home from a visit to Diana saying she wanted him to dress up in a satin costume with a floppy tie and be a ring boy at her wedding. He was distressed, said he wouldn't do it. I rang Diana, and she confirmed she's having the reception at your place. I gather Maria's organizing extra staff to help you to cope.'

Ellie grimaced. 'The reception was thrust upon me and as the invitations have gone out, I don't see how I can get out of it. How is Frank taking it? I know little boys don't like dressing up but . . . is he really upset about that, or about her getting married again?'

'He's distressed, full stop. We've had the dickens of a job getting him to sleep at night, ever since. If I didn't know better, I'd think he was afraid. But of what?'

'Ah. I think I know. Diana says Denis is taking a large house so that they can have all the boys with them in the holidays.'

A sigh. 'I'll have to ring her again. The wedding; well, if she really wants him to act as ring-bearer, then we'll go along with that. It doesn't matter so much if we postpone our own holiday for a few days, but I wouldn't want to change the existing arrangements for Frank. Maria loves him and he's doing well at school. He doesn't always see Diana at weekends, but when he does he comes back in such a state it's hard to calm him down.'

'I know. Diana isn't the wisest of mothers. Not everyone is gifted to be a wise and loving mother, though your dear Maria certainly is.' Here Ellie remembered Adelina Prior, who was nobody's idea of a loving mother, but who pretended to be exactly that.

'Stewart; there's something else. Probably it's nothing, but could you check on the house in Castlebar Road for me? The workmen must be nearly finished, but it's not been let out yet, has it?'

'Mm? Oh. Yes. Last weekend. It'll be in the next report.'

Ellie clutched the phone even harder. 'Who's the tenant?'

'I didn't deal with it myself, but I seem to remember it's a divorcee with four or five children, wants to take in her aged mum as well.'

'There's the usual clause about not subletting?'

'Of course. Is there a problem?'

'I just had a horrid feeling . . . Diana told me Denis was renting a house which answered that description, and I couldn't help wondering if it might be one of ours.'

'Why would he want to rent one of our houses? Oh.'

Ellie sat down with a bump, because she, too, could think of a very good reason why Denis might want to rent one of her houses.

Stewart was silent. She could imagine that he was thinking Diana had already been well provided for. When she'd married Stewart, her father had given them the money to buy a house, which had been sold at a profit when they divorced. Diana had used that money as deposit on a big house down here in London, which she'd divided into flats for sale, retaining the best one for herself. On top of that, when Ellie had inherited her aunt's big place the previous year, she'd made Diana a present of the semi-detached house in which she herself had lived for so many years . . . and which Diana had immediately rented out. Diana had done well out of what she'd been given, but had never been satisfied with what she'd got.

Ellie couldn't defend her daughter's past record, but she could excuse her present conduct to a certain extent. 'She says her present flat is too small for her and Denis together. I may be imagining things, of course, but suppose Denis *is* behind the let. Suppose he's trying to rent the property under a false name. Once he's moved in, he might think I wouldn't dare to turn my own daughter out. He could break the terms of the agreement by subletting, and naturally he wouldn't bother to pay any rent. He'd be well away, living in a six bedroom house in a good part of Ealing, while the Trust would be down the drain for thousands of pounds, when we might have let the house out to someone who really needs it.'

Stewart sounded as worried as Ellie. 'I'm sure you've nothing to worry about, but tomorrow morning I'll check the tenant's references and follow them up. I'll also get on to the bank to see that the cheque the tenant gave us hasn't bounced. It may be perfectly genuine.'

'I know. Put my fears down to old age.'

'I'd go back to the office and start on it now, except that

Maria's yelling that supper's ready and Frank wants me to read him a bedtime story.'

'You do that, Stewart. This can wait.'

She put the phone down and rubbed her forehead. Of course Stewart was right, and there was nothing in it. She'd just got a 'down' on Denis, that was all.

Now to deal with something else; she must get her house guest to talk about her mother, see if their stories tallied.

She was going back into the hall to collect her shopping when there came a knock and a ring on the front door. She hesitated. Would Rose hear it? Nobody was mentioning it, but Rose liked to have the volume on her television turned up rather too loudly nowadays. 'For company,' she said. Or maybe because she was getting a little deaf?

Ellie opened the front door, only to have a large wreath of red roses thrust into her arms. 'Sign here.'

'We haven't ordered—'

'You want them taken to the crematorium? You should have said.' An elderly man, delivering in a florist's van. He checked his clip board. 'It says, "For Mia." This is the right address, isn't it?'

Ellie signed and took the wreath through into the kitchen quarters. Luckily neither Rose nor Mia was there. The wreath had been beautifully made from the new flower shop that had just opened up in the Avenue, but there was no way Ellie was going to let Mia see it. She put the wreath in a black plastic bag and dropped it outside the back door.

First lilies, then roses. It was harassment, wasn't it? Ellie retreated to her study, shut the door, and rang the police station. Needless to say, the DI was not available, but Ellie left a message with the dependable – she hoped – DC Milburn, asking her to collect the wreath and to investigate.

She looked through the pile of correspondence Pat had left for her, checked the latest emails, and tried to concentrate on work, while all she could think about was Mia.

Where was the girl to live? Would she ever be capable of earning a living wage? Would she have to exist on social security payments for the rest of her life? What could she make of her life in future?

That is, if she had a future. That wreath . . . Oh, this was all nonsense, of course. Let the police deal with whoever was making these threats. They did amount to threats, didn't they?

Ellie retrieved the M & S bags from the hall and carried them up the main staircase to the first-floor landing.

Now for something completely different; trying on new clothes was bound to make them both feel better.

Tuesday afternoon

Die, witch! Die! I'm dropping hint after hint, and if they don't work then I'll have to move on to other measures.

You can't be allowed to live. I don't know how you can bear to wake up every morning and look at yourself in the mirror. You're living on borrowed time, and sooner rather than later you're going to pay for it.

You encumber the earth, you snail, you slug.

I shall brush you out of the way, as I would banish a bat or a gnat.

SIX

Tuesday afternoon

Ellie knocked on the door. 'Yoo-hoo! It's only me.'

She opened the door into what had once been Rose's bedroom and which was now supposed to be Mia's. Only, the girl wasn't there.

Ellie could tell Rose was alone downstairs, because she'd turned the volume on the telly up high. So where was the child? Perhaps in the good spare room which was where Ellie had meant her to sleep? It was a beautiful room, overlooking the garden at the back of the house. No Mia.

Ellie began to panic. Had the girl gone out? But where, and with whom? She had no money for bus or taxi. She'd told them she wouldn't leave the house. So where was she?

Ellie's imagination ran riot . . . Someone had mounted a ladder to Mia's room and carried her off . . . A dark shadow lurking behind the huge old painted wardrobe along the corridor might be a man in black, with arm raised to strike. It was getting dark, so Ellie switched on lights. *Dear Lord, keep her safe.*

The door to Thomas's quiet room was ajar. It was a bare little room with just a couple of chairs in it and a Victorian wool picture on the wall: the Good Shepherd carrying a lamb to safety. Thomas went there when he needed to talk to God in peace and quiet. Would Mia want to go there?

Yes. Well, thank the Lord, she was there and safe. She was sitting in Thomas's big chair, her feet not touching the ground. Her eyes were closed and she looked relaxed. Was she asleep? Should Ellie leave her be?

Ellie didn't think she'd made any sound, but Mia started, rubbing her eyelids. 'Sorry. Did you want me for something?' She slid to her feet, trying to smile. 'You don't mind me coming in here, do you? It's a sort of chapel, isn't it? For Thomas?'

'For everyone. I sometimes come up here, too, to be quiet. I brought back some clothes from Marks & Spencers. Would you like to see if anything fits?'

'I've no money. I can't afford to—'

'Then you'll allow me to lend you some till you get your finances sorted out.'

'I suppose that's all right, if you let me keep all the bills. I've been thinking, I really don't want to go down to the bank. Can I borrow a computer and go online, see if my account is still OK? I should have some money left from my grant at university.'

'Come into the spare room where there's a full-length mirror. I ought to have asked you what you wanted, but anything you don't like gets returned, no problem.' She began to take clothes out of the bags and lay them out for Mia to see. 'Try these jeans first. See if they fit.'

Mia shucked off the baggy pants she was wearing and tossed them aside. Her legs looked perfect, showing no sign of the beatings she'd experienced.

'Not a bad fit,' said Ellie. 'I wasn't sure about the pocket detail. What do you think?'

'I like it.' Mia surveyed herself in the mirror. 'You got the length right, too.'

Ellie held out a T-shirt. 'I don't think you can go wrong

with a plain white T-shirt. Blue and white suits you. I must admit I've always liked blue and white, ever since I was a child. What colours did your mother like to dress you in? Pink, I imagine?'

'Mm.' Mia stripped off her much-worn and washed sweat-shirt. Her arms were clear of scars, too. She wore no bra, but had on a cotton vest. A vest? What young person nowadays wore a vest, especially in summer? Ellie did, nowadays, feeling a chill around the kidneys without one. But young people? Gracious!

Mia pulled on the proffered T-shirt and looked herself over, back and front. 'Mummy used to dress me to match her when I was very little – mostly in pink, as you say – but Daddy used to like me in blue. He bought me a lovely blue outfit once, which I wore all the time till I grew out of it.'

Ellie held out another T-shirt. 'Is that one a bit big for you? I can always change it. How did your father die?'

Mia tried the next T-shirt on. As she lifted her arms, Ellie noticed some scars on her breast, above the line of the vest. Mia had lost all self-consciousness by now.

'I like this one even better. What do you think? The blue trim—'

'Is pretty, yes. Would your father have approved?'

'He was lovely. I cried buckets when he . . . but we don't talk about that, do we? What's next?'

'One of those cropped tops. I think young girls wear them over their T-shirts nowadays.' Ellie handed it over. 'What did he do for a living?'

'He illustrated children's books. I loved them. There was a brilliant pop-up of Noah's Ark, and another of Hansel and Gretel.'

'Try this.' Ellie handed over a pretty flower-printed dress, wrap-around style.

Mia held it up, shook her head. 'Not my style. Why do you want to hear about my father?'

'Curiosity, I suppose. I really wanted to know about your mother.' Ellie produced a pale green dress with a low neck-line and tiny buttons down the front.

'I've never worn that colour, but . . . yes, it might suit me.' Mia didn't move to try it on, but sat on the bed with the dress over her knees. 'Ursula brought me my bridesmaid's dress. It's beautiful. I can't bear to look at it. I hung it up in the wardrobe here.'

'You don't want to talk about your father?'

'There was a fire. Mummy had taken me to the cinema, which we never did – except for just that once. It was long past my bedtime. When we got home the house was on fire. He was in the bedroom he used as a study. He'd been drinking, she said. But he didn't usually. Mummy cried buckets, but I didn't. I couldn't believe I'd never see him again. I was twelve years old.'

'Misadventure?'

Mia looked away. Looked down at her hands. Looked back at Ellie. 'That was the verdict, but now I wonder if she killed him. I know she'd hit him several times, but you know how it is when you're a child, you accept what's happening because you don't know any better. She didn't want me bringing friends home from school to make the place untidy. Well, I didn't have any friends. Neither did he. We did as we were told, and so long as there was enough money for her to go out and have a good time, it wasn't a bad life. She was always on at him to do more, but he was a gentle soul, you know . . . always smiling, until . . .

'Yes, I think now that she killed him. Poured drink over him and set a candle to burn down, something to start a blaze while we were out. The people we went to stay with were friends of hers who worked for the Priors. She went to work for him, and then she married him and I was sent away to boarding school till I'd learned some social graces. You understand that I was at an awkward age, no help to her socially, and getting too old to pass off as her younger sister.'

'I understand.' Ellie held up a grey-green sweater, which Mia seemed to like but made no move to take. There were tears on her cheeks.

Ellie said, 'You take after your father in looks?'

'And temperament. If I'd been more like her, perhaps . . . Do you know, she even used to bleach my hair when I was little, to look like her? I was always a sullen, ungrateful little wretch who showed her up in company, though I did try, you know. I really did try to please her.'

'What happened when you failed to please her?'

'She'd slap me and say, "Don't you dare let me down in

front of my friends."' Mia took the sweater off Ellie and held it against herself as she looked in the mirror. 'This is such a pretty colour. Stepdad Prior hardly noticed me at first. She told me to be quiet as a mouse and keep out of his way in the holidays, so I did. It was only after I left boarding school and was at home, going to day school, that he started looking at me in an odd sort of way. Sort of clinical. Only, not. Even more when I started at uni. I suppose I know why now.'

'You met Ursula at university?'

Mia smiled. 'She's really something, isn't she? She transformed my life. I'd never had a real friend before.' Something tawny dropped down from the top of the wardrobe, landing behind Mia and making her scream and jump. 'Oh!'

'It's only Midge, our cat. He disappears for hours and comes back when he feels like it or hasn't been able to scrounge food elsewhere. Watch out for him. He can open any door that has a handle on it, though he can't manage knobs.'

Mia held out her hand to Midge, who hunkered down at a safe distance from her, eyes on her face. 'Why won't he come to me?'

'He divides the human race into three. Some people, like my daughter Diana, hate cats; he won't go anywhere near her. Others – like Thomas – provide him with a nice warm lap to sit on. People like me and Rose are tolerated so long as we feed him as and when he requires it. He's working out which kind you are.'

Ellie set out her remaining purchases: packs of panties, an underslip, a short, creamy nightdress and a caramel-coloured, shower-proof jacket. She removed the flowered wrap-around dress and put it back in one of the bags.

Midge finally made up his mind that Mia was an acceptable addition to his household and rubbed himself across her legs. Mia smiled, stroking him.

Ellie risked one last question. 'Did you love your mother?'

Mia shook her head. 'I knew I was supposed to, but I didn't, not really. One day I realized that she didn't love me, either. We were trying to cross a busy road and she had my arm in her grasp and she pulled me . . . and then slapped me. I hadn't done anything. I tried never to do anything to annoy her.'

'I understand. Would you like to show me the dress Ursula made for you?'

Mia got it out of the wardrobe, lifting layers of tissue paper to reveal it in all its glory. It was a long dress in lavender blue, in a soft uncrushable material. There was a low cut neckline, long tight sleeves, a ruched bodice, a gathered skirt.

It wasn't particularly fashionable.

It was timeless.

'Beautiful,' murmured Ellie.

'She says I must have my hair done and perhaps wear some make-up. She's making a little tiara of silver wire and crystal beads for my hair, and she's ordered a posy of white flowers for me to hold. She showed me the sketches she'd made for her own dress. They're wonderful. I know I'll never be a bride myself. I'll never be a bridesmaid again, either. This is definitely a once and for all event.' She tried to smile. 'When I put the dress on, I looked in the mirror and didn't recognize myself.'

'That's just it. You are stepping out of the past, leaving it behind. You can remake yourself now into whatever you want to be.'

'I'm still "me" inside.'

'Yes, you carry with you everything you've learned about human nature to date, the good and the evil. You can choose to stay in the past, if you wish. Or you can move forward.'

'When I was at my aunt's I didn't really care whether I lived or died. I was worn out. Now I'm daring to hope that I might have a future, but every time I think that, I have to remind myself that it may never happen. Perhaps I'll never even make it to the wedding.' She put the dress back in the wardrobe. 'I wonder who my mother's got in her sights now. She won't want to stick with Daddy Prior.'

Ellie remembered the letter signed 'Adelina Rossi, ex-Prior, née Parham'. 'You think she'll divorce him?'

'Of course. She'll take him for what she can get and then . . . Who will she go after next? Someone even richer, with even more to offer? She's a honeypot, you know. Men flock to her, they really do. She used to be stunningly beautiful. I used to sit on a little stool and watch her dress and make herself up, wishing I could be more like her. But I'm not like her, and I never will be.'

'Be grateful for that,' said Ellie. 'I must tell you she knows you're back in Ealing and says she's just as much an innocent

victim as you. How can she be innocent? She did know you
were locked in your room and abused, didn't she?'

'She never came in to see me. At least, I don't think so.'
Mia rubbed her forehead. 'I was drugged, things are hazy, but
I thought I heard her voice outside my room one day, asking
when they planned to move me on. I think it was her voice.
Yes; because who else could it have been?'

'You told the police that she knew all about it?'

'I don't know. Those weeks in hospital and afterwards . . .
they're a blur. I remember people coming with a camera and
me answering their questions. I know I had to stop once or
twice because I was crying so much. Did they ask me about
her? I suppose they did, but . . . I'm not sure.'

Ah, so that was why Mrs Prior had managed to get bail;
Mia had not been specific enough about her mother's involve-
ment.

Tuesday evening

Ellie was restless. She wanted to talk to someone, but all the
other members of the household were otherwise engaged. Mia
was cooking supper, Rose was dozing in front of the television
set, and Thomas was muttering over some paperwork. So Ellie
went through the hall to potter in the conservatory.

Rose was right; there was not a great deal in flower at the
moment. How about introducing some gerberas? A brilliant
bougainvillea might be fun, or perhaps something striking in
the form of a gardenia, in full flower? Or a collection of strep-
tocarpuses? Or should that be streptocarpi? She must look up
what flowers Ursula had ordered for her bouquet. Perhaps that
would give her some ideas.

She drifted on into the garden, which she rarely dared to
do nowadays. She loved flowers and had worked hard in the
garden of the semi-detached house in which she'd lived most
of her adult life. The garden in this big house was larger and
offered more scope for trying out various planting schemes,
but she never entered it without feeling like a trespasser because
when Rose had gone to look after Miss Quicke she'd taken
over the garden with a vengeance. She hadn't altered the basic
layout – which was basically a large rectangle of lawn
surrounded by herbaceous borders – but she'd filled every

spare inch of ground with the wildest possible combination of flowers. Miss Quicke hadn't known one plant from another, but had indulged Rose in her enthusiasm. It was Miss Quicke who had added the conservatory at the back of the hall, to provide Rose with somewhere to grow tender plants in the winter. Only, since Rose had become rather frail, both garden and conservatory had begun to look a trifle neglected.

The air felt heavy. Maybe there would be a storm later? But as of now the annuals were signalling that they needed help. Ellie wielded the hosepipe for a while; a pleasant occupation in the early evening. The Busy Lizzies in the borders revived, as did the petunias. Even the geraniums perked up, and the edges of the lawn turned from yellow to green as she moved along. Then she got busy with the secateurs, dead-heading roses and herbaceous plants. Mindless tasks. Soothing.

Thomas came out to join her, carrying a large green folder. Shirtsleeves rolled up. Surfacing from work. He got himself as far as the garden seat and collapsed.

'What a week! Light of my life, I fear I've been neglecting you, what with the conference and the tidying up afterwards. You left this on my desk. It's the file for Ursula's wedding, isn't it? When do they start moving furniture around? You won't need to upset my study, will you? I must say, Ursula's been most businesslike. I'm sorry I missed her when she called.'

Now was the time to tell him about Diana's plans. If she could find the words. 'I missed her, too.' She took the file from him and leafed through it. 'She's a good girl, wants to give us as little trouble as possible. She even wanted to pay for moving the furniture and cleaning up afterwards, though of course I'll cover that. And she's asked for all the bills to go to her. Unlike some.'

He didn't pick that hint up. 'I must remember to put the time of the wedding rehearsal in my diary. Six thirty on Friday evening, isn't it? I'd better check. Do we give them a wedding present?'

'She said no. She said our allowing them to hold the reception here was more than sufficient, but I'd like to give her something. Which reminds me that Diana—'

'Ah. Before I forget. There was a phone call from her

just now. She's sending somebody round to see you tomorrow
morning, didn't say what for.'

'She's getting married again.'

He looked at his watch. 'To that man she's been living
with? She'll expect a wedding present, I suppose, even if
Ursula doesn't. I wonder if I've got time to ring someone.'
He got to his feet. 'What sort of wedding present does one
give when someone like Diana remarries? Something disposable for another short-term marriage?' He went off into the
house, humming to himself.

Ellie sat on, holding Ursula's file.

Thomas was no doubt right. She couldn't see Diana's
second marriage lasting any longer than her first. If as long
as that. Stewart had been patient and kind. Denis was neither
patient nor kind. If Ellie were a betting woman . . . but she
was not.

She stepped through the open doors into the conservatory
and was startled to see a small grey figure turn from the plants.
It was only Rose, fingering the earth in a pot to see if it needed
water, but for a moment Ellie could have sworn she'd seen
the ghost of her aunt. It didn't help that Miss Quicke and
Rose were of similar build and that Rose seemed to think her
old employer was still hanging around.

Rose was shaking her head. 'It's very close, isn't it? Do
you think there'll be a thunderstorm? Miss Quicke says not,
but it does feel like it, doesn't it? She also says you must take
extra care when you leave the house.'

There was no point arguing with Rose at such times. It only
upset her. Ellie said, 'I'll take care.'

'Mia's turned me out of my own kitchen, said to tell you
supper will be five minutes. You can see what I mean about
a visit to the Garden Centre, can't you? We're a little short
of glamour in here if this is where they want to take the photographs. They could take them in the garden, but if the weather's
on the turn that'll be a washout.'

Rose produced an envelope. 'I forgot. This came for you,
it was lying on the mat in the hall, but I don't think it's junk
mail. Looks more like a birthday card, and it's got your name
on it.'

It was a Deepest Sympathy card. 'Thinking of you in your
loss.'

Ellie's first idea was to tear it up and thrust it into the garbage. But no. She must report it to the police.

'Rose, did anyone come from the police to collect the black bin bag I left outside?'

'Were they meant to? You should have told me. I saw a bag outside this morning and it had some dead flowers in it. I was going to empty them out on to the rubbish heap at the back of the tool shed, but they were stuck into an Oasis, so I put the whole lot out for collection as it's dustbin day. Was that wrong?'

Ellie was annoyed with herself. Of course she ought to have warned Rose. It wasn't Rose's fault that the flowers had been put in the dustbin. She made herself smile. 'Not to worry. Not important. I'll tell the police about this card in the morning.'

Wednesday morning

'Thomas, before you start work, I have a confession to make.' She'd slept better last night, but was still inclined to get flashbacks to the accident.

'Light of my life . . .!' he protested, throwing keys and money into his pockets. 'Can't it wait? I'm meeting someone up in town for a coffee and a chat. I did warn you, didn't I?'

Thomas had officially retired from running a parish, but editing a national Christian magazine brought him into contact with all and sundry – and very sundry some of them could be, too.

'No, it can't wait,' said Ellie. 'I didn't want it to happen but it has, and I feel thoroughly upset and ashamed of myself that I didn't tell you before, but with Diana sending people round this morning, you're bound to find out.'

'You look five years old. Whatever have you done? Broken the best china teapot?'

'I wish. Diana intends to hold her wedding reception here. This Saturday. She didn't ask me. She told me. The invitations have already gone out.'

'Ah.'

'On the same day as Ursula, but in the afternoon.'

'I think I'll find myself something else to do that afternoon. Out of the house.'

'Wish I could, too. She's having a sit down meal for fifty,

followed by a disco in the evening for a hundred people. She's sending all the bills to me.'

'Perhaps we could go away for the night? No, no. Of course we can't. She's your daughter.'

'I'd love to go away for the night. Perhaps we can. She won't want us around, casting gloom over the proceedings, and I can't find it in me to bless this marriage. Any advice?'

He stroked his beard. 'My love, what can I say, except that every family has a member of the awkward squad, and we just have to cope with them as best we can. Tell me what you want me to do, and I'll do my best to oblige . . . except that marry them in church I will not.'

'Registry office at two. All fixed.'

'Then all I can suggest is that you get out your finest feathers, book yourself a facial and a massage and whatever else it is that women do on these occasions. Get as much enjoyment out of it as you can.'

'I was so looking forward to Ursula's wedding, and now – it's all spoilt.'

'No, it isn't. We will both beam with happiness during Ursula's wedding and be civil at Diana's. Right? Now I must go or I'll be late. I'll put in a spot of prayer about it. Mia's coping all right? She looks a lot better to me. New clothes, ordering Rose out of her kitchen, cooking us a delicious supper.'

'I have to see her mother some time. Mrs Prior's pleading innocence.'

'Mm. Sounds unlikely.' He tore out of the house, checking his watch as he did so.

Ellie dithered. What should she do next? Ah, ring the police to report latest developments. She did so. WDC Milburn was not free to take her call, so Ellie left a message, apologizing for the loss of the wreath but reporting the arrival of the sympathy card.

WEDNESDAY MORNING . . .

He wasn't the sort to bite his nails, but he was beginning to understand why people did. The suspense was killing him. She had all that money, which she didn't need but he did. So why hadn't she died as she ought to have done?

They said an Englishman's home was his castle, but modern houses are not equipped with drawbridges or portcullises to repel boarders. She had to come out some time, and as soon as she did, he'd hear about it. And if she didn't come out, why . . . tradesmen, friends went in. He would find a way to get to her, sooner rather than later.

There were only three days to go.

SEVEN

Wednesday morning

Ellie couldn't make up her mind. She needed to visit Mrs Prior, but she also needed to be around when Diana sent people over to talk about her wedding reception. She rang Diana on her mobile. 'Sorry to interrupt, but what time am I to expect your caterers and so on?'

'The Party Planner will be with you at half past eleven to tell you what needs to be done. Oh, and sometime today I'll be coming over to have a fitting for my wedding dress. Probably this afternoon.'

'I was planning to go out.'

'Don't argue about it, Mother. I can't possibly have the fitting at home or at the office, or Denis will see it.'

'Why not at the dressmaker's?'

'Don't be stupid, Mother. I haven't time to go all the way up to Bond Street. Luckily the fitter lives in Ealing and will come to me on her way home.' The phone went dead. Diana could be very abrupt.

Ellie shrugged, found Mrs Prior's letter and dialled her phone number. 'Ellie Quicke here. You wanted news of Mia?'

'You might as well come over straight away. I have to leave the house this afternoon.' Down went the phone. Oh well.

Ellie rang the cab company, ordered a car, popped into the kitchen to make sure Mia and Rose were content to be on their own for a while – which they were, with their heads together over a recipe – and made for the front door. Only to be stopped by the phone ringing.

It was Stewart. 'Sorry to trouble you, but you know that house we talked about last night? I asked my assistant Elaine about it and don't like what she told me. I've got an appointment out first thing, but then I'm going to pop into the office, see what I can get out of the files, and bring it on to you. If that's convenient.'

'Sure. I'll be out for about an hour. See you after that.'

Her minicab arrived and she got in, glad to be out of the house for a short while. Mia's presence was a bit deadening, wasn't it? Ellie didn't regret asking the girl to stay, though it did look as if she'd be around longer than had been intended. Ellie couldn't see the girl being ready to leave for some time. Where would she go? What would she do?

Dear Lord, over to You on this one. I haven't a clue. By the way, could You make sure the police are checking up on the wreath and the sympathy card?

Now, I must call in on the flower shop, see if they can tell me who sent lilies and roses to Mia.

The cab turned off the road into the winding drive that led to the Prior's house. Ellie had only seen it in the dark before and was impressed. It was long, low and white, twenties-style, immaculately maintained and with an expensive, chauffeur-driven car in front.

Ellie asked her cab driver to wait, as she hoped not to be long. The front door of the house opened and a man in an expensive business suit emerged, turning his head back to speak to someone inside. The chauffeur leaped out of the limousine and held the door open for the suit wearer.

The suit had been handmade in a silk mixture. The man inside it gave Ellie a long stare and, ignoring the open door of his car, waited till she approached.

'You are Mrs Quicke? I trust you bring Adelina some good news about her unfortunate daughter. I would not have left her alone with a stranger, but she insists that you mean her no harm. You understand that she is very fragile? She has been hurt so much already.' So saying, the suit got himself into his car and was driven away.

Fragile was not a word Ellie would have associated with Mrs Prior, who now appeared in the doorway. 'Come in.' An order, not a request.

Ellie obeyed. She followed her hostess through a square

hall into a white drawing room, which gave her time to observe that losing a few stone had wrought a wonderful change in Adelina. Her hair was still blonded, but her hairdresser had achieved a softer, looser cut which was very becoming. Her face and figure had been slimmed down by heaven only knew what rigorous diet, and she was now as glamorous a figure as you could wish to see. Probably down to a size fourteen and aiming for twelve. She was upholstered in black, with a low neckline and short sleeves, and sported a deep tan which might or might not have come out of a bottle.

Ellie could now understand why Mia had described her mother as a beauty and a honeypot; she had a remarkable presence and oozed sex.

'Sit,' ordered Adelina.

Ellie sat. The chair was large and deep. If she sat back in it, her feet wouldn't reach the floor, so she perched on the edge.

'You have some good news for me, I hope? Mia is with you?' Her voice was low and deep. Hadn't Shakespeare said that a low voice was an excellent thing in a woman?

Ellie nodded.

'Does she intend to stay long?' The woman seated herself in a low armchair and crossed a pair of remarkably fine legs.

Ellie tucked her own legs under her chair. 'That's up to her. At least until after Ursula's wedding on Saturday.'

'This whole business –' the woman waved a hand sparkling with rings – 'has been most upsetting. Poor Mia. If only she had called out to let me know that she was being treated so badly. I can't forgive myself for not having realized . . .! But there; my husband that was, and her brothers, assured me that Mia was ill and didn't wish to see anyone. I imagined measles, or chicken pox. It was the most dreadful shock to discover what had really been going on.'

Ellie gave the woman almost full marks for her sorrowful act. What an actress! The businessman who'd just left must have been easy meat.

Adelina produced a tissue and applied it tenderly to the corner of each eye, without in any way disturbing her make-up. She even managed a sniff. 'Perhaps the worst of it is that I've been forbidden to help my daughter in any way, even to phone her or send her a letter. Of course I don't

blame you, for how were you to know? But I even have to
pack up and leave my lovely home, just because she chooses
to stay with you, instead of returning to her mother's arms.
It is very hard.'

Ellie's eyebrows were almost up to her hairline. 'It must
be. And to think of your dear husband and those handsome
boys of his in jail. Devastating. I assume you visit?'

'Well, no. My solicitor advises . . . and they've been moved
around a bit. The boys, I mean. Some trouble. I really don't
wish to know the details. A quarrelsome pair. I knew the eldest
had a short fuse, but really . . . No, I really can't subject myself
to . . . And I've divorced Mr Prior, naturally.'

'Naturally. So where do you plan to go when you leave
here?'

'A kind friend has offered me sanctuary in a flat in the
Barbican. Do you know it? Very fine views, I believe.'

'Close to his office, no doubt.'

The woman stared at Ellie. 'I trust you aren't hinting at
anything untoward? I'm sure my friend would take that badly.'
The mask was off; Adelina shed the 'poor me' role to reveal the
strong personality beneath.

'So, how may I help you?' asked Ellie.

'I need to know how my daughter is doing, what medication she's on, what therapy she's taking.'

Ah. The woman wanted to know this so that she could
build a case against Mia, prove the girl didn't know what
she was doing or saying when she accused her family of
rape? Above all, prove she was unfit to give evidence against
her mother?

'She's taking her time,' said Ellie, 'recovering. I don't think
you'd guess what she's been through, to look at her now.'

This was not what the woman wanted to hear. 'I understood she's very confused about the tragic events of last New
Year's Eve.'

Ellie looked at her watch. Now she'd discovered what the
woman was after, she couldn't get away fast enough. 'She's
fine. I'm afraid I have to go. Another appointment.'

'With her doctor? I would welcome his assessment. Will
you accompany her? Is she using our old family doctor? I
could ring him, make an appointment for her, make sure he
understands the position.'

'Thank you,' said Ellie, getting to her feet with some difficulty since her chair was so low, 'but that won't be necessary.
Let me have your new address in due course, won't you? Is it
going to be necessary to put this house on the market?'

'I've arranged a private sale already. Of course I get this
house as my share of the divorce settlement, plus alimony.'
The woman kept pace with Ellie on her retreat to the front
door. Now she laid a be-ringed hand on Ellie's arm. 'I won't
offend you by saying that I'd make it worth your while to
keep me informed but, as a mother yourself, you must realize
what I'm going through.'

'Undoubtedly,' said Ellie, wondering what would have
happened if Diana and Mia had changed places at birth, and
mentally reeling at the thought. If Diana was hard and greedy
now, what would she have been like if she'd been taught the
ways of the world by this woman? The mind boggled. Perhaps
there was something to be grateful for in the present situation,
after all.

Once out in the drive, Ellie took a deep breath of fresh air.
A white van had arrived in her absence, parked with its motor
idling at the side of the house. A tradesman?

As Ellie walked down the drive the van started up behind
her. She saw her cab driver look up, startled. A glance over
her shoulder made her realize that the van was bearing down
on her on the wrong side of the drive.

She wouldn't have enough time to reach her cab before . . .

She tried to catch the van driver's eye, but the windscreen
was tinted.

She looked around, wildly, giving way to panic.

The van was almost upon her.

There were low growing shrubs on either side of the drive.
She took a dive into them as her cab driver screamed, and the
van thundered past.

She'd landed in a pittosporum. A pretty, curly-leaved pale
green shrub much favoured by flower-arrangers. Reasonably
springy.

She extricated herself with some difficulty, helped up by
her shocked cab driver.

'You all right?'

She tested her arms and legs. 'I've lost a shoe. Can you
find it?'

'Let me see, let me see. Whatever did that man mean, driving like that, he should have his licence taken away.'

'Did you get his number?'

'Why would I bother with his number? He is just a white van man, and they are two a penny in London, no? Ah, here is your shoe, a little bit of earth inside it, but not to worry, it is all right to wear. Can you walk?'

She could. She got back inside the cab and found her mobile phone. Tried the police station. Learned that DI Willis had just started a week's leave. Learned that WDC Milburn was not in that day. Left a message for them to call her. Discovered she was trembling.

'Is all right now?' The cab driver was anxious. 'Not a scratch on my car. Is it good idea to tell the police? I can say nothing, nothing at all. I was almost asleep, I swear it. Then I heard the van and I screamed and you heard me and saw what was happening. I saved your life, no?'

That wasn't how Ellie remembered it, but she wasn't going to argue. She nodded.

'So where to now?' The driver was anxious to get rid of her.

She had intended to do something else this morning. Something to do with flowers. She shook her head. She couldn't remember. She ached all over and needed the loo. 'Take me straight back home, will you? And thank you.'

She got back home in time to see a rolled-up carpet being carried through the hall by a couple of hefty lads. The long mahogany table in the dining room had been moved to stand against the wall, and there was her ex-son-in-law, laying out his laptop and some paperwork. Stewart was a big man who liked space around him, so they usually talked business in that room, rather than in her study at the end of the corridor.

Was the carpet going to be put in her study, or in Thomas's? Thomas didn't want his room disturbed, did he? She rushed along the corridor, to make sure the men knew that. No, it was going in her study. Somehow or other. Oh well.

She returned to the dining room saying, 'Sorry, sorry,' and trying to disentangle herself from the bag she'd been wearing on a strap across her body. She was conscious of a blinking light on the answer phone in the hall, indicating that there was at least one message for her. Tough. It would have to wait.

Rose came across the hall with some coffee for Stewart and nearly dropped the pot when she saw Ellie. 'Now what? Are you all right?'

'I fell in a bush. Quite all right. I'd love some coffee, too. But first I must wash my hands. Stewart, would you give me five minutes?'

A good wash in hot water. A few scratches to add to those she'd collected the other day. Perhaps a new bruise or two. Her shoe didn't look too bad. A bit dusty. She brushed herself down, did some deep-breathing exercises. Found she was still shivering. This would never do. Stewart was a busy man. She mustn't keep him waiting.

She held on to the washbasin, and closed her eyes. *Dear Lord, I don't understand what's going on here. Two vehicles trying to run me down in a week. It's a bit much, don't you think? Although, of course the first one was an accident, and this one was probably some stupid fool wanting to give an older woman a fright.*

On the screen behind her eyes she replayed Monday's tragedy: the sprawling pushchair, the spinning wheels, the toddler, the body of the young mother. *Oh, make it go away! Please!*

She was going to hyperventilate. No, she wasn't. Breathe deeply, that was it. And again.

Please, Lord! Keep me calm so that I can help those who rely on me. There's so much to do at the moment – not that any of it is really important in terms of global warming and wars and suchlike. I know it's trivial stuff really, but, well, if you could keep an eye out for me, I'd be grateful. Amen.

She was smiling as she went into the dining room. 'Sorry to keep you waiting, Stewart.' She found herself a chair and drew it up to the table. 'Sorry about the mess. We're having to clear the decks for the wedding, you know. Oh, I am stupid. Of course you know all about it, don't you? How your Maria can keep the cleaning business going while being a successful wife and mother, I don't know.'

'They tell me women are good at multitasking.' Smiling. 'She has a really good assistant now to help her, worth her

weight, you know? We both owe you so much, we're delighted
to be able to repay, even in such small matters . . .'

'You're a lucky man, Stewart, and I'm lucky to have both
of you as friends.' Before they got maudlin, she moved on to
business. 'You have some news for me about the house in
Castlebar Road?'

He had his laptop out, and not one but two mobile phones
on the table. 'The letting was handled by Elaine. The paperwork says that the prospective tenant is a Mrs Summers,
divorced, large family, wants to take in an aged parent as well,
understands there can't be any subletting. She gave two references and a cheque for the deposit, intending to move in at
the end of this month.

'It sounded all right, but I trust your instinct so I did a spot
of delving. We have Internet banking, so I looked to see if
Mrs Summers' cheque has been cleared yet, and it hasn't. It
may be some glitch or other. It may not. I will enquire further.

'Then I turned up her application form. Mrs Summers'
current address is in Oak Tree Lane. The houses there are
small, two- and three-bed cottage types. You wouldn't normally
expect to find a large family in one of them, but at first I gave
her the benefit of the doubt; perhaps it's because she has a
large family that she needs to move to a bigger place? On the
way over here, I detoured to call at the house she'd given as
her current address. A Sikh family live there now. No Mrs
Summers, and they don't know of any Mrs Summers in Oak
Tree Lane, either.

'She gave two references. The first was a doctor in
Pitshanger Lane. Maria has a friend who attends that surgery,
so I asked her to check that they knew a doctor by that name.
She says not. She says that that particular doctor retired a
couple of months ago and is now living in Cornwall. The
second reference was from a magistrate on the Isleworth
circuit.' He indicated his mobile phones. 'I'm waiting for a
call from him now.'

His phone trilled, and he answered it. 'Yes, I did leave a
message for you. Sorry to trouble you, but we've had your
name given to us by a Mrs Summers . . . Yes, Summers. As
in winter and summer, but with an "s" on the end. She says
that . . . You don't know anyone of that name? Are you sure?
Yes, of course you're . . . Yes, I must be mistaken. I'm so sorry

to have troubled . . . Oh, your husband passed away last year?
I am sorry to hear it. Yes, it must be very disturbing . . . Again,
so sorry.' He put the phone down, shaking his head.

Ellie helped them both to some more coffee. She felt she
needed it, even if Stewart didn't. He was twisting a pencil
around his fingers, rapping the table with it, then jotting down
sums.

Ellie said, 'You will, of course, turn Mrs Summers' application down. A false address, false references, and we've yet
to discover what happened to her cheque. The house goes
back on the market. It's not worth turning the matter over to
the police.'

Stewart shook his head. 'There's no obvious link to Denis.
It might not be him behind it. There are other large properties on the market that he might be trying to rent, but I've
worked it out that he could make a fine living out of that
house if he got it rent-free and sublet rooms. The point is;
does Diana know?'

Ellie sipped coffee, trying to clear her head. 'No, I don't
think she does. If she had gone to you asking to rent one of
our largest houses, alarm bells would have rung all over the
place, wouldn't they? I don't think even she would think I'd
give them a place like that rent-free. Diana told me that it was
Denis who was getting them a large house, and I think she
spoke the truth; this is something Denis has thought up for
himself. You didn't see this Mrs Summers yourself? Can you
ask Elaine what she looks like?'

'Will do. One thing, though. Mrs Summers must be a real
person, and she must be local, because she presented a cheque
in the name of Summers. OK, so it bounced, but she's got
a chequebook with that name on it, right? Banks don't hand
out chequebooks without making sure the person concerned
really does live at the given address. Also, she gave references from people who do or did live nearby. Suppose I
check how many people with the surname of Summers are
in the phone book?'

Someone knocked on the front door and at the same time
rang the bell.

'Heavens!' Ellie jumped to her feet. 'The party people for
Diana's wedding reception! Can you manage without me
for a bit?'

She shot into the hall and opened the front door, to admit a stately figure carrying a silver-topped cane, dressed in a bright pink shirt over grey jeans, and crowned with a mass of carefully curled yellow hair. Gay as a lark.

Behind him came a downtrodden-looking little man carrying folders and clipboards which kept slipping from under his arms, and a woman holding not one, not two, but three mobile phones.

'Behold the hour and the Party Planner arrives! Let me introduce myself. Freddie Balls, the man of the moment. You'll be Mrs Quicke, I assume?' He revealed blindingly white teeth in what was supposed to be a welcoming smile. The smile quickly morphed into a downturned mouth. 'I thought the hall would be bigger than this.'

'Oh,' said Ellie. 'Diana did measure it.'

He frowned. 'If anyone can work miracles, it is I. Show me the reception rooms.' He turned to the room from which she'd come and threw open the door. On seeing evidence of a meeting in progress, he reeled, the back of his hand to his forehead. 'Is this all the space I have to work with?'

Ellie suppressed a giggle. 'Would you like to see the drawing room?' She felt sure he'd call it the 'drawing room' and not the 'sitting room'. She opened the door and let him take in the splendour of the big room, furnished with antiques from many periods.

His eyes were small, bright and quick. 'If all the furniture were removed from both rooms, and my own tables and chairs brought in, then we might, possibly, be able to seat fifty people for supper. But it would not be politic to divide the sheep from the goats, would it? Those in one room would envy those in the other, and whichever way we looked at it, communication would be difficult. No, impossible. I cannot be responsible for such a social disaster. My reputation would not permit it.'

Ellie set her teeth. 'I am not prepared to clear these rooms of furniture; in fact, most of the items are too large and fragile to shift. I suggest you downsize to a buffet supper, served in the dining room, and forget the disco. I am hosting another wedding party earlier in the day for a buffet lunch. We are dismantling the dining room table this afternoon and storing it down the corridor, and bringing in a number of small tables and a lot of chairs. I imagine that arrangement may serve for the evening event as well. After supper they can all go home.'

He swelled like a toad. 'I do not arrange such makeshift affairs. First Slave!' He turned on his luckless girl assistant. 'Get the client on the phone.'

The front door bell pealed again. Rose shot out of the kitchen and opened the door to let in a middle-aged woman with a brutal haircut and a dress sense that her daughter Ursula must often have deplored. Colour and shape all wrong, wrong, wrong.

Ellie stifled a moan.

Mrs Belton was not amused to find the hall full of people. 'Mrs Quicke, I've come to check on the arrangements for my daughter's wedding, and I don't understand—'

'I was asked to be here at eleven,' said the Party Planner, beaming charm down upon her – to no avail.

'Did I ask you to explain yourself?' said the middle-aged woman with the bad haircut. The Party Planner gaped. Mrs Belton had a commanding presence, which was about the only thing her daughter Ursula seemed to have inherited from her.

Mrs Belton turned to Ellie. 'May I ask what is going on here? My daughter told me I had no need to fuss, but naturally a mother wishes to be involved. Of course if I had *my* way, the reception would have been held in a hotel, which would have been far more suitable, but—'

Ellie held up her hands. 'Mrs Belton, Mr . . . er. We need to talk. Mrs Belton, I offered to hold a small reception for your daughter here in this house next Saturday. Unfortunately, my own daughter Diana, without consulting me, appears to have arranged to hold her own wedding reception for a much larger number of people here that very same day. I have no idea how this can be managed.'

She turned to the portly Party Planner. 'You've seen the rooms and understand the . problems. May I leave you to produce a solution while I show Mrs Belton around?'

Wednesday noon

Rat poison worked well on animals, and nowadays she was nothing but an animal that needed to be put down. Put her out of her misery. Right.

He had plenty of rat poison from the shed at the bottom of the garden, which hadn't been cleared out since his father died, yonks ago. He'd looked at some cakes in the bakery but they weren't quite right for it.

Chocolates, now. She'd had a sweet tooth in the old days, hadn't she? What was it she'd liked best? Coconut ice? Suppose he were to cut a bar in half, hollow it out a bit, stuff it with rat poison, and seal it up again with a hot knife? No one could tell the difference. He'd experiment with it tomorrow.

EIGHT

Wednesday noon

Ellie ushered Mrs Belton into the dining room, and shut the door behind them. 'This is where we'll set up the buffet. For thirty people, right?'

Mrs Belton was displeased to find Stewart on the phone and papers littering the table. 'This is an office, not at all suitable for a buffet lunch.'

'As the Queen said about Buckingham Palace, this is a working institution, not a show house,' said Ellie. And to Stewart, 'You'll let me know if you come up with anything?'

Stewart nodded, making notes on a pad as he listened on his phone. Ellie explained to Mrs Belton how the room would be rearranged for Ursula's reception. Returning to the hall, she found the Party Planner deep in converse with his cohorts. Ellie ignored them all to lead Mrs Belton through into the sitting room at the back of the house. She closed that door behind her, as well.

'The drawing room. We thought we would take out the smaller pieces of furniture and put in some extra chairs. Ursula has booked a caterer, who will be responsible for the drinks and the service. She's also arranged matters with the florist, and has a friend who is to take the photographs. All I've done is organize a cleaning agency to help move some of the furniture beforehand and to clear up afterwards.'

'A poor sort of do.'

Restraining herself with some difficulty from hitting Mrs Belton, Ellie opened the French windows on to the garden and led her visitor out that way. 'We might spill over into the garden if the weather is fine.'

'If she'd followed my advice and gone to a hotel, she could have doubled the numbers, and then I might have been able to invite some of my colleagues from work.'

Ellie knew that Ursula had wanted only a small, family wedding, so didn't reply. She opened the doors into the conservatory. 'We thought we could have the photographs in here. We will, of course, lend Ursula a bedroom in which she and her new husband can change into their going away outfits.'

Mrs Belton sniffed. 'It seems a paltry affair to me. Those people out there in the hall . . . Who are they? At my friend's daughter's wedding – a very upmarket affair I might add – there was seating for a hundred and twenty with a proper dance afterwards. They had a top florist, too. Superb arrangements. Now that's the style of things I expected for my daughter.'

'Yes, but she wanted—'

'She's made her own dress, if you please, and insists on having that poor girl Mia for her bridesmaid, though I told her that her cousin would expect to be bridesmaid and would really look the part, but would she listen? No, she wouldn't. She's far too fond of having her own way, and I don't envy her husband if he thinks to rule the roost.'

'I'm sure that—'

'Ursula tells me I need worry about nothing but turning up on the day looking nice, and that is all very well, but how does she know the way these things should be done? Has she made preparation for pieces of wedding cake to be sent out afterwards, for instance? Who is printing the order of service? What provision has been made for taking care of the wedding presents which will no doubt be brought here on the day?'

'No doubt she's thought of those things, too. She knows how hard you work, and she wants to spare you as much trouble as possible.'

Mrs Belton had been born discontented. 'If his people are so keen to pay for the reception, they might at least have done it in style.'

The words, 'You ungrateful cow!' sprang to Ellie's tongue. She swallowed them with difficulty. She even managed a smile as she said, 'Ursula didn't want a big splash. She wanted a small family "do". Something intimate, with only her best friends and family around her.'

She thought of the long talks Thomas had had with the young couple, during which they'd explored all the problems they might face in their new life. They'd told him they wanted to make their commitment to one another before God in church. She thought of Ursula making time to see Mia, in the middle of her important job interviews and the preparations for her wedding. She thought of the love and trust between the couple. If anyone was going to start their new life off the right way, these two would.

Mrs Belton sniffed. 'Well, all I can say is, I've been almost ashamed to send invitations to my dearest friends.'

'Console yourself,' said Ellie, leading the way out, 'she'll make a beautiful bride.'

Surprisingly, the hall was empty of people. Ah, but out of the dining room came the leaves of the long table, hoisted aloft by two burly men, and behind them came not one but two of the cleaning team, carrying another leaf between them. They disappeared down the corridor. Ellie hoped they'd remember not to put anything in Thomas's room, but hadn't time to check.

As Ellie showed Mrs Belton out of the house, Stewart appeared in the dining room doorway. Ellie brushed one hand against the other. 'Phew! Peace at last. Sorry about that, Stewart.'

'They've left me a couple of chairs, but I've been warned they're next to go. The Party Planner is in there –' he indicated the sitting room – 'waiting to speak to you. Before I go, I must tell you there are only two Summers in the Ealing phone book. One lives in that road just above Oak Tree Lane. The other's in one of those flats on Eaton Rise. I rang both. One is a man in his eighties, who thought I was his carer coming to put him to bed – very confused as to the time of day. The other answered the phone to a background of children screaming. I made up a story quickly, asked if she were the Mrs Summers my mother used to know, and she said she didn't think so. She apologized for the noise, said she was looking after some children for the day.'

'A childminder? Denis has four children, but they're surely a bit old for child-minding?'

'Agreed. I underlined the name and address in the phone book. It's too late to do it today, but I'll get on to the bank first thing tomorrow about her cheque and let you know the result. And now, if you don't mind, I promised to take the family out to Kew for a picnic this afternoon.'

Ellie said, 'Go, man, go!' He laughed and escaped.

The door to the sitting room opened, and the Party Planner beckoned her in. 'A word, Mrs Quicke?' He was shaking his head. 'I am considered the very best in the business at solving problems, but here we are faced with a veritable mountain of troubles.

'One: Diana's caterer insists she was asked to provide a sit down meal for fifty, and she either cannot or will not alter the menu at such short notice. So, if you wish to change it, you will be charged the full amount for a set meal with three wines and champagne, plus the amount she must charge per head if you downgrade to a buffet. She requires access at noon on the day of the event, so that her staff can lay the tables with all the appropriate silverware and decorate with balloons, party favours and so on.

'Next: the florist has already designed displays for the hall, the dining room and the drawing room, to complement the bride's bouquet. These displays are somewhat larger than usual, if I may say so, but the client has agreed the designs and the flowers have already been ordered.

'Third: the wine merchant requires refrigerated space for his stock, plus ice. Two hundred bottles to start with. And a secure bar from which to serve drinks throughout the evening.

'Fourth: the photographer wants a good half hour to take his still pictures, while his assistant will of course be making a video of the event from first to last. This means the caterer must set back the hour of the evening meal by that amount of time, which she refuses to do.

'Fifth: the wedding cake must have a suitably strong table to stand on, and we've been told it should be situated in the hall under the biggest of the floral displays. The grandfather clock will have to be moved, of course.

'Lastly: the disco in the evening will require to be set up

at least an hour beforehand to account for the lighting effects, the testing of the equipment, the correct placing of the speakers, and so on.

'Mrs Quicke, even if we strip out all the furniture from the whole of the ground floor—'

Ellie put her hands to her head. 'We can't possibly do that. Some of these antiques are fragile, they were in my husband's family, and the clock repairer said that the grandfather clock in the hall must never be moved.'

'Mrs Quicke, I do most strongly advise you to rethink. The combination of drink and disco in the evening will play havoc with your mahogany and carpets.'

Ellie gasped. What he said was all too true. 'I didn't realize.'

'Sit yourself down,' he said, handing her to a chair and revealing a consideration for her welfare that she found soothing. He patted her hand. Close to, she could see beads of sweat on his forehead, and she realized the bright yellow hair was a wig. Underneath all that gaiety was a kindly, middle-aged and probably balding man.

He said, 'Why have you let out your house for wedding receptions, if you are not prepared for what happens on these occasions? Let me guess; you haven't even bothered to insure against loss and damage?'

'I never thought of it.'

'Then think of it now. I can arrange it for you, if you wish.'

'Thank you, yes. Please do. I am hosting the first reception as a favour to a friend. It is a small, private occasion and I hadn't anticipated any loss or damage. As to the evening event, this was wished upon me by my daughter whose eyes, if I may say so, are bigger than her stomach. Could we not have a small three piece band and not a rowdy disco? Then people could dance in the hall and sit out in the other two rooms.'

'Mrs Quicke, I sympathize, but you are a lady who has let time slip by without realizing it. A disco it has to be, nowadays. It's already been booked. If you take my advice, you'll lock up all the bedrooms except one in which to dump coats, and remove all knick-knackery and valuable china.'

'Oh, dear. What am I to do? This house is not at all suitable for such an event. Could I pay for some hotel rooms somewhere?'

'At this late stage? Everything will have been booked up
months ago. I, who am in the business, can put my hand on
my heart and tell you to think again.'

It was too much. Ellie was a much stronger, more decisive
person than she had been when her first husband died. She had
learned how to cope with tasks which she would have considered beyond her in the old days. She had mastered simple jobs
on her computer, she had made a new circle of friends, learned
how to manage her finances – with help – and given advice to
others which had proved acceptable and sensible. She had
managed, through networking in the community, to right certain
wrongs and bring a few villains to justice. Now and then she
had even been able to counter her daughter's wilder schemes.

But this business of Diana's wedding was all too much.
Tears threatened. She sniffed. She told herself she was over-
tired, that she had been shaken up by everything that had
happened these last few days. She told herself to be strong,
but it was no good. She began to weep, at the same time
apologizing for her weakness.

'Oh, what am I to do? Oh dear, don't take any notice of
me, I'm not usually like this.' She looked round for her handbag
to find a hankie.

He got to his feet, using his cane to help himself up, and
walked over to the open French windows. 'Mrs Quicke, I am
not *the* Party Planner for nothing. I know how to solve your
problem. It will require a great deal of hard work. Time is
not on our side, but I have the solution! We must have a
marquee on your lawn!

'We will set aside the dining room to receive coats. I will
arrange for some racks to be delivered to hang them on in
safety. You will lock the door to this drawing room, and lock
the French windows as well, so that no one can enter this
room. The receiving line will be held in the hall. Bride and
groom, parents, best man, bridesmaids. The photographs will
be taken there, of course.

'From there the guests will proceed through the conservatory into the marquee, which will be laid out with tables for
fifty people. Cables will carry power from the house for
lighting, and for the disco. A side entrance will lead direct to
your kitchens, which will be where the food comes on to the
premises, ready cooked and ready to serve. There is a back

entrance, I assume? The wines can also be kept chilled there. The bar? We will set it up at the back, beside the exit to the kitchens. Are you with me?'

'Yes, indeed. But, a disco in my garden at night? Whatever will the neighbours say?'

'You will send round a note asking for their understanding because this will only be for one night. If you finish before midnight, there should be no complaints.'

Ellie went to stand beside him, taking in the depth and width of the garden. 'The beauty of your scheme is that the two parties can be kept separate and no damage done to the house. How Ursula's mother would have loved a big "do" in a marquee, and how Ursula would have hated it. I'm very fond of that girl, and she deserves a quiet family wedding. A marquee here for Diana – splendid. It solves all our problems. However can I thank you?'

'By paying my fee, which will be enormous.' He smiled and winked to show he was only joking, but she thought he was worth whatever money he chose to ask.

She said, 'I'll gladly pay your fee, and double it if you'd agree to mastermind both weddings. I'll fetch you the file Ursula has given me and, if you agree, you can act as Master of Ceremonies throughout the day.'

'You do me too much honour. Slaves!' His assistants rose from chairs in the background. 'Take notes. We must get on the phone at once. We need a wooden framework to cover the lawn, and on this we need a sufficient number of boards to act as a dance floor. There must be no skimping, no rocking. Then we need a marquee. I will measure up; I don't trust anyone else with such details. Tonight we burn the midnight oil, working out a timetable for everything.'

His eyebrows worked overtime. 'Mrs Quicke, you will have a copy of my schedule tomorrow morning, and so will your daughter. If there is any quibbling, remind her that she who pays the piper, calls the tune.'

Ellie fetched the file for Ursula's wedding and gave it to him. He glanced through it and said, 'Is your phone number here? And your mobile number, please.'

She wrote down the numbers. 'I rarely have my mobile switched on. I only use it for emergencies.'

'This is an emergency. Please leave it switched on at all times.'

Properly cowed, Ellie produced her mobile phone from her handbag and switched it on.

'Slaves! To work. Where is the measuring tape? Not that one, you fool! The larger one.'

Ellie left them to it.

The house lay quietly around her absorbing their busyness; Mr Balls was giving orders to his slaves in the garden. She could hear Thomas's deep tones; he must be on the phone in his study. The cleaners were now in the drawing room, removing all the valuable silver and china, rolling it in bubble wrap and storing it in wooden boxes.

From the kitchen came the sound of Capital Radio, not as loud as Rose usually had it . . . and yes, the chirrup of Rose's voice and Mia's sweeter tones. There came the clash of pans as they cooked something for lunch or supper. The grandfather clock ticked away, oblivious of the recent threat to its safety. Ellie put out her hand to touch its silky wooden surface. 'You shall not be moved.' She laughed at herself.

As she relaxed, various parts of her body began to hurt. She'd been tossed around rather too much for comfort these last few days.

Her mind went into overdrive. Was Mia right in thinking that she'd been the target of that hit and run on Monday? A hit and run which had taken the life of a young woman and left two children motherless? The lilies, the wreath and the sympathy card surely meant that she had been the target?

Ellie let herself down on to a hard wooden chair, thinking that she ought to take some paracetamol for her aches and pains, aware that she was not thinking too clearly. Had she drunk more than her usual quota of coffee that day?

If Mia had been the target of Monday's hit and run, then how to explain the attempt of the white van to run Ellie over today? Well, someone might have thought that Mia would be visiting her mother and had lain in wait for her to emerge from the house. As soon as he saw a female figure, he went for it, not realizing till too late that he'd mistaken his victim. Did that make sense? Sort of.

The house phone trilled at Ellie's elbow, and she jumped. The answer phone light was winking, telling her that a couple of messages had already been recorded for her. She lifted the receiver and recited their phone number.

'Who is that? You rang me earlier. Who are you? What's going on?' A woman's voice, neither young nor old.

'I'm afraid I—'

'This is the number that rang me. Look, no messing. What's this all about?'

Light dawned. 'Are you Mrs Summers? I think my business manager may have contacted you earlier. He was trying to trace someone who's applied to rent a place from our housing trust. Would that be you?'

'It might be.' Cautiously. 'Is there a problem?'

'I'm not sure. Look, could I drop round to see you for a moment?'

'I'm not really at liberty to . . .' Her voice faded away as she shouted at someone to shut up for a moment.

Ellie could hear boys' voices in the background. Several boys. Unbroken voices, but tough. Top of primary school age? Could it possibly be that Denis's children had been farmed out to this woman to look after during the school holidays? Having met Denis's young hooligans, Ellie was of the opinion that, if this were true, the woman deserved a medal for services beyond the call of duty.

Mrs Summers returned to the phone. 'I'll be free this afternoon after two and before half past three. Why don't you drop round then?'

'I'll try.'

Mr Balls and his slaves passed by, smiling and bowing, miming that he'd phone her later. Ellie smiled back. What a relief to have him take over! They let themselves out of the house as Ellie pressed the play button on the answer phone.

Two messages. The first was from Diana saying she might not be able to get over till after four. The second was from WDC Milburn, saying she'd tried to reach Mrs Quicke but was off duty till Monday morning, and please to leave a message if it were anything urgent.

Thomas appeared, smiling and relaxed after a good morning's work. 'You're looking tired, my love. Are the cleaners being a pain? I see the dining room's been cleared already. Remind me to remove my stereo from the sitting room and store it under my desk. Have you had something to eat yet? Will you treat yourself to a nap after lunch?'

She cranked herself upright, thinking that at least his

sanctum appeared to have been respected. So far. 'I have to
go out again. Oh dear, I wish I hadn't said I would.'

'Food up!' Rose, all smiles. 'Today we're having one of
Mia's aunt's favourites: a sausage-meat and onion pie.'

Wednesday afternoon

Ellie didn't mean to fall asleep after lunch. She sat down and
closed her eyes for a moment, only to hear the grandfather
clock in the hall chime three. She jerked upright. 'Oh dear!'
She'd been meaning to go somewhere, but where?

She remembered. Ouch. She was going to be late. Mrs
Summers lived the other side of the Avenue, didn't she? The
address; where was it? Stewart had left it for her, but what
had she done with it? She found it and tucked it in her purse.
Would she have time to walk there? Probably not. She phoned
for a cab, and then dashed into the kitchen to see if there was
anything the cooks wanted her to buy for supper. The kitchen
had been scrubbed clean and tidy, the dishwasher was reaching
its final spin, and there was no sign of Rose, who was probably having a nap, or Mia – who might be anywhere. Well,
probably not out of the house. Ellie left a note to say she'd
be back by four and got to the front door as her cab drew up
outside.

The road in which Mrs Summers lived was not far from
Ellie's old house. She got the cab driver to cruise along, looking
at the numbers on the gates till she located the right one. Was
this it? It was a small semi-D, three bedrooms, in pristine
condition. Oh, except that the gate had recently been torn off
its hinges, and various shrubs in the front garden had been
trampled into the ground.

Ellie envisaged a herd of elephants – no, children –
rampaging through the garden, shattering everything in their
path.

The cab driver said, 'You want that I wait for you, Mrs
Quicke?'

Ellie hesitated. How long was she going to be?

A well-known figure came out of the house, using his
remote to unlock a large car parked nearby. He was
scowling. A well-built man, a man wearing his forty-odd
years with panache, a man from whom you would not buy

a used car. He had a smile as false as National Health teeth, but at the moment it was nowhere to be seen. Denis the Menace. The big car swallowed him up and he drove away, still in a temper.

Ellie shrank back in her seat. She told herself there was no reason to be frightened, but for some reason, she was.

'Summat the matter, missus?'

'Not really. Yes, do wait for me. I won't be long.' She'd better have backup. If this Mrs Summers were in league with Denis, then it was only sensible to keep the driver waiting.

She rang the doorbell. Sweet chimes. She couldn't place the tune, but thought she might recognize it if she heard it again. The house was quiet. The boys had departed. She was, of course, arriving after the time slot she'd been allocated. Perhaps Mrs Summers had also gone out already?

A woman opened the door, saying, 'Forgotten something? Oh.' She stepped out, looking down the road. 'Oh dear. Has he gone already? He was going to give you a lift.' Mrs Summers was a skinny woman in a skimpy dress. She had a mess of taffy-coloured hair and was in her early forties, aiming to look thirty. She wore a lot of heavy gold rings and two gold bracelets, plus hoop earrings.

Ellie said, 'I know you from somewhere, don't I?'

'Probably. I used to work part-time at the 2Ds Estate Agency, and you came in once or twice, didn't you? I'll give him a ring, tell him you've arrived at last. He'll come back for you, I'm sure.'

'Don't bother. I've got a cab waiting for me outside, and I'll catch up with Denis later.'

'Well, come on in, then.' The woman was nervous, perhaps embarrassed, but not showing signs of guilt. 'Like a cuppa? Sorry about the mess.' She led the way into a through lounge and dining room, sparkling with new paint and the very latest wallpaper. The furniture was also expensive and up to date, but showed evidence of a recent rough house . . . or of four bully boys tearing the place apart.

Mrs Summers picked up a cushion and chucked it back on to the sofa. 'I'm looking after my ex-boss's kids in the mornings.'

'You have my sympathy. I've met them.'

The woman laughed, reddening. 'Oh, they're not so bad,

really, and Denis said he'd compensate me for them wrecking my vegetable patch.' She gestured to the French windows at the back, which were open and gave on to a garden which looked as if a tornado had burst through it. Runner-bean sticks had been torn up, with the plants still clinging to them. Marrows had been trampled into mush. Ripe tomatoes had been thrown against a circle chalked on the fence.

Ellie said, 'Oh dear.'

Mrs Summers pulled a face. 'Yes, but Denis and I go back a long way, and he's promised to make good any damage. Since my hubby passed on and the work at the agency dried up, I've been at a loose end. Might as well keep busy, don't you know? In the afternoons I've even been doing some cold calling on the phone. Tiring, that. People are so rude, you can't imagine. I usually pop over to see my sister in Islington on Wednesday afternoons, which was why I asked you to call earlier. Their mother collects the boys at one, takes them for tennis lessons. Then Denis dropped by specially to give you a lift back home.'

'And to pay you?'

'Well, not exactly. At the end of the week, he said.' She had put most of the cushions back on the chairs by now and gestured for Ellie to be seated. She met Ellie's eyes with only a trace of embarrassment. 'It's about the house you called? He said there wouldn't be a problem, but if you've found out already . . .' She shrugged. 'There wasn't any harm in it, was there?'

WEDNESDAY AFTERNOON . . .

Furies take it! Why hadn't the woman turned up when she was supposed to? Once he'd got her in the car, he could have made her see things his way. He hadn't thought she was the sort to be late for an appointment, either. Had she somehow stumbled on the truth about the house let? No, how could she? Could the Summers woman have let him down?

If she had — he ground his teeth — he'd make her pay for it. And for refusing him a loan, too. How dared she!

He must see her again. Tonight, after she got back from wherever . . .

NINE

Wednesday afternoon

Ellie said, 'I wouldn't agree with you about there being no harm done, Mrs Summers.' She picked up an orange which had rolled under her chair, and restored it to a bowl of fruit on the window sill. The flat-screen television was about the only thing in the room that hadn't been upended or thrown around. 'Tell me how you got into this.' The sympathetic tone of voice worked.

'Well, Denis asked me to help him rent a big house locally, somewhere he could have the boys to live with him. He didn't want to go through the agency because he wanted it to be a surprise wedding present for Diana.'

'So she doesn't know anything about it?'

'Not yet, no. He said he'd never got on well with you so you might refuse to let him have a house which you owned, if you knew it was him who wanted it. That's why he asked me to be a go-between. I thought it was all rather a lark, I must say, until I realized how much I'd have to lie for him, and I'm not sure even now . . .' An ingratiating smile, appealing for understanding.

'Start at the beginning. He showed you the particulars of one of the houses belonging to the Trust and asked you to check it out for him?'

'It seemed ideal for him. I dealt with someone called Elaine, whom I didn't know, and told her I'd take it from the end of the month. She explained there was a clause about no subletting, and that was all right because I knew Denis wanted it for him and his children. So I made up a story that I had a big family and wanted to bring my aged parent in as well. Elaine wanted a deposit, and I knew what to do about that because I'd already discussed it with Denis.

'He couldn't pay the deposit or it would have given the game away. I could have paid it for him because my dear hubby – who passed away last year – left me quite well off,

but it was for rather a lot of money and I do have some
common sense so although Denis wanted me to pay it for
him, I didn't want to do that. Denis said he was going to
transfer the money into my account with a bit extra for all
my trouble, but that it would take a couple of days. So then
he suggested that I make out the cheque myself with the wrong
date on it, which is what I did. He said that if the bank spotted
it, then I could give them another cheque with the right date
on it, because by that time his money would be in my account.'

'Of course,' said Ellie, feeling rather faint. 'And has it?'

'Give it time. It'll be all right when it does, won't it? I
mean, it doesn't matter now you know who wants to rent the
house, does it?'

'Or perhaps he hasn't put the money into your bank account
yet. Do you have Internet banking? Would you like to check?'

An indulgent smile. 'Oh, he wouldn't let me down like
that.'

Ellie sighed. Of course he would. 'And the two references?'

'We had such fun, deciding who to name. My doctor's just
retired, and Denis knew of a magistrate who'd died. All I had
to do was remember their names and addresses. It was such
a laugh.' Her voice ran downhill. She shot a sideways look at
Ellie. 'I shouldn't have done it, should I? Have I broken the
law?'

'Possibly, but I don't think anyone's going to prosecute.
You gave Denis your bank-account details, I suppose? So that
he could transfer the down payment into it? Was there much
in your current account?'

'A good bit. Some bonds have just matured, and I'm trying
to decide what to do with them. Do you play the stock market
at all?'

'I'm not clever enough for that. I'm wondering if Denis
has emptied your bank account.'

She laughed, all jagged nerves. 'Don't be silly, he wouldn't
do that!'

'I hope he hasn't. Just check, will you?'

Mrs Summers unlocked an old-fashioned bureau and produced a laptop. 'I have to keep this out of sight, or the boys
will wreck it.'

'Very sensible.'

Click, click. Whirr. Tap tap. 'No, it's all there, what should be there, I mean. Denis's cheque isn't in yet; I have to give it time to clear, you know. Oh, how could you give me such a fright! Denis would never, ever do anything like that. Not to me.'

'I'm glad to hear it.' Ellie got to her feet, checking the time by her watch. The clock on the mantelpiece had been turned on its side and had stopped some time ago. 'If you'll take my advice, you'll make sure he pays you in cash for child-minding, and perhaps you'd better take out some insurance against further damage to your house and garden.'

'Oh, you are funny!' A trill of laughter. 'I'd trust Denis with my life. Won't we just laugh, when I tell him.'

'I hope you're right.'

Mrs Summers bridled. 'As if . . .! I wonder you dare to cast aspersions on his character!'

'I'll let myself out, shall I?'

She returned to the cab and sank on to the seat with a sigh of relief. 'Thank you for waiting. Back home, please.' Something was bugging her. A murmur, a tremor in her handbag? Whatever could it be? Ah, she remembered she'd left her mobile phone on, at the request of Mr Balls. 'Yes? Mrs Quicke speaking?'

The fruity tones of the Party Planner. 'Mrs Quicke, I have done a preliminary recce through the two files and there is one duplication which you might be able to correct. Both brides have chosen the florist in the Avenue. Your friend's daughter Ursula has asked for modest bouquets for herself, her bridesmaid, buttonholes for the ushers and bridegroom, and for two smallish flower arrangements to go on the buffet. She has not asked for anything else. Is that your understanding, as well?'

'That's right. We thought we might go to a garden centre to get some more plants for the conservatory, to make up.'

'Well, your daughter Diana has asked for much the same as Ursula – only larger and more expensive in each case . . . though nothing, of course, for the buffet. Instead, she has asked for six floral arrangements, one for each of the tables for the sit-down meal, plus two more for the top table. She's also ordered an extremely large display for the entrance hall. You get my drift?'

'Combine the two in some way?'

'I understand Diana has ordered a bridal arch. If that is delivered early enough, it would be a nice backdrop for the reception line at the earlier event and for the photographs. Also, the table arrangements for Diana can be used first in the dining room for Ursula's buffet, and dotted around the drawing room to replace the knick-knackery which you have already removed for safety reasons; and may I say what a pleasure it is to deal with a firm who take such good care of your furniture and effects.'

'You mean that if I can get the florist to agree, Ursula will get a really beautiful backdrop for her photographs and more flowers everywhere, which she hasn't had to pay for? I'm impressed, Mr Balls.'

'May I leave it to you to coordinate the flower displays? I must admit that I am having some difficulty tracking down a marquee of a suitable size, though I do have a lead on one which I am hopeful we can lay our hands on. However, it is almost impossible to find enough decking for a wooden floor at such short notice. I have both my slaves working on it as we speak, but I must tell you that it is not going to be easy.'

'Let them eat grass. Sorry, I meant, they can dance on the lawn, can't they?' It would also be less expensive. Millionairess or not, Ellie was shuddering inwardly at the thought of how much this was all going to cost her. Almost all her money had been put into the Trust, leaving her ample for everyday purposes, but not for this. Thomas contributed to the household expenses and made her a generous allowance as well – which he really had no need to do. But he couldn't be asked to help pay for Diana's wedding. And there was Mia to be looked after, as well. Ellie would have to do some hard thinking about where the money was to come from.

Meanwhile, the Party Planner was humming to himself. Finally, he said, 'Yes, I see no reason why we shouldn't do without decking. The lawn would recover in time, and it would simplify matters enormously. It is a pleasure to work with you, Mrs Quicke.'

He shut off his phone, and Ellie redirected the cab driver to the Avenue. She had thought of calling in at the flower shop, but no; it was closed. Wednesday afternoon, of course.

What next? Oh. Hadn't Diana threatened to have a dress fitting that afternoon? No doubt Ellie would be footing the bill for that, too. Diana's dress for her first wedding had been a pretty meringue: a huge skirt, a lace veil, bare shoulders. Fashionable at the time, and costly enough.

What would she choose this time round? Something even more expensive, of course.

It was *much* more expensive.

Ellie was greeted by Rose as she entered the house. Finger to lip, Rose threw her eyes upwards. *'She's* here. In the guest bed room with the fitter. Ordered me to provide her with a drink, but the fitter said, "Not when wearing my dress," so I didn't.

'But you don't need to worry about Mia, because Ursula's here in the kitchen, working out if Mia can bake something special for the party, which is keeping Mia happy I must say, and Ursula's brought her some delightful sandals to wear and an iPod with her favourite music on it and all sorts of things that a girl needs to feel pretty. Isn't she a clever girl?'

Disentangling this, Ellie dropped her voice to a whisper. 'I need a word with Ursula—'

There came a summons from above. 'Mother, are you there? What kept you? I need you here, now. I keep telling the woman that I need the dress to be tighter, and she *will* argue with me, which is quite ridiculous!'

Ellie exchanged despairing glances with Rose and obediently mounted the stairs.

No, it was not a meringue. Perish the thought. It was a shimmering sheath of oyster-coloured silk, hand embroidered with crystal beads around a shockingly low cleavage – shocking because Diana didn't really have much to boast about in that direction. The rest of the dress was spangled with beads of the same oyster colour. There were thin straps over the shoulders which left Diana's arms bare, and there was a train. Of course. The dress followed the lines of her body without clinging to it, so that when she moved, the beading caught the light. It would be, as Ellie understood at a glance, hideously expensive.

'Tighter!' demanded Diana. 'Mother, take a seat over there. Don't come between me and the mirror.' She did a quarter turn so that Ellie could see her back view. The dress was cut away down past her waist and held in place only by a couple of straps, anchored by buckles of what looked like gold.

'The dress must flow!' insisted the fitter. 'It is designed to suggest, rather than flaunt!'

'Tighter!' insisted Diana, who had always known what she wanted, and usually got it. 'Mother, you agree? Since you're paying for it, you might as well have some say.'

'Any tighter and we'll be able to count your ribs, dear,' said Ellie, unaccustomedly tart. 'How much is all this going to cost me, may I ask? I've been down this road once already, remember, and frankly I can't afford to be so extravagant this time.'

'Oh, three choruses of hearts and flowers! Everyone knows you're rolling in money.'

'The Trust has plenty, true. But I can't see myself asking them to pay for your wedding. I personally have a reasonable but not lavish income, which does not allow for expenditure at this level.'

'Get Thomas to stump up, then. He only married you for your money, didn't he?'

Ellie drew in her breath sharply. How could Diana even think that! Ellie controlled herself, just. 'I think you'd better pay for your dress yourself.'

The fitter said, 'No dosh, no dress.'

Diana reassured her. 'It's perfectly all right. Mother's bark is worse than her bite.'

Ellie said, 'Not in this case.'

'Nonsense! How could I possibly afford it? I skimp every day as it is—'

'Only because you're supporting Denis as well. Did you really have to take him into your flat when his wife threw him out?'

'What else could I do? Besides, he's getting us a wonderful big house to live in.'

'Have you seen it yet?'

'Not yet.' She wasn't worried about it, either. 'It's good you reminded me about the flat. I'm putting that on the market, of course. Difficult to sell, in this recession. Can you get the Trust to buy it off me?'

'No, I can't. You keep it. You may need it.'

Diana pulled a face. 'Such a poky little place. Denis and I are falling over one another all the time, which is another reason why I had to have the fitting here, where there's more room. I shall stay here the night before the wedding, of course, so you can tell little orphan Annie to find herself another cushy berth.'

'I'll do nothing of the kind. If you must stay here, you can have little Frank's room, and by the way, I hear he's most unhappy about the wedding. Don't you think it would be a good idea for you to spend some time with him, explain things, listen to his fears?'

'I'll get Denis to talk to him.'

'That, Diana, is not a good idea. Frank is frightened of Denis.'

'What nonsense.'

'Diana, I insist.'

A shrug. 'Oh, very well.'

'Good. And by the way, your Party Planner says you'll have to have a marquee in the garden to house your reception, as our rooms are not suitable for such a large party. More expense.'

Another shrug. 'You can afford it.'

'Keep still, please!' said the fitter.

Diana smoothed the dress down over her hips. 'That reminds me. We're only inviting a couple of witnesses to the registry office, so Denis and I plan to exchange our vows here, before the sit-down meal. I thought Thomas might pop on a surplice and preside.'

'Now that he will not do! No, Diana; you go too far.'

'Ask him nicely. I'm sure he'll do it to please you.'

'I think not.' Ellie walked out of the room, telling herself to keep calm, that it wasn't the end of the world, that worse things happen at sea and so on. She needed to go to some place quiet to recover.

Soft orchestral music was coming from somewhere. Ellie looked over the banister down to the hall below. Thomas's much-loved stereo had been turned on in the sitting room, and a figure in a peach-coloured dress was dancing to its beat, twisting and twirling, barefooted on the parquet floor. She held a pair of high heeled sandals in one hand; she was graceful, almost ethereal, her eyes unfocused, absorbed by the music and the movement. Her hair had been cut shorter and curled closely around her head, and she was wearing a discreet amount of make-up.

Mia was happy.

A sudden movement startled the girl, and she stopped dancing to look at someone who'd come along the passage past the dining room. The music continued to play so Ellie couldn't hear what was being said, but she thought she detected Thomas's deep tones. The girl nodded once, twice. Then, moving like a sleepwalker, she passed out of sight, leaving the music to play on.

Ellie made her way downstairs, turned off the stereo and went into the kitchen to make herself a cup of tea. There was a big tote bag on the table, and from it spilled the things which Ursula had brought for Mia. Another pair of sandals, some make-up, a pretty jacket. How thoughtful of Ursula, and also, how good of her, as she must be living on the remains of her student grant, and perhaps was even in debt. Most students ended up in debt, didn't they?

Rose had retired to her own room for her afternoon nap.

Ellie made herself a cuppa, sat down with it in her hands, put both her elbows on the table, and gave way to tears. She cried softly, because she didn't want to disturb Rose. She told herself that she had no real cause for tears, that she was just annoyed by the way Diana was behaving, not even asking her mother to be a witness at her wedding, and then there was the horrific expense, and she didn't know how she was going to manage it, but manage it she must. Then Thomas had lured Mia into his room and the girl had gone without a hint of alarm, when she'd been shying like a frightened horse if any other man came near her, which meant . . . which meant that Thomas was much better at dealing with Mia than Ellie.

Which meant that she was being self-indulgent, self-pitying, sorry for herself, call it what you like. Crying like a baby for no good reason. She ought to be thanking God for all His goodness to her, instead of crying.

Well, she did thank God, and on the whole she trusted that He'd see her through her present set of crises. She knew she ought to be able to dump the whole lot of problems in His lap in a sort of 'over to you' fashion. If He couldn't solve them, nobody could.

Which made her laugh. For in the cosmic scale of things, her problems were really nothing, were they? There were wars

and floods and famine happening all over the planet, and here
was she, wailing away over trivialities.

*Dear Lord. Sorry. Stupid of me. I do trust You, really I do.
Please give me the right words to say, show me how to deal
with my troublesome daughter, the money problem, some way
to help Mia.*

*Oh, sorry again. I ought to have started with praising You,
and I gave You a shopping list instead. Well, I do praise
You for the wonderful world you have made, for the beauty
of the skies and the clouds, the wonder of the myriad flowers,
the loving kindness of so many people. I thank You for keeping
me alive, and I do hope You mean to keep on looking after
me, because it seems as if I've got rather a lot of work on
hand. Amen.*

She mopped herself up, looked at the clock, peeped into
the oven to discover that her largest casserole was at work
there . . . beef stew, by the scent of it? Mm. Wonderful. With
dumplings, perhaps? All right, perhaps not the perfect
summer's evening meal, but the sky had clouded over and it
looked like rain, so why not? The vegetables had been prepared
and were cooking already: carrots, peas and potatoes.

Ellie had nothing to do but fret.

In came Mia, exclaiming that they'd been looking for Ellie
everywhere, but Ursula had had to go eventually, and wasn't
it a shame that they'd missed one another? And here came
Rose, fresh from her nap, rosy-faced and relaxed, saying that
supper was ready. It was easier to push problems away and
eat, than to continue to fret about them.

Thursday morning

After breakfast Ellie called a meeting to brief everyone on
what was going to happen next. 'It's going to be chaos for a
few days, but if we keep our heads we'll get through it all
right.'

Thomas rubbed his beard. 'I have to stick around today.
I'm expecting some phone calls. Is there anything I can do
to help?'

'I really don't know. Mr Balls, the Party Planner, should
be able to sort out any tangles, but there may be times when
he'll need to ask about power points and all that. I'm afraid

there's going to be all sorts of people coming into the house, putting up the marquee, and running cables around. Then there's the cleaning team and the men bringing in the tables and chairs . . .'

'Bacon butties and tea needed all day,' said Rose. 'Can do. Right, Mia?'

'If I'm going to make canapés for Ursula's buffet, I'm going to need one or two things from the shops. Mrs Quicke . . .?'

'Give me a list.'

There was a rumble of lorries turning into the driveway, and everyone jumped to attention. First the Party Planner rang the front doorbell and came in, trailing his two slaves. The marquee arrived, with the men to assemble it. Mr Balls was pleased with himself, for not only had he managed to find a marquee, but also some flooring upon which the partygoers could dance in the evening. More men arrived, propping the front door open to carry poles and tent and then boards through the hall and out into the garden through the conservatory.

By the time the dishwasher had been set going, another two lorries appeared: electric cabling, and lighting, plus the cleaning team to polish floors. Then came a further lorry bringing tables and chairs for the buffet. The cleaners and the furniture people argued about who had the first crack at the dining room.

Ellie was distracted, didn't know what to say or do. Her usual ability to make decisions seemed to have deserted her. She was aware of it, and despised herself accordingly.

Mr Balls cut the Gordian knot. 'The cleaners can do the reception rooms first. The furniture can be unloaded into the hall, leaving a passage through to the conservatory for everyone else.' And so it was done. The tables and chairs for the buffet were terribly in the way, but what else could they do? Thomas slid through them somehow, carrying his beloved stereo to safety in his study. And slammed the door behind himself.

Ellie said, 'Mind the grandfather clock,' though no one seemed to be listening. There was something the matter with the clock. Somebody's cap or hat had landed up there. Ah. It was Midge the cat, surveying everything from a safe distance.

How on earth had he got up there? Was it worth while trying to get him down?

Ellie decided it wasn't and made her way down to her own

study – where she was met with a mountain of furniture which
had been removed from the reception rooms. Edging her way
round a rolled-up carpet and the leaves of the dining table,
she managed to make it to her desk. Pat was already there,
huffing and shaking her head. Pat was not amused.

'Dear Pat, I know, I know. But can you cope, somehow?
It's only for a couple of days. Oh, and could you run off some
notes to be delivered to the neighbours? Something to the
effect that Mrs Quicke's daughter is getting married on
Saturday and the music at the party afterwards may be rather
noisy. We apologize for any inconvenience. You'll know what
to say better than me.'

Pat raised her eyebrows and booted up her computer in
silence.

Oh. We're going to get the silent treatment, are we? Right.

Ellie decided to get out of the house and make herself
useful. She'd get the bits and pieces which Mia needed for
her cooking first – better take an insulated bag to transport
them in – and then visit the new flower shop to discuss the
flower arrangements for the two weddings, and at the same
time find out what they had to say about delivering scary
bouquets to Mia.

Ellie hadn't been inside 'Stems' before. It was an upmarket
flower shop which had no truck with mixed-bunches-for-a-
couple-of-quid. The proprietor was a young woman with long
flowing hair, who was making up a professional-looking posy
of pink and white roses as Ellie arrived.

'Can you spare a minute? I'm Mrs Quicke. I believe you're
supplying flower arrangements for the two wedding receptions at my house on Saturday?'

The proprietor was happy to bring up the details on her
computer, and she produced a scrap book showing Ellie photographs of work she'd done in the past for similar occasions.

'We understand that the first wedding on Saturday – the
Belton one – is to be done on a shoestring. I will arrange the
flowers in church on Friday; one large floral arrangement by
the altar, and one by the font. The bride's bouquet and buttonholes for her family and the ushers will be delivered to Mrs
Belton's address the same day, but the bridesmaid's bouquet
is to be delivered to you. Then, moving on to the buffet on

Saturday morning, I am to prepare some of my glass candelabra wreathed in ivy, plus six small table decorations. The
colour scheme throughout to be white and lilac.'

Ursula had been as good as her word and had directed the
invoice for her event to be sent to herself. Ellie nodded.

'Now, as to the second wedding, the colour scheme is to
be all gold and white. We'll use some more glass candelabra
for the top table and for three of the smaller tables. They, too,
will be wreathed with ivy, but will have white and gold flowers
entwined in them as well. The candles will be gold, of course,
to match the other decorations. On three of the tables, by
contrast, we'll have low arrangements of white hydrangeas,
with gold ribbon puffing up between each one. There is also
to be a bridal arch, which is going to be delivered today
because it comes straight from the nurseries. The bride's
bouquet and buttonholes for the men to be delivered to you
on Saturday morning, together with the invoice.'

'Agreed,' said Ellie, feeling rather faint and reaching for a
chair. 'Now, do you think you could include some puffs of
gold ribbon in the Belton bouquets? Let me tell you why.'

As Ellie explained that there needed to be some rational-
ization, the proprietor frowned, obviously thinking that she
was going to lose money on the deal.

So Ellie said, 'I see you have a good selection of unusual
flowering plants for sale, and I shall need some more plants
to brighten up what we have growing in our conservatory at
the moment. I had intended to make a trip to the Garden
Centre, but if we can come to some arrangement about hiring
or buying some from you for the day . . .?'

Suggestions as to the appropriate plants were made and
accepted. When the proprietor was nicely softened up, Ellie
said, 'By the way; I've recently received a sheaf of lilies and
a wreath of red roses from your shop. Can you remember
anything about the person who ordered them? I assume it was
the same person on both occasions, though of course I might
be wrong.'

'It was a young man, who stuttered a bit. I thought perhaps
it was the first time he'd ordered flowers for anyone.'

This was odd. Who on earth could he be? 'There are three
women currently living at my house, and we weren't sure . . .
Did he say who they were for?'

'He wrote out a card, didn't he? Didn't he address it properly? We shall have to look out for that, make sure it doesn't happen again. My father does my deliveries. He's retired and likes to have something to do. Did he get the wrong address?'

'No, I don't think he did, but it's a bit of a mystery, all the same. Did the man pay by cheque or card?'

'Cash. He was . . . I don't know . . . a little strange. He kept muttering something. A poem, I thought.'

'How was he dressed?'

A shrug. 'Like any other young man, casual clothes, a bit scruffy. Unruly hair, dark, a bit too long. Honestly, I didn't think I'd ever be asked to—'

'No, of course not. You've been a great help. May I leave you my phone number? If he ever comes in again, may I ask you to let me know?'

Thursday morning

He didn't think he'd made a bad job of it. The coconut ice looked as if it had never been touched by human hand, hiding its secret well. He'd had to discard the original wrapping paper which had got torn when he'd taken it off. His mother had had some cling film in the kitchen. He experimented with that. It was difficult to handle, tending to stick to itself at just the wrong moment.

Finally he achieved a bar that looked reasonably well wrapped. He would have put a bow on it, but hadn't the knack of tying ribbons. That sort of thing was for women with nothing more important to do. Somehow the resultant pink block didn't look impressive enough to please. It lacked presence.

Perhaps if he put it in one of his mother's glass dishes and wrapped it round with cling film again it would look more like a present? He told himself he was doing the right thing. Vermin needed to be exterminated, didn't they? And she was nothing but.

TEN

Ellie bought the things Mia needed for her cookery and walked home, thinking hard.

Who was the young man who'd sent flowers to Mia? One of the students who'd once formed part of the Priors' social circle? According to Ursula, Mia hadn't had a boyfriend before she was abused. At that time Ursula herself had been engaged to a lad called Dan Collins but, after he'd sided with the Priors and refused to help her look for Mia, she'd sent back his ring and refused to have anything more to do with him. And now was going to marry someone else.

Could Dan still be carrying a torch for Ursula? Mm, yes. Would Dan know anything about these threats to Mia? Ellie would ask him. Later.

Her house was in chaos. Mr Balls was conducting an orchestra of shakers and movers, of sparks and chippies, all working at the top of their voices. Midge had disappeared from the top of the grandfather clock, for which Praise Be.

Ellie took evasive action as two workmen in dirty overalls carried some piping through the hall and followed them to discover the Party Planner, standing in the conservatory. 'Mr Balls, how is it going?'

'Very well, dear lady.' He put his arm round her and gave her a hug. She stiffened. He wasn't gay at all! Oh.

Smiling nervously, she disengaged herself and circumvented a stack of chairs to disappear into the kitchen . . . to find that Rose had turned up the radio to deafening level to drown out the noise in the garden. Mia was hooked into her own MP3 player, cutting rounds out of dough and laying them on baking sheets to cook.

'Now don't you be looking out of the window,' said Rose, taking the insulated bag of goodies off Ellie. 'We're only serving tea and coffee on the half hour in future, and we've run completely out of biscuits, so Mia is making some more as we speak.'

'Midge?'

'Hiding under my bed. He thought the visitors would like him hanging around, until he came across one who didn't. He's all right, though. It's only his pride that's hurt, bless him.'

'Thomas?'

'He says if he's wanted, I'm to knock three times on his door and he'll let me in. Pat came in just now to say she can't stand the noise and is going to deliver some notes to the neighbours, whatever that may mean.'

'Oh, good. In that case, I'll just make one phone call and get out of here.' She evaded Mr Balls in the hall, sending him a smile but not allowing him time to talk to her . . . and reached the sanctuary of her office in safety. Her chair had been smothered by a huge pile of fabric – were those the dining room curtains? Don't ask.

She dialled the police station and asked for DC Milburn. Out. Away. Gone for a walk. Unavailable, anyway.

However, the policewoman had left a message for her. 'All suspects still in jail, duly accounted for. Mrs Prior has been informed that she must leave this part of Ealing, and has now removed herself.' End of message.

Fine. As if Ellie didn't know that already. Oh well.

Someone in the garden outside dropped a clanger. More voices were raised. Ellie put her hands over her ears and hoped the lawn would survive. She told herself she was only in the way at home and might as well make herself useful elsewhere.

So she looked up Dan Collins' address and went to see what Ursula's ex-fiancé might have to say about Mia's current problems.

The house looked much as Ellie remembered it: a large Edwardian structure, running downhill. But this time – surprise! – a middle-aged to elderly man was sweeping the front path. His hair was scanty, but had been ginger at one time. He wore a tatty old shirt and even tattier trousers. The sort of garb a householder might wear when doing odd jobs around the house or when working on an allotment.

Ellie smiled at him as she passed.

He said, 'Afternoon,' and smiled back.

'Mrs Collins at home?'

'Dottie? Yes, she's in the back somewhere.'

So he called Mrs Collins by her first name? Interesting. Ellie rang the doorbell, peering into the front window to see if she could spot Dan, whose room that used to be, but the curtains were drawn across.

Mrs Collins – 'Dottie' – opened the front door. She was no spring chicken, but wasn't giving up without a struggle. She'd had a perm recently, and her fair hair had been tinted pink to match a strapless cotton top and tightly-fitting skirt. When she saw who was standing there, Mrs Collins did not look pleased. 'What do you want? More trouble for Dan?'

'May I come in for a moment? Something's come up, and I wondered if Daniel might be able to cast light on it.'

The odd job man appeared at Ellie's elbow. 'Is there a problem, Dottie?'

'It's all right, Ginge.' Short for 'Ginger'? 'This lady's an old friend, sort of. Come in, Mrs Quicke. Mind the paint pot. Ginge is helping me out with a spot of this and that.' And probably with 'how's your father', too. Mrs Collins had the sleek look of someone who'd acquired a new partner late in life.

Ellie followed Mrs Collins down the corridor and into the sun lounge at the back. It was reasonably tidy now, with his and hers La-Z-Boy chairs facing the television, and the big table pushed well back. It seemed that Ginge was making himself very much at home.

'I had a spot of trouble letting my rooms after what happened in the spring, what with my boys being mixed up in it because they were friends of the Priors. It's turned out quite well in the end, but I had to alter my rule about only having students.'

'Ginge is one of your lodgers now?'

'Cuppa? A bit early for anything else, or is it?'

'Cuppa would do me fine. Is Dan around?'

'Got a new girlfriend, down the club. Nobody wanted anything to do with a building that Mr Prior had named after himself, so they changed the name to The Place from Prior Place, and the flats are selling, slowly, but moving at long last. As for the Health Club, they made Dan manager and call it Collins Health Club. He's down there from first thing till last. Making it pay, too. That's what sticking by your friends can do for you.'

'Even if they're in prison?'

A shrug. 'The building was up and empty, so why not get it moving, employ your friends, make some money?'

'It's what Dan always wanted, isn't it? A job in the Health Club?'

'Being made manager, though, that was tricky at first. He's not the brightest at the books, but then the Priors brought in this blonde. She's a sharp blade, I must say, and they work together a treat. He moved into her place, one of those new flats up by the Green, last month. I miss him in a way, of course, but now Ginge's got his room, so it's an ill wind, isn't it?'

'I'm glad to hear everything's worked out well for him,' said Ellie. 'I know he was upset when Ursula broke off their engagement but we were agreed, weren't we, that it was a case of their having got together too young for it to last?'

That wasn't quite what they'd agreed, but it was the right thing to say. Mrs Collins, unasked, brought a plastic box of wine from the kitchen and poured out a couple of glasses. 'That Ursula, she's a nice girl. She came round a couple of weeks ago to tell me she was getting married to someone else. Asked if I thought Dan would like an invitation to the wedding. I said he was well over her now, so she agreed to let bygones be bygones. Besides which, his new partner wouldn't have like it, and she's a terror when roused, she is.'

It sounded as if Dan had exchanged one strong-minded female for another. Ellie sipped wine and said, 'Mm,' which was all that was required of her.

Mrs Collins took several sips and wiped the back of her hand across her mouth. 'I'd have been glad to give Ursula a wedding present, but things being as they are, and after talking it over with Ginge, I decided it wouldn't be the right thing to do. But I wish her luck, with all my heart.'

'She's a good girl.'

'Not right for Dan, though. This new partner of his . . . Well –' a frown – 'she's older than him. Been around the block a couple of times, I wouldn't wonder. Not exactly love's young dream.'

'I wonder where the Priors found her?'

'Some smart lawyer-type produced her. Everything goes through him, nowadays.'

Ellie set down her glass. 'Which reminds me; I know Dan never looked at anyone but Ursula in the old days, but I wondered if he could think of someone who was interested in Mia Prior before . . . before everything went wrong. Someone who might now wish her harm?'

'That poor girl. Rotten what they did to her. That is, if it's true, and we can't say it was or it wasn't yet, can we? Not till it comes to trial. Though why they have to lock them all up just on her say so, I really don't know, when it might have been only a spot of rough housing going too far, if you see what I mean. Too much slap and tickle, and her taking it the wrong way.'

Ellie suppressed a shudder. She'd seen Mia's injuries, and they'd gone well beyond 'slap and tickle'. 'Mia's recovering slowly, but someone keeps sending her messages saying they want her dead, which is giving her the heebie-jeebies.'

'Serve her right, if she made it all up. Getting that fine family, that never harmed nobody, into trouble. Anyway, they can't do nothing from where they are at present, can they?'

Ellie set her teeth. 'Her injuries were very real, Mrs Collins, and it is possible that some friend of theirs might be trying to intimidate the girl, trying to frighten her enough to withdraw her testimony. I wanted to ask Dan if he can think of anyone who might be lurking in the background, someone willing to help the Priors out.'

Mrs Collins poured herself another drink. 'All the Prior's fine friends disappeared overnight, didn't they? That's why they had to change the name of the building and of the Health Club. Mud sticks.'

'Dan stuck to them.'

'You're not suggesting that he would—'

'No, I don't think he would.'

'No, he wouldn't.'

Were they both trying to convince themselves? No, Ellie thought not. Dan simply wasn't the type to think up such things. What about his new partner, though? Mm, if she were employed by the Priors, she might be acting for them in more than one capacity. Except that the girl in the flower shop had

specified an untidy young man, not a woman. On another
tack . . .

'Did you ever meet one of Mia's boyfriends in the old
days?'

'She didn't really have one. She liked the boy who went
over the balcony and got himself killed, but he only had eyes
for Ursula, who didn't encourage him, I'll say that for her.
She didn't look at anyone but Dan in those days.'

'Dan might know of someone? It's really important,
Mrs Collins. We think someone from Mia's past is still
around and anxious to see her dead. I realize it's a long
shot, but would it be possible for me to speak to Dan about
it some time?'

'I suppose.' Another shrug. Mrs Collins emptied her glass.
'He usually drops in with his dirty washing after the
weekend. Says the new girl won't do it, so I have to. They
never really grow up, do they? I'll ask him to phone you,
shall I?' She got to her feet. 'Well, I must be getting on.
Ginge likes a spot of tea, something with chips. I tell him
he'll have me putting on weight, and he says he likes to
have something to get his hands on, if you see what I mean.'
She giggled.

'Of course. And thanks.'

So that was that. Ellie called in at the bank, and she was on
her way home when she clapped her hand to her forehead.

You silly fool. Missing what's under your nose. Ursula
would know who might be targeting Mia. She's intelligent
and observant; she'll be able to give us some idea who to look
for. She's been in and out of the house all the time, seeing to
Mia, and I've never once thought of telling her what's been
going on.

All right, all right, I know she's busy with the preparations
for the wedding . . . though come to think of it, I ought to be
putting her in the picture on what's going to happen with the
Party Planner.

I don't want to alarm Mia unduly. I wonder if I can ring
Ursula on her mobile, arrange to meet her somewhere outside
the house?

Ellie picked up her pace, looking at her watch. She'd reached
the Green around the church by now. Should she take time

to run over to the police station to see if DI Willis was back from leave? And what – if anything – DC Milburn might be doing? Had the police picked up the Sympathy Card and wreath? No, the wreath had been put out with the rubbish, hadn't it?

Ellie told herself she shouldn't waste valuable police time by reminding them of things which they already had in hand. No, of course not. And that was nothing to do with the fact that DI Willis intimidated her. She sat down on one of the benches by the church and got out her mobile. She rather thought Ursula's number was somewhere in its interior workings, but how did you discover . . .? Ah, got it. She was pleased with herself. Now, how did you make the call? Ah, splendid. Except that her call went to voicemail, and Ellie hadn't worked out precisely what she wanted to say.

'Ursula? This is Ellie Quicke here. I need to talk to you about the wedding, and about Mia. Perhaps away from the house? I know you must be terribly busy, but . . . could you ring me?'

She switched the phone off. Then remembered that Mr Balls wanted her to leave it on all the time . . . and of course Ursula might get back to her soon. She switched it back on. She sat back, trying to relax. The sun was warm on her face, the grass at her feet well mown, the stonework of the Victorian church glowing. Someone's phone trilled. With a start, Ellie realized it was hers. 'Hello?'

'Mrs Quicke? Ursula here. You wanted an update? Mia's fine, I think. Coming along nicely. Thomas has let her use his computer to check her bank account, and it seems the Priors haven't stopped her allowance and it's been piling up all these months. She didn't want to take it at first, but we talked some sense into her, and she realizes she'll have to use it to pay some bills – you've been getting some bits and pieces for her, haven't you? – and keep her afloat till she decides what she wants to do with herself.' Ursula's voice was like herself, alto-sax. Wasting no words.

'That's fine,' said Ellie, 'but look, I need to talk to you away from the house. I'm near the Avenue. Could you spare time to join me for a bite to eat? My treat.'

'My father and his family fly in from America today, and I have to meet them at Heathrow Airport this afternoon, but I know you wouldn't ask if it weren't important. It is important, isn't it?'

'Yes. The Sunflower Café, half an hour?'

Thursday noon

Ursula was on time. A tall, strongly-built girl with long honey-coloured hair. Not an anorexic Hollywood chicklet, but someone who could blaze into beauty. Today she wore a skimpy flowered top over a black vest and leggings, and looked a million dollars. Her hair had been tied back in a knot, but it wasn't coming apart like most people's did. In fact, Ellie concluded that part of Ursula's 'presence' was her grooming. She looked older than she really was. She looked as if she could hold her own in any company.

She was wearing a stunning engagement ring, a sapphire surrounded by diamonds. Probably old. Something his family had cherished for generations?

Ellie handed over the menu and said to the waitress, 'I'm having sausages and mash. I need carbohydrates.' And to Ursula, 'You look as if you've had some good news?'

Ursula said, 'A ham salad for me.' And to Ellie, laughing, 'Does it show? Congratulate me; I've just landed a wonderful job, helping to choose the jewellery and accessories for a big fashion firm. I'm floating on air.'

'You've told Sam?'

'On my way out of the interview. He's thrilled for me. I start as soon as we come back from honeymoon. It'll be chaos, getting into the new flat and everything, but I don't care if we do sleep on a mattress on the floor at first.'

'That's the spirit. I remember when I married first . . . No, no. You won't want to hear about that.'

Ursula smiled. 'Some time you'll tell me, but not now. You haven't asked me to meet you so urgently without a good reason. Mia's all right, isn't she?'

'Yes, she is. I won't keep you long, but first let me tell you what's happening on the wedding front.' She proceeded to give Ursula a word picture of Mr Balls and his two slaves, and what they were going to do to keep the two wedding receptions apart.

Ursula was fascinated and appalled. 'If I'd known, I'd never have accepted your offer to hold the reception at your place. I wonder if it's possible even now to shift it somewhere else?'

'Certainly not. I'm looking forward to seeing you wed and to giving you a good send-off. Neither Thomas nor I would miss it for the world. We want to give you a wedding present, too, if you'll allow us to do so.'

Ellie passed over an envelope containing some of the money which she'd just collected from the bank. 'We'll give you something for your new home later on, when you've settled in and found out what you need, but for now this is to help with expenses. Your father and his family staying over, that sort of thing.'

Ursula pushed the envelope back. 'No, no. Something for the flat later; that would be wonderful. You've given me so much, Mrs Quicke. When I asked you to find Mia, I didn't really believe you could do it. I'd been surrounded for ever by men and women who believed that corruption was acceptable, that you couldn't fight it. I was on the point of accepting it, too. Then I met you and Thomas and understood it was possible to stand up for what I believed in at heart. You don't realize it, perhaps, but you and Thomas sort of shine. That sounds a bit silly, but—'

'No, you're right. Thomas does shine.'

'You do, too. It was like turning a corner and seeing that there was a different road to travel down. A harder road, maybe. But one that made me feel more comfortable in myself. Now I look back and shudder when I think how near I was to giving up. My dear Sam is the same. I know that in the years to come there may be times when he'll stand up for the truth, against the odds, and refuse to compromise. Perhaps his sense of humour will help him through difficult situations, and perhaps not. Perhaps his integrity may count against him, and may even block his way up the career ladder, but he's not in this life for wealth and power, and neither am I. And remember, if I'd never met you and Thomas, I'd never have met Sam, either. So please, don't try to give me money.'

Ellie put the money back in her bag. 'You're right, of course. Sorry.'

Ursula gave one of her blindingly white smiles. 'So how are you coping with two weddings at once? And how is Midge the terrible cat managing?'

'He's very annoyed, but on the scrounge for titbits at coffee times. Mia is preoccupied, cooking up a storm, which I think is a good thing. She really is a good cook, isn't she? Your wedding certainly is doing wonders for her confidence. It's the best possible way to ease her back into a social occasion. She loves her dress. You are clever, Ursula.'

Ursula drew in a sharp breath. 'Not clever enough to have seen what the Priors intended to do with her. Not clever enough to have stopped it.'

'Now don't beat yourself up. I don't see how you could have known what would happen, and you got her out of it, didn't you? And rescued her from that harridan of an aunt in the country.'

'Poor old biddy. She'll probably have to go into a home now. She'd become totally dependent on Mia to keep her going. I feel sorry for her.'

A smile. 'But not sorry enough to leave Mia with her.'

'No, not that.' Ursula laughed. Their meals arrived. 'And now for the bad news?'

'Ah. Well, someone – we don't know who – seems bent on terrorizing Mia. I'm not referring to the car accident last Monday, because I really don't think that was anything but chance.' Ellie filled Ursula in on the delivery of the lilies with its threatening message, the Sympathy Card, and wreath.

Ursula ate her salad, her eyes flickering this way and that, considering possibilities. 'Have you checked with the police? Who's still inside, and who's out on bail?

'I asked the police to do so. Mr Prior and his sons are both still in jail, as is their friend, the councillor. Mia's 'uncle' Bob is dead. Which leaves—'

'Mrs Prior. I can see her sending poisonous messages, but surely she's not allowed anywhere near Mia, is she?'

'She summoned me to say that she had Mia's best interests at heart, which I beg leave to doubt. However, I don't think it's her. She's got a nice big fish to fry, a wealthy businessman, and is moving out to the Barbican . . . to live under his "protection" no doubt.'

'Miaow,' said Ursula. 'Though you're probably right. Incredible to relate – since she's as old as my mother – Mrs Prior is still a sex bomb, isn't she? She reminds me of Mae West. A little.'

'So who is doing this? Can you think of some hanger-on of the Prior crowd who'd want to upset Mia now?'

Ursula finished her last mouthful. 'There's one or two, but . . . no. They're camp followers, good at obeying orders, but not exactly . . . there's a different mindset behind this nastiness, isn't there? A sympathy card, lilies, a wreath. Dan might know, or know who to ask.' She contemplated the idea of asking Dan in silence. Finally, she shook her head. 'I don't think I can ask him.'

'No, but I might. Mrs Collins said she'd pass on a message that I wanted to speak to him. He's got a job as manager of the Health Club, you know.'

'Glad to hear it,' said Ursula, signalling to the waitress. 'Two coffees? Oh, did you want something else? Sorry, I'm always jumping the gun.'

'That's fine. A latte.' Ursula had always been a bossy boots and probably always would be. Luckily, her fiancé was one who could cope.

Ursula put her elbows on the table and rested her chin on them. A characteristic pose. 'I suppose you could always ask Silly Billy. Stupid name. He's not silly, really. Just . . . a skin too few? Mummy's boy? He used to follow Mia around with his tongue hanging out, but he wasn't part of our crowd, really. He might have noticed something, but . . . No, I don't suppose he noticed anything. Not really bright enough, if you know what I mean?'

'He was in love with Mia?'

'I wouldn't put it that strongly. "Love" implies . . .' she thought about what the word love meant to her, and her expression softened. She shook her head. 'No, he's a pathetic little creature, worshipped her from afar. Might have got round to sending her a valentine card, perhaps. She was always kind to him, never brushed him off. He's the only other person I can think of who might have spotted someone who wished her harm. Dan would know where to find him, I suppose.'

'What's his full name?'

'Billy, William. Can't remember.' She finished her coffee and looked at her watch. 'I've got to get out to Heathrow to meet the family. You'll excuse me, won't you? Let me know if I can do anything else to help.'

'I'll see you at the wedding rehearsal tomorrow evening.'
Ursula landed a kiss somewhere on Ellie's cheek and fled.

THURSDAY AFTERNOON...

*Worry was a killer. He was a killer. He'd killed the problem,
stone dead. If only she'd agreed to lend him what he needed . . .
but she'd been as tight-fisted as a miser. So she'd had to die.*

*Carefully he entered the numbers into his laptop. Checked
them over. Sent.*

*Whizz! Waited a few minutes. Strode up and down. Considered
what still needed to be done. He hadn't left any traces, had he?
No.*

*He returned to his laptop. Money received. His shoulders
relaxed, and he breathed deep and hard.*

Good. He'd made a killing there, too.

ELEVEN

Thursday afternoon

Ellie paid the bill and was just wondering whether to take
the bus or a taxi to the Health Club when her mobile
phone trilled.

It was Thomas. 'Sorry to disturb you, Ellie. Can you get
back here, pronto?'

Ellie immediately thought the worst. 'What's happened?
Someone's hurt?'

'We're all fine, and Mr Balls tells me everything's going
to plan, but you're needed.'

Thomas didn't send out an SOS unless there was real trouble.
'Ten minutes.'

Whatever could have gone wrong? Some precious piece
of furniture smashed by workmen? Should she call a cab?
No. It would be quicker to walk. She walked. The sun had
come out, but the day was humid. Not the best day for
walking fast. She told herself to take it easy, worse things
happen at sea, nothing could be that traumatic if Thomas,

Rose and Mia were all right. Of course, the house could be on fire. No, Thomas would have said so. Wouldn't he?

She turned into her road and looked for fire engines. There were none. Well, good. She hadn't really thought . . . Of course not.

A lorry backed out of her driveway. She couldn't even be bothered to see what firm it was from, but took out her keys to open the front door. It had been double locked and bolted. Why? She hurried round to the kitchen. That door was also locked and bolted. She rapped on the door, and after a pause it was opened by Rose, who looked flustered but seemed to have the usual complement of arms and legs.

'Inside,' said Rose, unusually terse.

The kitchen was a large one but old-fashioned by today's standards. Rose liked it that way, and who was going to argue with Rose? A pine table occupied the centre, and round it there were now grouped Thomas, Mia . . . and four boys whose ages Ellie estimated as seven to eleven. Eating sandwiches and drinking squash. Denis's boys? Of course.

They turned blank faces to her, but didn't speak.

Mia was idle, which was unusual for her.

Thomas had a large pot of tea in front of him and the largest of large mugs. He poured tea into a cup and handed it to Ellie, indicating that she sit down beside him.

The boys watched her. Wary. Chewing. On closer inspection, it looked as if they'd been sleeping rough. Or roughing someone else up?

There was a rapping on the back door and Rose went to see who wanted admission. She murmured something, and the man – whoever he was – disappeared.

Thomas said, 'Ellie, let me introduce you to the General, and his troops. General, say hello to the lady.' The eldest boy muttered something around his sandwich, keeping his eyes on her the while.

'Second in command, and therefore called the Major.' The next biggest boy bobbed his head at Ellie and said, 'Howdedo.' Well, sort of.

'Third in line, the Captain.' This boy managed to clear his mouth long enough to say, 'I want some more drink.'

'And last, but not least, the Lieutenant.'

The General had cleared his plate. 'We've finished, so give us our stuff back.'

'In a minute,' said Thomas. 'First of all, I want you to thank Mrs Quicke for allowing you into her house and giving you something to eat.'

Mumble, mumble. The Captain reiterated his demand for more drink. Rose refilled his mug in silence.

'Now,' said Thomas, who could apparently control small boys as well as parish congregations, 'I'd like you to tell Mrs Quicke how you came to be here.'

The three youngest boys looked at the General, who shrugged but vouchsafed.

'Dunno. She weren't there like she should have been. At first we thought she was hiding, and we went all over the house, but she weren't there. Except she might of been in the bathroom, I suppose, but it's locked. There's a separate toilet downstairs so we used that. We kicked around for a bit, but there was nothing much to eat, and we had no money to buy stuff with. So we went up by the shops, but they didn't let us in, not all four of us at once, so we couldn't nick anything much. Then we got really hungry and phoned Mum, but she was just off to have her hair done and said we'd better go round to Dad's work. So we did, but he weren't there. Diana wouldn't give us any money, but said she'd give us a lift to you and you'd look after us. Only that man there—'

'Meaning me,' said Thomas. 'Chief of Staff, if you please.'

A wriggle. 'Well, Diana dropped us off at your door and we came in, and the man with the wig squealed when he saw us and—'

'Mr Balls,' said Ellie.

'He went and got your man with the beard—'

'Chief of Staff, War Office,' said Thomas.

'And he took all our electronic games and mobiles off us and wouldn't give them back till we'd had something to eat. We want them, now!'

Ellie tried to disentangle this. 'When did your mother drop you at Mrs Summers' place?'

Another shrug. 'Early. This morning. I want my game. Now!'

The Lieutenant began to kick his chair, rhythmically. Annoyingly.

'Another round of ham sandwiches, anyone?' said Rose.

All four boys switched their eyes to her and nodded. Mia and Rose began to assemble more food, while Ellie spoke in a low voice to Thomas. 'I saw Mrs Summers yesterday afternoon. She planned to go over to her sister's later, but she was definitely expecting the boys back today. Am I imagining things, or is there something sinister about the locked bathroom door?'

'As ever, you go straight to the heart of the matter. I've tried ringing the Mrs Summers in the phone book, but there's no reply. I tried Diana, but she's out of the office on some job or other, and so is Denis. Both their mobiles are switched off. I left messages.'

'How on earth did you subdue them? I thought they were feral.'

'I renamed them, which I thought might instil a sense of discipline, and removed their electronic gadgets. They're to get them back after they've eaten in peace and quiet. They were famished, so that worked for a bit. What do we do next? Because they're occupying the kitchen, Rose hasn't been able to feed and water the multitudes outside, which makes the workmen unhappy and Mr Balls threaten to resign.'

'Now that really would be a horror story. I'm so sorry, Thomas. You shouldn't have had to deal with this.'

'My treat. At least I can do something to earn my keep while all around me are busy preparing for the weekend.'

'Shall we call the police to take them away?'

'On what grounds? Antisocial behaviour? Yes, but they haven't actually behaved badly here.'

'Only because you stopped them. If let loose, these boys are capable of reducing a normal house to rubble in fifteen minutes. I've seen what they can do at Mrs Summers' place.'

'So, do we ring the police?'

'Have we enough evidence to start panicking? I think maybe I ought to call a cab, take them back to Mrs Summers' place and see if that bathroom door is still locked. Maybe she barricaded herself in there against them.'

Thomas grunted. 'I'll take you. I'm not leaving you at the mercy of these young hooligans.'

'Who's a hooligan, then?' chanted the General.

His brothers took up the chant. 'Hooligan, hooligan!' They banged on the table and kicked chair legs.

'Quiet!' thundered Thomas, and they were quiet, but started giggling and shoving one another. They'd been fed and watered, and their energy levels were up to normal again.

'Out of the kitchen, please, and stand in line!' said Thomas, opening the back door. 'General takes the lead, followed by other ranks in order. Quick, march! Left, right, left, right. That's it. Now march on the spot. Left, right, left right. Rose, Mia; sorry about this. You're both stars. Left, right, that's it, lads. Halt! General, show me how to salute. Not bad, not bad. Now the rest of you, salute the General. Could be better. Now into the back of my car, all of you. Yes, all of you. No, not in the front! That's where my wife sits. And belt up. All of you. We don't move from here till I see you are all safely belted up.'

The General objected. 'There are only seat belts for three in the back.'

'That's true. Well, Lieutenant, you're the lucky one who can sit in the front next my wife. And belt up. Everyone safely in? General, you're to see there's no fighting in the back, right?'

Thomas drove smoothly along. The youngest boy cuddled up to Ellie under the passenger seat belt. He had long lashes and looked grubby. He also smelt. Oh dear. He yawned. There was perhaps four years difference between him and the General, and the gap in age was telling on his stamina. He drowsed against her, and she put her arm around him to hold him safely as they drew to a close outside Mrs Summers' house.

The gate was still off its hinges. One of the curtains in the front bay had come adrift. Ellie eased herself out from under the sleepy boy and stepped out of the car on to the pavement. The General, the Major and the Captain followed suit. The Lieutenant started awake and joined them, rubbing his eyes. Thomas locked the car up with his remote.

'Boys, has anything changed since you got here this morning?' asked Ellie.

'Nothing.'

'Well, we booted things about a bit.'

'That was in the back, though.'

Ellie shuddered at what they might have done to a garden which they'd already attacked once. 'How did you get in, if she wasn't here to let you in?'

A shrug. 'Front door was on the latch.'

Thomas walked up the path and pushed the front door open. They all huddled into the hall behind him. A sticky hand stole into Ellie's, and she held it tight.

'Hello, there!' said Thomas. 'Mrs Summers?'

They listened. Silence. A murmur of traffic not far away. An aeroplane took off from Heathrow Airport – would Ursula have met up with her father and his second family by now? A bluebottle hit a window. Water dripped somewhere.

Thomas threw open doors. Ellie and the others stayed in the hall. Returning from the kitchen, he shook his head at them and went up the stairs. The Lieutenant shuddered and pressed close to Ellie.

'Mrs Summers? Are you there?'

No reply. Ellie expected none. She knew, guessed, suspected . . . so did the boys, apparently. They turned watchful, apprehensive, excited eyes towards her. She smiled at them all. 'Let Thomas investigate. He's the biggest.'

'Chief of Staff, War Office,' said the Major, and the General nodded. Let Thomas do it.

Thomas came back down the stairs, taking out his mobile. 'Would you lot like to get back into the car for a moment? I'm not sure there's anything much to worry about, but just in case, we'll call the authorities. The first to hear a police car coming gets mentioned in despatches. Right?' He used his remote to unlock the car from the front drive, and Ellie shepherded them back into it.

'Can we have our games back?' asked the General, in what was a polite voice for him.

'Definitely,' said Thomas, producing them from about his person. 'Now, General; you're in charge. Keep them quiet and occupied, right? Like a General should, looking after his men.'

The General saluted. So did Thomas. A small miracle.

Ellie stood by the car as Thomas rang for the police. He'd turned away so the boys shouldn't hear, but she heard all right. '. . . Yes, that's the address. She was supposed to be child-minding today but didn't appear. The bathroom door's locked. Yes, a proper old-fashioned lock, but there's no key in the lock. You can hear water dripping inside . . . No, water isn't flooding out of the bathroom, but the landing carpet's wet . . . No, I tested it. It's not blood. Just water . . .'

He moved away, and she heard no more. She leaned back against the car and closed her eyes. The early evening sun was warm on her face. She ought to have brought her sunglasses. Another plane went by, far overhead. A big one. She wished she knew more about planes. No, she didn't. Not really. She'd enough to remember without worrying about different makes of planes.

This couldn't have anything to do with Mia, anyway. Could it?

No, it couldn't. Ellie had been going to call on Dan Collins this afternoon, but hadn't. How dare Diana dump her fiancé's children on Ellie like that? Ah, but Diana thought she could get away with anything where her mother was concerned, didn't she? She was right, because Thomas had coped. Wonderfully.

The General got out of the car. The Major and the Captain were busy on their games consoles, and the Lieutenant was asleep.

Ellie roused herself. 'We must ring your mother, tell her what's happening.' She got out her own mobile. 'Tell me the number.' He told her, and she fumbled it.

'Let me,' he said, and did it for her.

Ring, ring. 'Is that . . .? Mrs Quicke here. Yes, Diana's mother. We have your boys with us at the childminder's, but there appears to be a slight problem—'

A sharp, crystal-clear voice. 'Nothing to do with me. They're his responsibility in the holidays.' She shut off the phone.

Ellie did an eye-roll and redialled. 'Mrs Quicke here. Don't ring off! We're waiting for the police at the moment, but—'

'What have they done now?' Alarm. 'Surely the woman can take a joke.'

'No joke. I think you'd better get over here.'

'I can't. I'm at the hairdressers. I won't be finished for another hour.'

Ellie counted to five. 'Are you willing for my husband and myself to act as responsible adults when the children are questioned by the police?'

'What? What have they done now? I'll murder them.'

'They're witnesses, not suspects. Can you get Denis to come?'

'What's that? Witnesses? I don't believe this! Listen, Denis won't pick up the phone if he knows it's me.' Pause. 'Let me know how you get on. I'll come as soon as I'm through here, but you must realize that I can't leave in the middle of a perm.'

'I realize that.' Ellie shut off the phone.

The General sighed, long and hard. He wasn't too clean, but that might be just a boyish talent for collecting dirt. His shorts were torn. And there were yellowish stripes on the backs of his legs.

Ouch.

Ellie's mind made a couple of giant leaps. 'Is it your father who hits you, or your mother?'

Shoulders lifted to ears. Eyes downcast. Scuffed shoes scuffled.

Ellie insisted. 'Him?'

A nod.

Ellie remembered what the boys had done to the house the previous day. 'Did your father tell you to wreck the place?'

A hunched shoulder. An averted face. 'No. She did. She said that this was one of Dad's squeezes, and we could be a bit rough if we liked. So we did. No harm in it.'

Humph! 'What does your mum think about the wedding on Saturday?'

A grin. 'She says it'll make him a biggy, no . . . a pygmy. Then she'll be rid of him for good, and we'll have the house to ourselves and a lot of money.'

A 'pygmy'. Now what was that in adult terms?

He was shifting from foot to foot, pressing his legs together. Oh. She looked around. Where could he go? Would it be all right for him to use the facilities back in Mrs Summers' house? Probably not, if it were a crime scene.

A police car drew up. As if by osmosis, heads appeared in windows nearby, and a woman next door opened her door to see what was happening. A mistake. Ellie propelled the General to the neighbour's open door, and asked if he might use the toilet. Neighbour nodded and indicated a way through to the back of the house. The boy shot inside.

Ellie called out after him. 'Wash hands and face afterwards.'

The Major and the Captain presented themselves at her side. The neighbour shrugged, and said, 'Why not? Straight through, last door on the right.' And then, 'What's going on, then?'

Where was the Lieutenant? Still asleep? No, he was out on the pavement, bleary-eyed. Was that a dark stain on his pants? Oh dear. Seeing his brothers disappear into a strange house, he followed them up the path. Thomas met the police officers and spoke to them. Ellie gesticulated to Thomas, miming that the boys were going in next door for a moment. He nodded and ushered the police into Mrs Summers' house.

Ellie smiled at the neighbour. 'Sorry. The boys were bursting. I'll clean round the toilet and washbasin after them.'

The neighbour nearly cricked her neck, trying to see what was happening next door. Another police car drew up. Walkie-talkies at full pitch.

The General presented himself in the hall, more or less clean and heaving a sigh of relief. The Major and the Captain followed, ditto. The Lieutenant was slower.

'He does it in his pants sometimes,' said the General.

Ellie met the eyes of the helpful neighbour and iterated, 'I'll clean up after them. Have you seen Mrs Summers today?'

'Is there something wrong? No, I haven't. I've seen these boys around before, haven't I?' Neighbour folded her lips, and Ellie could guess what had not been said.

'Rampaging, were they?'

The General said, 'It was a battle. It was cool.'

'I don't think Mrs Summers thought it was cool.'

He shrugged, and the Major and the Captain shrugged, too. 'Can we go and see her now? Is she all bluggy?'

'No, and no. We don't know that anything's happened to her, anyway.'

The Major picked his nose. 'She might of gone to sleep last night in the bath and left the tap dripping.'

Ellie was intrigued. Perhaps the Major was the one in the outfit with brains?

'Why do you say that?'

'The milk was on the doorstep this morning. She hadn't taken it in.'

The General nodded. 'We drank it for our lunch. And ate the rest of the bread and jam.'

'And the cornflakes,' said the Captain.

'But there weren't any biscuits left in the tin,' said the Major.

All three sighed. 'That was a long time ago.' They switched

their eyes to the neighbour, who reacted exactly the way they intended.

'Oh, you poor things! No lunch? Now, what can I find for you to eat? A fry-up would be quickest, with a couple of rounds of toast each.'

The Major kicked the Captain, who had opened his mouth to ask for something else. 'We'd love that!' said the Major. 'You are so kind.'

Ellie perceived that the boys knew exactly which buttons to press when it came to impressionable middle-aged women. She herself was not so impressionable. Or was she? 'The Lieutenant?' she asked.

'Probably crying because he's done it in his pants,' said the General, and followed their hostess down the hall into a well-appointed kitchen.

Ellie found the youngest boy in the toilet, which was now awash with splashed water, dirty towels, and a lot of toilet paper strewn around the place. The Lieutenant was sitting on the loo, dirty pants around his ankles. Crying.

Ellie washed out his pants, cleaned him up, dried the pants roughly on the cleanest of the remaining towels, scrubbed him down as much as she could without stripping him entirely, put his pants back on and sent him out to join his brothers.

She popped her head round the kitchen door. 'Have you some rubber gloves I could use, and something to clean the toilet?'

'Bless you, yes. Cupboard under the stairs.' The woman was ladling out piles of scrambled egg on to plates awash with sausages, bacon and baked beans. 'Boys will be boys, won't they? I had four myself, and they've got five between them and two more expected in the autumn, and I know they keep you on the go. Now, tea all round?'

'Any coca cola?' enquired the Captain.

Ellie was astonished and pleased to see how well the boys could behave when they put their minds to it.

She also knew there was going to be an account to be settled when they'd finished. She returned to cleaning up the toilet. Through the party wall she could hear thuds and the occasional shout. And more walkie-talkies.

When she'd finished cleaning, their hostess pressed a most welcome mug of tea into her hands. 'Two sugars? You look as if you need it. Sit down. I sent the boys to play in the garden.'

Ellie shuddered at the thought of what destruction they might wreak there, but their hostess was ahead of her. 'I told the eldest he was responsible for their behaviour, and he said he'd see that they didn't do any damage. I've kept an eye on them and they're playing five-a-side or whatever. They'll do.'

Ellie looked out of the window and saw that this garden had been laid out with small boys in mind, for a football net had been set up at the end of the lawn, and there were not one but two basketball hoops bolted on to a high fence.

'Excuse me a moment,' said their hostess and disappeared into the toilet; no doubt to check on its cleanliness. Satisfied, she returned to pile dirty dishes into a dishwasher. The moment of truth had arrived. To pay for all this, Ellie must now be prepared to Tell All.

Their hostess was a comfortable-looking sixty, dressed in Marks & Spencer clothing, with blonded and permed hair and an air of competence. The sort of person who paid her bills on time and kept a sweetie jar filled for visiting grand-children. Her bright eyes were set in wrinkled lids. She'd seen most things in life, but was still optimistic.

'The name's Marge, by the way. The children aren't yours?'

'Ellie Quicke. No. They got landed on us – on myself and my husband Thomas, who's next door. He's the one who called the police when we couldn't make the childminder hear us. Mrs Summers was supposed to be looking after the children for the man she used to work for—'

'The estate agent?'

'That's right. Their mother was busy today. In fact, she's at the hairdressers at this moment, which is why she couldn't help. The boys arrived early this morning, the front door was open, they got in, couldn't find Mrs Summers anywhere, noticed the bathroom was locked, spent the morning killing time then went to look for their father, who was out of the office at the time. So my daughter – his partner – brought them over to us to look after. We thought the whole thing was a little odd and came to investigate.'

Shrewd eyes. 'I've seen you before here, haven't I?'

'I called to see Mrs Summers on Wednesday. Yesterday.

Yes. The place was a mess. The boys had got a bit above themselves, I gather.'

'That they did. If they'd been mine . . . but I reckon they get enough of that at home. You noticed that the eldest and the youngest have both been beaten recently?'

Ellie nodded. 'The father, I think. The youngest probably because he wets his bed. The eldest . . .?' A shrug. 'Possibly getting big enough to challenge his father?'

'Mm. Likely. One of mine used to get beaten regularly. Different father, you know? Scarred him for life. The only one of them that never married. My fault, I suppose. My old man was playing away, so I thought I could, too. Turned out to be a mistake. I had to throw him out in the end; my husband, I mean. More tea?'

'Thanks. Yes. What do you make of Mrs Summers?'

A wry face. 'Stupid girl. Thinks she's still eighteen and can get away with it. Has male visitors, who come out checking their ties. She likes them big and fair-haired, says it's because she's missing her husband. Well, no need to go that far, is there? She's dead, isn't she?'

'I don't know. It doesn't look good. When do you suppose . . .?'

'Mm. Been thinking about that. I saw her about six, I suppose. She was picking up bean sticks in the garden, clearing away broken plants. They'd slashed the heads off everything in flower, little monkeys that they are. She was upset but playing it down.'

Both women turned to look out of the window, but the boys were playing reasonably happily together, with the General telling them 'what'.

'What time was that?' said Ellie. 'She told me she was going over to visit her sister after I left.'

'She didn't go. She said her sister had cancelled, had a dentist's appointment. I popped out to get the washing in and we had a word over the fence, but I didn't stop to chat because I was cooking supper for my youngest-but-one who comes over from work once a week to see I'm all right, and I usually give him a bite to eat. Sometimes he stays for the evening, but he went early last night, got a darts match on. I saw him off and noticed the big car was back, the one belonging to the estate agent. You know about him, do you? He comes by maybe once a week, puts in an hour's hard grind, and goes again. He left about seven or half past, I suppose. I heard him go. Her front door sticks a bit in hot weather, needs a good bang to get it shut.'

Ellie was disappointed. 'It was open this morning, so it can't have been him who killed her – that is, if anyone did. Someone must have called later.'

'Or he banged the door shut from the inside so's I'd think he'd gone, when he hadn't. He left it open when he did go later on, so's I wouldn't hear him.'

As one, they lifted their mugs and drank.

Ellie said, 'Why should he kill her? Surely it was to his benefit to keep her alive and child-minding? But . . . Oh. I just thought . . .'

'She had money, didn't she? Told everyone about it. Boasted. Silly woman.'

'She told me she'd given him her bank account number. I queried it with her, but she said he'd never do her down. I wonder if that money is still in her account?'

'Give you two guesses.'

'We don't *know* anything yet.'

'Want a bet?'

Both women laughed, then sobered. Ellie said, 'The police will want to talk to you.'

'I'm not going anywhere.'

Thursday afternoon

He'd covered his gift in some pretty paper from the drawer in which his mother used to keep all sorts of bits and pieces useful for wrapping up presents for birthdays and Christmas. She'd said her oddments of paper, string and tinsel always came in handy, and so they had. He'd even stuck a pink rosette on top of the packet, just the sort of thing the witch would like. There! It looked harmless.

But the contents – he hugged himself with glee! – were lethal.

TWELVE

The police did indeed want to speak to Marge and Ellie, and to the boys. But they took their time getting round to it. Ellie and Marge moved into her big living room which – as in Mrs Summers' house – had been knocked through into one. From there they could see the coming and going of cars outside, and keep an eye on the boys in the garden. Marge opened a window so they could hear better.

'That's the paramedic,' said Marge, as a man rode up on a motorbike. 'Come to look at her. He won't be able to pronounce her dead, so they'll call the doctor next. Do you fancy a bite to eat, although I'm not sure exactly what I've got left in the fridge? All this excitement makes me hungry.'

'They'll send for the brighter bobbies next, won't they?' said Ellie. 'And no, thanks, kindly meant, but we're having supper back home.'

'Suit yourself.' A pause. A clink of bottles. 'You wouldn't say no to a small sherry, would you?'

'I'd better not. It would make Thomas jealous if he smelt it on me while he's stuck with the police. He's driving, you see. Ah, here comes the doctor.'

'And some of what you call the brighter bobbies. Not off the local beat.'

'I recognize one of them.' Ellie sighed. 'He's a Detective Inspector now, but I wouldn't have called him one of the brighter bobbies. Unfortunately.'

'The one with the sticky-out ears?'

'I wish I'd had that sherry you offered me. But no, better not. That particular policeman would accuse me of being drunk.'

'He'd better not try that on me.' Sipping away, Marge glanced up the garden. 'They'll be wanting their tea soon. Boys that age, you can't satisfy them.'

'They'll want their telly in a bit, I shouldn't wonder. I hope their mother makes it soon.'

They watched in silence as a large silver car drew up. 'Himself,' said Marge.

Denis, in a silvery-grey handmade suit, powered up the garden path to Mrs Summers' house, only to be stopped at the door by a uniformed policeman. Denis demanded entry. Was refused. Raised his voice. Demanded to see whoever was in charge. Refused to calm down.

Marge remarked, 'You realize he hasn't yet asked what all the fuss is about?'

'Because he knows. He hasn't asked where his children are, either.'

'Because he doesn't care? Do you think it would be worth while reporting those marks of abuse on the children to social services?'

'He's supposed to have moved out of their house and is now only responsible for them on certain days during the school holidays. Perhaps, if the mother knew the marks had been spotted . . .?'

'She must know. Some mother!'

'He can be intimidating, you know. I don't envy her, married to him. Ah, he's crossed the threshold.'

'He's running the risk of being arrested, pushing past a policeman like that.'

'He's a clever, slicky Dicky. He'll say he's worried sick about the children.'

Marge pressed a small sherry into Ellie's hand, and she took it. Marge said, 'You don't like him.'

'He's marrying my daughter Diana on Saturday. And no, I don't like anything about him. He's a sneaky, pushy, cut-throat, cut corners sort of man. Hard.' She thought about it, and added 'Large.'

Marge gulped, and giggled. 'Your future son-in-law. Can't we pin the murder on him?'

'We don't know that it is.'

They knew all right.

Presently Thomas came round to knock on Marge's front door and was let in. He looked tired. Marge offered him a sherry and he said, 'No, no. I'm driving.' But looked as if he'd have liked to accept. She got him a coffee instead, while he explained what had been happening.

'They had to break down the bathroom door. It was locked

on the inside, and the key was on the floor. Probably it had been pushed under the door after . . . after. The police told me to stand back, but I could hear what they said. She was in the bath, half-clothed. It looked as if she'd just slid under the water. Her feet were dry, sticking out by the taps. She'd a bad bruise on her chin. They reckon she was knocked out, dropped into the bath and left to drown.'

Marge coughed. Her eyes watered. 'That's not nice.'

Ellie shuddered.

'Are the boys all right, Ellie?'

Ellie waved to the French windows, through which they could see the boys playing tag on the lawn.

Thomas gulped coffee and shook his head. 'Bad business. Ellie, you told me once about a particular policeman who hadn't treated you well, someone with big ears. I think it might be him.'

'It is. Made inspector last year.'

'Mm. Makes you wonder how they select . . . Well, no doubt I'm being judgmental.'

'He likes the limelight. He called in the boffins, I suppose? What happened when Denis arrived?'

'He pushed his way in – typical – and demanded to know where his children were. I said they were next door with my wife, but he didn't leave. Instead, he homed in on the inspector, demanding to know why he'd been summoned from an important meeting to look after the children when they weren't there. The inspector knew nothing of the children. I had tried to tell him, but he wasn't listening. Instead, he squared up to Denis, asking what he thought he was doing, forcing his way into the premises of a murder enquiry.

'Denis didn't like that. He used his superior height to get within the inspector's personal space and hissed at him. Hah! It's a toss up whether Denis reports the inspector for incompetence, or the inspector arrests him for impeding the police in the course of their investigations. I wouldn't take a bet on it, either way.'

He shook his head. 'Those boys made a good job of trashing the place next door. The inspector looked around and said that it was clear to him that someone had broken in and done the place over looking for valuables. Denis chipped in to say that he'd been keeping an eye on Mrs Summers because she used to work for him at one time, and he knew she'd been having male visitors at all hours of the day and night.

'That went down wonderfully well. The inspector was pleased to hear there had been all these men calling at the house and jumped to the conclusion that one of them must have had a fight with Mrs Summers and killed her, either when he was looking for valuables or in the heat of an argument.

'I did say that I believed the boys were responsible for the mess, but Denis, of course, contradicted me, saying his boys would never, ever, etcetera. The inspector turned a frosty eye on me because I was complicating an otherwise straightforward case. He said he saw no reason for me to hang around. I agreed with him. I told the DC on the door that the children were next door, and that I'd be joining them.'

'The eldest and the youngest show marks of abuse,' said Ellie. 'It's Denis, not their mother.'

Thomas stroked his beard, unsurprised. He looked at Marge, 'You had no trouble with them?'

Marge shook her head. 'They'll need feeding again soon, but I've been thinking, and I don't believe I've enough in the fridge to give them another meal. I was going to have baked beans on toast for my supper, but I gave them all I had to eat at teatime. What do you reckon to a takeaway?'

Ellie looked at her watch. 'Their mother should be here soon. I hope.'

There was a thud on the door, and someone rang the bell. Police? Yes. And Denis. As if they'd received a signal to present themselves, the four boys filed into the room, eyes downcast, hands behind their backs.

Denis was first into the room. He glared at his sons. 'What are you doing in here?'

The General quailed. 'She wouldn't come out of the bathroom.'

'So you went for help. Good lads.'

Four wooden faces, four sets of downcast eyes.

Denis noticed Ellie and did a double take. 'You? What brings you here?'

'Diana dumped the kids on us, without notice. No one could understand why Mrs Summers didn't let them in this morning, so we drove over with them to see what was going on.'

'You! Ellie Quicke!' The Inspector's large ears seemed to redden, as he realized who was sitting in the window with their hostess. 'You had to poke your nose in, didn't you!'

'No,' said Ellie in her sweetest voice. 'I looked after the boys while my husband phoned the police.'

The inspector huffed. 'I understand that you and your husband brought the boys back here, that you didn't see any intruders, and so left the house. Is that correct?'

Ellie debated saying that she didn't think there had been any intruders, felt the boys' eyes on her, and nodded.

The inspector swung back to Denis. 'I'll need a statement from the boys in due course, with a suitable adult present.'

'I'll do that,' said their father. 'No need for anyone else.' He swung back to the boys. 'It wasn't you who made such a mess of the place next door, was it?'

As one, the boys shook their heads, eyes wide with innocence.

At this inopportune moment Marge hiccuped, and then giggled.

Denis turned on her. 'What do you mean by that? Oh, I see. You're drunk.'

'Not drunk. I saw you there last night.'

Angry. 'Of course you did. I called to pay her for child-minding and to arrange for her to have them again today.'

Marge flushed. 'I know what else you used to do with her, and I know how much money she had in her account. Is it still there, do you think?'

He towered over her. 'What do you mean by that, may I ask? Are you daring to suggest that I had anything to do with her tragic death?'

'I don't know, do I?' said Marge, obstinacy itself. 'You might have.'

Denis turned to the inspector. 'Drunk. As usual.'

'Ears' nodded. For once, the two men thought alike. 'We'll have to take her statement, of course.'

'Of course,' said Denis, magnanimous in victory. 'I shan't sue her, even though you are the best witness I could possible have.'

They both laughed. Members of the men's superiority club.

Marge said, 'What, what?' Even her neck flushed a painful red.

Ellie wondered whether to tell the inspector what the boys had told her about trashing Mrs Summers' place. She opened her mouth to do so, and met four pairs of eyes begging her to keep quiet. She thought about the weals she'd seen on the boys' legs, and about the difficulties faced by children in a divorce situation, and shut her mouth again. Perhaps she would have a word with the boys' mother when things had calmed down a bit.

A shabby car drew up outside, and there was an altercation with a uniformed policeman outside.

'Mum!' cried the boys, and rushed to the front door, letting it bang to behind them in their haste to be gone.

A tall slender woman with a mop of pale yellow hair in a no-nonsense bob, counted the boys off and ushered them, mother hen like, into her car.

'Their mother,' said Denis. Dropping his voice to indicate he was telling a joke, he added, 'God bless her.'

The inspector laughed, as intended. Neither Ellie nor Thomas, nor Marge joined in.

'Ears' said, 'Mrs Quicke. Leave your address before you go.'

'You know where I live,' said Ellie, annoyed and frustrated.

He produced a notebook. 'Tell me again. We can't be expected to keep up with everyone's details, can we?'

Ellie gave her address and telephone number with exaggerated clarity, and got to her feet. 'Well, if that's all. Thanks for everything, Marge. We'll keep in touch, shall we?'

Thomas patted Marge on her shoulder. 'It was good to meet you. Thanks for the coffee.' And to the police, 'You have my statement already, right?'

Down the path they went and into Thomas's car. Ellie noted the dark patch on the passenger seat in front, where the Lieutenant had left his mark, and sat in the back. A policewoman was busy taping off Mrs Summers' house as they drove away.

'What do you think, Thomas?'

'It would take a monster to let the boys find their childminder dead.'

'But they didn't, did they? Find her, I mean. He'd locked the bathroom door after he killed her, and pushed the key underneath. He counted on the boys not actually breaking a door down, and they didn't. He lied about other things.

He knew about the mess the boys had made earlier on, because Mrs Summers told me he'd promised to make good the damage they'd done.

'She admitted that it was he who'd put her up to renting a big house from us with false references. She said that he'd asked her to pay the deposit herself – she'd plenty of money in her current account – but she'd refused, so he'd promised to transfer money into her account, to cover it. She was too trusting. She gave him her bank details.

'Given that he'd asked her for money once and been refused, I think he tried her again last night, and when she refused for the second time, he killed her. Once she was dead, he had until her body was discovered to empty her bank account.'

'Is he that cold-blooded? It's hard to understand.'

'So are the bruises on the backs of the boys' legs. They went to their mother willingly enough. She must know about the bruises, mustn't she? How can she bear to let the boys visit him?'

'It sounds as if she's between the devil and the deep blue sea. Does she have a job? What are the outgoings on the house she occupies? Didn't you say he put the boys into private education? Is she frightened of him? Perhaps she knows but is too frightened to say anything.'

He turned into their driveway and parked. There was only one other car there now; probably the Party Planner's. Something or somebody dodged behind the car, and Ellie put her hand to her heart. 'What was that?'

'What?'

'Not sure. A man hiding behind that car?'

Thomas went to look. Bushes rustled and shook. A figure broke out of them and ran off down the road. Thomas laughed. 'Someone caught short, perhaps, thinking our shrubbery offered a refuge? Which reminds me, I'll scrub that car seat out now before I forget.'

Ellie looked up at the front of the house and wondered what scenes of wedding preparation and chaos it might be concealing from the public gaze. The windows of the house seemed to wink back at her – recently cleaned, thank goodness – and she thought they might be saying, perhaps a little wearily, that they'd seen it all before, but would still be there at the end of the day.

She was grateful for this reminder; her worries looked trivial compared to the hundred or so years that this house had already seen.

One thing was for sure, she was never going to host another wedding reception here. Far too much aggro.

She let herself into the hall and had to fall back to avoid being trampled underfoot by a screaming mob. Someone pushed past her, yelling. A pile of boxes was knocked into by another person, and rocked dangerously till a third person pushed it back upright. A streak of ginger flew from the top of the grandfather clock and landed on a bridal archway of entwined summer jasmine and ivy, which sank in the middle and was only saved from crashing to the floor by the cat taking another leap on to a pile of tables, which then did slid sideways with a crash, followed to the floor by a stack of chairs.

Midge cannoned off Ellie's legs and bolted out of the front door and down the drive, ears flattened to head, tail bushed out to twice its normal size.

'Midge!' The cat vanished.

Ellie called over him, but he wasn't listening. Would he be run over? He didn't usually go out of the front door, did he?

Thomas, cleaning rags in hand, emerged from his car, spotted Midge's tail disappearing into the road and started off after him. Only to return, shaking his head. 'He'll be back when he's calmed down. What set him off?'

'I don't know.'

There was a babble of sound indoors. 'Have you got it?'

'Sorry, I didn't mean to push you, but—'

'Help her up! Are you hurt badly?'

'Oh, it's bleeding.'

Ellie took a deep breath, and went into the hall. She didn't get far, since her way was barred by cardboard boxes full of plants in full bloom. The mob reduced itself to Mr Balls, the Party Planner and his two slaves, plus Rose, who was sitting on the lowest stair, holding her wrist. And Mia, wide-eyed and breathing hard. The slaves looked the worse for wear. Over the banister came the heads of two of the cleaning team, eyes and mouths wide, who were supposed to be turning out the bedrooms in readiness for Saturday.

Mr Balls leaned against the newel post, wiping his brow with care so as not to disturb his toupee. One of his slaves was checking out the bloodied elbow of the other. Mia wept, sucking a cut finger.

Rose saw Ellie first, and got to her feet at the second attempt. 'So sorry, such a madhouse, I don't know what got into that cat, but he's been growling and getting in our way ever since the parcel arrived—'

'What parcel?'

'Can we help?' asked one of the cleaners, half way down the stairs.

Ellie waved her away. 'No, thanks. It's all right. You get on with what you were doing.' The cleaner withdrew with some reluctance. She didn't come across this much excitement every day.

Rose said, 'A wedding present for Ursula. Honest, we did our very best, but we don't even know who it's from, so how ever is she going to thank them for it?'

'I'll get a dustpan and brush,' said Mia, drying her eyes. 'It was an accident. I'll tell her. She won't create, I'm sure she won't.'

'It might have come from his side of the family though,' said Rose, brushing herself down. 'They might get upset, think we were careless, though goodness knows we put it in a safe place on the table next to the telephone, and when Midge knocked it off there we put it high up on that little ledge outside the cloakroom where you wouldn't think he could get at it, but somehow he did, and hooked it down and it smashed on the edge of that stack of chairs.'

'Never mind,' said Mia, returning with dustpan and brush. 'It wasn't anyone's fault, and Mr Balls and his assistants were really wonderful and I'll make it all right with Ursula, just you wait and see.'

'Dear Mrs Quicke.' Mr Balls puffed and panted. 'What a scene to greet your return, when really we were right on target, everything going well except for the shortage of cables but that will be put right tomorrow, I do assure you.'

Ellie felt rather faint. 'Yes, of course. But what about your wounded soldier?'

'It's nothing,' muttered the wilting female slave.

'Let me look,' said Rose. 'Oh, I'll just run it under the tap and then put a plaster on it. Naughty, naughty Midge. No dinner for him tonight.'

Mia bent over the mess on the floor, looking as if she might cry again.

Ellie took the dustpan and brush off her. 'Go and attend to that cut on your finger. I'll deal with this. We may find a label inside the package that will tell us who it's from.'

The parcel had been inexpertly wrapped in a layer of coloured tissue paper which looked as if it had been used before, and which hadn't proved to be much protection for the glass dish within. Ellie couldn't see any label, though she turned the mess over and over by pulling on the paper with her fingertips, once she'd got it into the dustpan. Something squishy and pink clung to the tissue paper.

'Who would send newly-weds an old-fashioned moulded glass dish?' Ellie wondered. 'Someone of the older generation, perhaps? Not even cut glass. Well, I suppose we must put it safely into some sort of container and keep it for Ursula to see. Perhaps she can make a guess as to who might have sent it. I'll find something with a lid on it in the kitchen.'

Mr Balls fanned himself with his clipboard. 'Dear lady, you are efficiency itself, and no great harm done, except to my nervous system. So, shall we have a quick run through what we have achieved today and what still needs to be done tomorrow?'

Ellie gestured with the dustpan. 'As soon as I've got rid of this. We don't want any more blood shed, do we?'

She took the sticky mess out to the kitchen, where Rose was busy putting a plaster on one of the slave's elbows. Ellie rummaged in the cupboard where she kept plastic boxes with lids from the freezer, and found an old ice cream carton which would do.

'Now where shall we put it? In a cupboard where Midge can't get at it?'

'In the larder. He can't manage that door knob.' Mia opened the door for Ellie and followed her down the two steps into a narrow, tiled room with a stone shelf running along one side of it, which had served the house well as a cold store before the advent of refrigerators. In old Miss Quicke's day, there had still been a meat safe at one end, with a mesh front to keep the flies out, but this had long been banished, and new shelves fitted to house Rose's fabled collection of chutneys and jams.

Mia took the box off Ellie, and opened the lid. 'I just want to . . .' She poked at a wodge of pink with one finger, and let out a hiss. 'It wasn't meant for Ursula. It was meant for me.'

Ellie took a closer look at the mess. 'What makes you think that?' She smelt it, and spotted a mass of blue speckles in the pink. 'Ah.'

Mia shivered, but didn't break down. 'That pink stuff is coconut ice. I used to love it, in the old days. But this doesn't smell right to me. What about those blue granules? What do you make of them?'

'They remind me of something, but I can't think what.'

'Something used to kill mice? We had mice at Prior Place one summer, and I seem to remember the man putting down some blue granules which the mice were supposed to eat. He made sure we had no pets around the place first. I think there's something nasty in that block of sweet stuff, and that Midge knew.'

Ellie put the lid back on the box and dropped it into a large crock which had been used in the second world war to house eggs pickled in isinglass, and which Rose occasionally used to keep bread fresh.

Mia replaced the lid on the crock and smiled at Ellie. 'Not to worry. I'm not going to faint or anything. In fact, you don't need to worry about me any more. I've done all the agonizing I'm going to do, and somehow all the fear has gone. For good, I hope. What happened before is all in the past. I'll probably continue to have nightmares for a bit, but one day, maybe, I'll even be able to sleep properly without waking up every half hour to make sure I'm not still in my old room with men coming at me to . . . No, no. That's all in the past. At the moment I seem to be bearing a charmed life, what with cars missing me by a fraction and poisonous sweets meeting a sticky end. Long may it last.'

'Indeed.' Ellie looked at her watch. 'It's a bit late to ring the police tonight. I'll do it in the morning. What a pity that Detective Inspector Willis is on leave. She left all details of your case with a Detective Constable who seems reasonably bright, but perhaps not quite up to dealing with something like this. And now, let's find a plaster for that finger of yours.'

THURSDAY EVENING...

*It was a juggling act. The money he'd downloaded into his
account would stave off trouble for a while, but the school fees
for the autumn were still outstanding. He cursed the day he'd
committed himself to a year's fees. If only . . . He ground his
teeth.*

*If only the stupid woman had agreed to lend him what he
needed. He'd said he could pay her back, but she wouldn't have
it. So he'd had to wipe her out, hadn't he? She'd given him no
choice.*

*It wasn't enough by a long chalk. Now, how to get to the
target? Perhaps there'd be an opportunity tomorrow. And if not,
he'd make one. He was not going to be beaten by a woman.*

THIRTEEN

Thursday evening

Mia's smile flickered and went out. 'It's stopped
bleeding already, see? I don't want you to keep on
worrying about me. I'm all right, really I am.'

There was a new serenity about her. It might not last, but it
was there. It was amazing that the girl hadn't buckled under
the knowledge of yet another attack on her life. Perhaps in the
future there would be less despair and more hope in her life.

'I'm so pleased,' said Ellie, and meant it.

Mia gave Ellie an awkward, hasty hug. Perhaps the first
time she'd touched someone of her own accord for months?
'It seemed for a long time as if the world was full of nasty
creepy-crawlies, but you showed me there are still good people
around. You and Thomas and Rose; and Ursula, of course.
And Ursula's Sam. You used to call him Hawkface, didn't
you? It's a good name for him. I don't suppose I'll ever meet
anyone like that, and I wouldn't have been right for him,
anyway, even before . . . even before.'

'Some day you'll meet someone who is right for you.' Banal
words, but it was what every woman wanted, wasn't it?

'Oh, I don't think so. I don't suppose I'll ever get married and have children, now. But as Thomas says, the fact that I'm still alive is something of a miracle, and I'm happy to wait and see what God wants me to do next.'

'Well, that's good.' Inadequate words to express a deep thankfulness.

Mia turned on her brilliant smile. 'It's you we ought to be worrying about now. Are your cuts and bruises hurting you? You look as if you could do with some of the tender loving care you've been giving me.'

There is nothing better calculated to make you feel weak and tottery than someone saying you don't look your best. All of a sudden Ellie realized she did indeed feel in need of a soothing cuppa and something to eat, plus a shower or a long deep bath with plenty of Radox in it. 'I'm fine,' she said. Of course. 'Now, what about Mr Balls and his team, and those plants in the hall?'

Where was Midge? How far might he have gone in his flight? Would he be able to find his way back, once he'd stopped running?

Mia led the way back to the hall. Ellie peered out of the front door to see if Midge had returned, but he hadn't.

The two women looked at the muddle of furniture and plants which had been left in the hall and quailed.

Mia said, 'The thing was that the furniture came first thing and wasn't too much in the way, but then the florist arrived just as the electricians were doing something important, traipsing backwards and forwards through the house. They didn't want anyone crossing their path, so Mr Balls said the delivery people could put the plants down wherever they could find a space, and we'd put them into place later. Which I suppose means now.'

Mr Balls emerged from the conservatory at this moment, trailing his two slaves after him. 'It is not our job to move furniture. No. Nor to attend to the floral displays. But, in view of the circumstances, we will set aside our own feelings to save the day.'

He stood in front of the bridal arch which had collapsed under the weight of Midge's dive to freedom and now looked like a capital 'M'. He sighed deeply. Then recovered to demand, 'Strong wire! Pliers! At the double!'

His two slaves scurried to obey him, and with a heave from him, and some nifty work from the two slaves, the arch was coaxed into resuming its former shape and dragged to stand before the doors into the conservatory. It looked stunning, and no one would guess how nearly it had been wrecked.

The cleaners streamed downstairs, demanding that Ellie approve what they'd been doing. She went back upstairs with them, to find everything fresh and clean . . . and that all her toiletries had been removed from her dressing table and bathroom, and stowed away. She didn't have many aids to beauty, but what she had she'd need, wouldn't she? Oh well, she supposed she could put up with it for a couple of days.

Was Midge back yet? As Ellie let the cleaners out, she went out to the road to call his name. No cat.

She returned to face Mr Balls, who didn't want comments; only admiration. She was, in fact, very willing to give it to him, because he really was an artist in his way. The florist had supplied a dozen gardenia plants which he proposed to arrange on the staging in the conservatory. They looked stunning, and the perfume was almost too much to bear.

Thomas appeared to add his words of commendation, but shortly made his escape, decoration not being precisely his thing.

The marquee was a revelation. Ellie stepped from the conservatory directly into a big tent. There was a small stage immediately to the left, beyond that there was an exit leading to the kitchen quarters, and beyond that a long table for drinks. Chairs and tables stood around in huddles to be put into their final places on the morrow.

Mr Balls and his team departed and quiet descended upon the house.

Ellie couldn't rest, but wandered around. The dining and living rooms looked strange with most of the usual furniture removed. Her footsteps resounded on the polished but un-carpeted floors. At least their old settee and the television had been left in its usual place, so they could watch something that evening.

At supper time Ellie went to call Thomas out from his study. His sanctum had not remained unscathed as he had hoped it might, since his stereo and various small items from the lounge and dining room had come to rest in and around his desk.

She said, 'I'm worried about Midge.'

Thomas switched off his computer and rubbed his eyes. 'I've got a bit behindhand today. Don't let me forget the wedding rehearsal tomorrow evening. I think I'd better go straight to the church from my afternoon meeting, which is up in town. Do you think Mia can get to the church under her own steam, or will you take her?'

'She seems a lot better, much calmer, but she hasn't been out of the house since Monday, so I'd better take her. We'll get a cab to the church, ask the driver to wait through the rehearsal and afterwards it can bring us all back here.'

'No need for that. I'll have my car with me and can bring us all back afterwards. As for Midge, he'll come back when he's hungry.'

Well, Midge wasn't his cat, was he? Ellie went on worrying about him.

Somehow or other, despite all the interruptions the kitchen had experienced that day, Rose and Mia had contrived a tasty supper of gammon steaks with apple sauce, new potatoes and fresh beans, followed by a chocolate and orange soufflé which was a total delight.

Rose, however, seemed abstracted, and eventually burst out with what was worrying her. 'Ellie, I know you're a really big businesswoman nowadays and of course I don't know the first thing about that sort of thing, but Miss Quicke caught me in the conservatory just now and asked me to give you a message.'

Rose's belief that Miss Quicke was still hovering somewhere around the house could be unnerving, but normally Ellie could take it in her stride. Today, however, it caught her on the raw, and she would have made a sharp retort but that Thomas said, 'Don't tell me. She thinks the marquee an abomination and can't abide all the comings and goings.'

'Oh, no. Not at all. She's finding all this most stimulating, though she thinks the marquee ought to have been used for Ursula's wedding as well. No, no. It's the finances she's worried about. Have you taken out some insurance, she says? And if not, she would advise you to do so.'

Thomas took this seriously. 'What does she think will happen?'

Rose shrugged. 'Everything from an Act of God to someone breaking the glass in the breakfront cabinet in the sitting room, I should think.'

'An Act of God?' Ellie repeated. 'Did she actually say that?'

Rose looked bemused. 'How should I know? Seconds, everyone?'

When the kitchen had been cleared and Mia had settled down to watch television with Rose, Ellie wandered around the ground floor, now and then checking the drive outside to see if Midge had returned. Thomas watched one television programme, then came to find Ellie, who was in the middle of the marquee, staring into the distance.

He put his arm around her. 'Cheer up. Midge will come back in his own good time.'

'Of course he will. I think I'll just ring Mr Balls to make sure he did arrange some insurance for the weekend.'

'My love, are you sure this is not all too much for you?'

'Do you mean, why do I take any notice of Rose's conversations with a ghost? It's not that, exactly. It's everything; the cost of Diana's wedding, and all the horrible things that have been happening, and those boys this afternoon. I have a nasty feeling that there's something bad waiting to move in on me – on us. I know it's not rational . . . Well, it is rational to dread Denis coming into the family, I suppose. Those boys of his are deathly frightened of him, and I don't blame them. Then Diana is such a fool; oh, not in many ways, but she does take short cuts at work when she shouldn't, and they never work out.'

'You think Denis is a short cut?'

'I don't know what I think about him, except that if she's difficult to deal with, he'll be far worse. Tricky. Cruel. I'm sure he murdered Mrs Summers, though they may never prove it.' She shuddered.

'Relax. Leave it to the police. And if he does marry her, we'll manage, somehow. Come and sit down. You're worn out.' He led her back to the sitting room and replaced her chair facing the television. His own La-Z-Boy had vanished, so he stretched himself out on the big settee and half closed his eyes. He fingered the remote, but didn't switch the television on again – yet.

Ellie rang Mr Balls. 'I'm so sorry to phone you so late, but did you remember to take out some insurance for the weekend?'

Mr Balls was slightly reproachful that she should have had to ask. He quoted a reputable insurance firm and said he thought he'd covered all eventualities, just in case. The cost would appear on his invoice.

'Thank you,' she said. And switched off.

Thomas yawned and relaxed. He checked the television listings in the newspaper. All he needed to complete the picture of a man peacefully taking his ease after a hard day's labour was Midge sitting on his stomach. Oh, Midge; where are you?

Ellie couldn't relax. 'Thomas, may I tell you what the boys told me today? The police seemed to have written off Marge's evidence because she'd had a glass of sherry, but I believed every word she said. As for the boys . . . Well, judge for yourself.'

She repeated everything she remembered, finishing with, '. . . And when I asked the General what his mother thought of the wedding on Saturday, he said she was pleased about it because it would make his father – a word he clearly hadn't understood – a "pygmy" or a "biggy".'

Silence. But it was a different sort of silence. Not restful. Full of uneasy suspicions.

She thought about what she'd just said. 'Pygmy' and 'Biggy'. If you put them both together they made another, very different, word.

Thomas evidently thought so, too. He sat upright, looked at his watch, frowned. Got out his mobile phone, shook his head and put it away again.

Ellie said, trying the word out, 'Bigamy? I asked Diana if Denis had got rid of his wife, and she said yes. But she can be very stupid about people, can't she? She thinks Denis is the answer to all her dreams. She'd believe anything he said, if it meant she could marry him; though why she should want to . . . All right, I know. Sex. But she wouldn't knowingly enter into a bigamous marriage, would she?'

'What time are they due at the registry office on Saturday?'

'Two o'clock.' A long silence while Thomas rubbed at his beard and considered various unpleasant alternatives.

'You could check at the registry office tomorrow?' Ellie said.

'Tell me again what Diana said about their making their vows before their guests. Didn't you say something about her wanting me to don a surplice and officiate?'

'Yes. She did, and I said you wouldn't do it. I have no idea whether she believed me or not. She always thinks that if she pushes hard enough, people will do what she wants.'

'We're building a scenario on the word of a ten-year-old who clearly didn't understand what he was told.'

Ellie was restless. 'I know, I know. You may say I should give him the benefit of the doubt, that I can't go round suspecting people of crimes they haven't even thought of, and I agree. I also know that every fibre of me detests that man and has done from the moment I first met him. Yes, I am prejudiced against him. I believe he murdered Mrs Summers, and I believe he abuses his children. Now he wants to marry Diana and everything inside me is screaming, "No!".'

'Suppose you're right. Why go through with a mock marriage since they're already living together?'

'I don't know. Maybe he really loves her.'

The words 'and pigs might fly' hung in the air, but were not uttered.

Ellie twisted her hands together. 'He may be feeling insecure about her love for him, and so wants her to make a public commitment.'

Double 'pigs might fly'. Make it 'elephants'.

'Yes, but Thomas, if I'm right, then his wife – his present wife – knows something is phoney about his intended marriage to Diana. She must do, or she wouldn't be saying its going to be to her advantage and that it will help her to get rid of him for good.'

'Have you had a word with her?'

'Do you think I should? Oh dear, I don't even know her first name. But if she's as terrified of him as the boys are, then I can't blame her for hoping he's going to come to a sticky end.'

'A bigamist would probably get a custodial sentence. If she divorced him after that she could keep the house, at least till the youngest is eighteen. But does he have enough of an income to give her alimony and to pay for the boys' schooling?

Didn't you say he's put them into private schools? Aren't estate agents supposed to be doing badly in the recession?'

'I know. I can't think what he's hoping to gain by this marriage.'

'If this did all go wrong, what do you think Diana will do?'

Ellie shuddered. 'That's one of her virtues; loyalty. You may think it's rather selfish of me, but I don't fancy having my daughter tie herself to a man who's then put in jail for bigamy. She might very well decide to stand by him and waste the best years of her life keeping the agency going while waiting for him to be released.'

'If you're right, she wouldn't be tying herself to him. A bigamous marriage is no marriage in the eyes of the Law. Ah, we're building bricks without straw. You may have misheard the boy. Denis's papers may all be in order and the marriage will be valid.'

Ellie threw up her hands, frustrated.

'All right,' said Thomas, being reasonable. 'Let's suppose he hasn't got his divorce through. So long as he doesn't go through with the appointment at the registry office, but simply has a commitment service and party here afterwards, then he's in the clear. No bigamy. Just a formalizing of an existing secular arrangement with his partner. Suppose you ring Diana, check if she's still expecting to meet him at the registry office on Saturday. If he's made some excuse and cancelled it, then we'll be that much nearer to understanding what's going on.'

Ellie reached for her mobile phone, and got through to Diana. Background music. Television? Was Denis there?

'Diana, it's me. Mr Balls and his team have worked wonders. He's excellent, isn't he? Just a thought; are Thomas and I invited to the registry office on Saturday, because the timing's a bit tight . . .? No? You only need two witnesses and they're coming from the office? Right. Tell me; do you have to make sworn declarations about being divorced nowadays? You from Stewart, I mean . . . You did? And Denis, too? . . . No, no problem; just that you dumped his boys on us today and it was tricky, not knowing what to say to them about the wedding. Are they invited? . . . They're not? . . . No, quite understood. What's his wife's name, by the way? She came to collect them, but I didn't have a chance to . . . Valerie? Oh. Right. Yes, she'd been at the hairdressers . . . Yes, yes.

Fine. Yes, of course. What's that? You want a cheque for the dressmaker? Oh. Yes, I suppose so. Let me have the bill in the morning. By the way, you're not intending to wear that dress to the registry office, are you?'

She switched off. 'Their date at the registry office is still on. Diana's bought a special outfit for the civil ceremony, but paid for that herself, alleluia! They both made a declaration that they're free to marry again. He must have forged his divorce papers.'

'Now we don't know that for certain. It's possible he got them through in time. After all, he's been living with Diana for . . . what? Six months now? More?'

'Yes.' Ellie stared into the distance.

'It's probably all right.' He didn't sound convinced, but he reached for the remote and switched on the television.

Ellie couldn't sit still to watch with him. She wandered out into the shadowy hall and from there into the conservatory. Mia was there, watering the plants that had been delivered that day.

'Thank you. I'd forgotten all about watering them in. They look good,' said Ellie, thinking how much the girl had come on these last few days.

Mia touched the petals of a luscious gardenia and smiled. She was wearing a dusky pink dress which suited her. It wasn't one that Ellie had bought for her; presumably it had come from Ursula. 'Rose suggested I do it. She's good with plants, isn't she?'

'Yes,' said Ellie, thinking about a host of other things, none of them pleasant.

Mia did a twirl and stepped out into the marquee, holding up her arms, almost floating along. She sang, '"See me dance the polka" . . . Not that I ever did, of course. Dance the polka, I mean. Before supper I was worrying about the grass getting trodden down under the dance floor, but a good watering afterwards should help it return to normal.'

Ellie took a chair from a nearby stack and set it down to sit on. It was very quiet. Maybe she could think more clearly here.

Mia drifted around the marquee, listening to music from her MP3 player. Finally, she got herself a chair from the stack and sat down beside Ellie. 'You look worried.'

'I was thinking that you've filled out just these last few days. Good food and a rest have worked wonders.'

'And you, and everyone. Do you know, I've even begun to think about the future for the first time since everything went wrong. Such plans I have in my head!' She laughed. 'All stupid, of course. But it's true, I do feel so much better.'

'Who do you think it is who's trying to hurt you now?'

A shrug. 'My mother, I suppose. Although . . .'

'Not quite her style?'

'No. I really can't think . . . Someone who believes it might help their old friends . . .? Except that I don't think I know anyone who's got that sort of mind.'

'Ursula suggested someone who might know. She called him "Silly Billy".'

'Oh, him.' An indulgent smile. 'Poor Billy. Not quite all there, you know. Brilliant at maths, I believe; probably autistic. Socially he was always on the outside, you know? Some people made fun of him. He couldn't help it. He was brought up by his mother, single parent, kept to herself, didn't talk to neighbours. He grew up the same way. Then his mother died, and he sort of lost his way in life.' A quick frown. 'I suppose he might have noticed something, but getting him to talk about it might be another matter.'

'He was always hanging around your group?'

'Mm. He wasn't invited to the parties, of course, but he'd ask to walk me to the bus stop or the library, and he'd sit beside me if I happened to be on my own. I was sorry for him.'

'It might be worth asking him if he's still around. Do you know where he lives?'

'My brain's gone all stupid. What was his surname? Bright? I think he was able to keep his mother's flat on after she died, but where was it? Acton way? I could ask Ursula, I suppose. Oh, I know who'd be able to tell you – Ursula's old boyfriend; Dan Collins. Is he coming to her wedding?'

Ellie shook her head. This was the second time Dan's name had come up. Perhaps it would be a good idea to have a word with him in the morning. She yawned. Yes, it had been a long day. The sun had gone down and shadows were creeping around the marquee. Tomorrow someone was going to hang strings of fairy lights around the walls. Pretty.

Mia called out a goodnight and climbed the stairs to sleep in the room above Rose's bed-sitter. Thomas emerged from the living room, turning off lights, yawning. Ellie went to the front door and called Midge's name. No reply. No furry touch on her ankles.

She hoped the cat would return some time that night. Most of the windows overlooking the garden were kept open at the top in this hot weather, and he could get in as and when he pleased.

Tomorrow would be another busy day.

Thursday night

That had been a narrow escape. The big man with the beard had very nearly caught him. Not that he'd been doing any harm, watching the comings and goings from behind the laurel bush. Such a busy time. He'd noted down the licence numbers of all the vehicles that had come to the house. Two of the vans had unusual numbers, that he'd have found interesting on any other day.

He'd asked one of the electricians if he'd take the packet in for him. 'Sure,' the man said, without even looking at him. Probably thought he was the postman.

Then he'd waited. And waited. How soon would she taste it and die?

The hours wore on, and still there was no sign of an ambulance being called.

Perhaps she'd leave the sweet until after she'd eaten supper? He wasn't sure he could wait that long. He needed three good meals a day and though he'd brought sandwiches and a flask for his lunch, he really needed a good cooked meal at night. That was what his mother had always taught him, and he knew it was the right thing to do.

Then that fiend with the beard had jumped on him, and he'd fled. Out into the road, heart thudding. Round the next corner and away. Out of breath, leaning against the gatepost of a house in the next road.

He couldn't afford to be caught. He'd go back home and eat, and then . . . and then perhaps he'd see if they'd left a window open somewhere. He wouldn't feel right till he knew she was dead.

FOURTEEN

Friday morning

Still no Midge. Ellie had thought she'd heard him scramble up on to the window ledge sometime in the dark hours, but he didn't seem to be anywhere around today. As she took in the newspapers – was the local paper there, as well? It was – Ellie told herself that she had much more important things to think about than a missing cat, but the worry didn't go away. Just went underground.

Rose came in through the back door as Ellie went into the kitchen. Rose was frowning. 'I thought I heard someone scrambling over the fence late last night. I hoped it might be Midge, but he's nowhere to be seen.'

'He'll come back when he's good and ready,' said Ellie, hoping it was true.

Rose shook her head. 'I think someone was trying to get into the house at the back, because there's footprints under all the downstairs windows this side. They couldn't get far because of the tent being in the way.'

'Any damage?' said Thomas, yawning as he joined them. 'It was probably some down-and-out looking for a place to sleep.'

Rose exchanged glances with Ellie. Neither of them was happy about this solution, but neither could think of a better one. Rose prepared breakfast while Ellie worked out what food they might need to buy for the weekend; fish for tonight, perhaps? Something light to eat after the wedding rehearsal. A joint of meat for tomorrow evening after the weddings, or perhaps a chicken? They'd been invited to partake of Ursula's buffet, but not to sit down with Diana's friends in the evening, so they'd need something.

Mia came in, puzzling over the Party Planner's file. 'There's an awful lot to do still.'

Rose poured tea, looking over Mia's shoulder at the paperwork. 'What does the decorator do, anyway?'

Mia flicked through sheets. 'The decorator hangs drapes around the inside of the marquee and strings lights around. She brings covers for the chairs, which will be all in gold to match the ribbons that she twines round the poles that hold up the tent.'

She looked up. 'It says here that there will be favours provided by the wedding party for each guest, wrapped in organza and tied with gold ribbon to match the decorations. Is anyone doing anything like that for Ursula?'

Ellie took the file and looked for herself. 'I don't think so. Ursula's doing it on a shoestring. It's not mentioned here. I wonder—'

'If I could arrange something for her?' Mia's eyes were bright with excitement. 'How would I go about it?'

'It's a bit late to start now,' said Thomas, reaching for the toast. 'But –' and here he patted Mia's shoulder – 'it's a splendid thought. What would you like to do?'

Ellie noticed that Mia hadn't even flinched when Thomas touched her. Bully for Mia. And for Thomas.

Rose was in a dream, fingers fluttering in the air. 'Of course, it should be Ursula having the expensive 'do' in the marquee, with dancing and all, and Diana stuck with a buffet in the dining room. How about some boxes of Belgian chocolates, tied up with ribbons to match Ursula's bouquet and Mia's bridesmaid's dress? That's in lavender, isn't it?'

'Or why not pop into that nice shop "Present Company" in the Avenue,' suggested Ellie. 'They would know what sort of thing might do. I've heard of little containers of bubbles – you know, the sort you blow into the air. Doesn't that sound good? Maybe they'd have confetti, too. Or perhaps some rose petals?'

Mia clapped her hands in delight, and then sobered. 'How can we get enough in time? And some lavender ribbon? I could put the ribbon on, couldn't I?' She frowned, and chased the frown away. 'Oh, but I haven't any credit cards or cheque-book; I lost them all when I was escaping from the family. Ursula made me ring the bank to say I was back in circula-tion and they confirmed I've still got a good balance in my account, but I have to go in personally and sign this and that in order to get some more cards and some cash.'

'Let me lend you some.' Ellie was so pleased she'd had the

forethought to get a float from the bank the other day. Now where had she put her handbag? Ah, on top of the fridge. She got out some notes and gave them to Mia, who jumped up to give her a kiss.

'Oh, thank you. You're always rescuing me, aren't you? I'll go to the bank after the wedding's over, I promise I will. I'm getting braver by the minute, aren't I? Now, if I got a minicab, I could go to the Avenue and make them wait while I got enough favours to go round. Couldn't I?'

'I'll come with you,' said Rose. 'I know where to get the ribbon. It shouldn't take long. I'll tell Mr Balls that his slaves can make free of the kitchen while we're out.'

'I'm out of here,' said Thomas, getting to his feet while finishing his second mug of tea. 'This house is no place for a sensible working man today. Mia and Rose; I'll drop you in the Avenue, and you can get a taxi back with your purchases, right? Ring for a black cab from outside the station, rather than wait for a minicab. I've got an errand to run at the registry office –' and here he flicked a grin at Ellie – 'to check up on something. I'll leave the car in the Town Hall car park and grab a sandwich for lunch somewhere after my appointment up in town. Then I can pick up the car on my way back and take it over to the church for the rehearsal at a quarter to six. Mia; Ellie will bring you over in a cab. Right, everyone?'

'Can I come to the rehearsal, too?' said Rose, brightening up.

'Of course,' said Ellie. She gave Thomas a special smile. He hadn't dismissed her worries about Denis, after all. He was going out of his way to check up on the paperwork. Good for Thomas. And Mia was actually planning to leave the house? Wonderful.

The three left in a flurry, which gave Ellie a chance to rescue the local *Gazette* from where she'd hidden it. It would not be a good idea for Mia to see pictures of the accident on Monday, even though she was so much better now. The story was on the front: *Tragic Accident – Young Wife Killed – Two Children left Motherless.* The picture showed Ellie helping Mia to her feet, the wrecked pushchair and the big black man standing beside Ellie, gazing off the edge of the picture to where Ellie knew the young woman had been lying. Thankfully, there was no view of the actual body.

Ellie sat down with a bump, hands shaking. The shock, the blood, those two wonderful women working on the toddler, the wreckage . . . the baby wailing.

She sniffed, told herself to stop crying. It had been an accident.

She reached for some scissors to cut the picture and the story out of the paper.

All their names were there. Some hadn't been spelled correctly, but that didn't matter. Mia's name was given as 'May' and she was reported to be Ellie's daughter. On the other hand, they'd got Ellie's name right, as well as the name of the road in which she lived. Leon's, too. Apparently, he'd been discharged from hospital the same day. Good. She must check how he was doing and find some way of rewarding him for saving her life.

Then she noticed something which lifted her spirits. 'The children are being cared for by relatives.' What a relief! She hoped they'd be much loved.

What did the police have to say about it? Nothing Ellie didn't know. A dreadful accident . . . A stolen Volvo . . . Joyriding which had got out of control. Anyone who had seen anything, etcetera, contact the police on, etcetera.

Ellie took a deep breath. It had been an accident, not attempted murder. It was all in the past. It had happened; she'd survived and so had Mia. Best not to think about it. There was plenty else to think about, wasn't there?

Such as getting in some food for the weekend. Then Mr Balls must be let in and listened to. As Ellie stacked breakfast plates in the dishwasher, the first of the vans rolled into the driveway. Electrician, decorator, florist or members of the cleaning team?

Ellie opened the front door to let them in and picked an envelope up off the doormat – the bill for Diana's wedding dress. Then came a box of favours for Diana's wedding; chocolates, by the look of it.

Mr Balls arrived with his two slaves, the doorbell continued to ring, and workmen to trample through the hall. The decorator arrived with a stout youth carrying bags of this and that. The electricians came. Ellie warned the cleaners that the polished floor of the hall was going to need polishing again that evening.

After fifteen minutes of smiling and being helpful to everyone – who probably wished her out of the way in any case – she escaped to her office. Pat was there, sniffing. Pat didn't like all this disruption. Well, neither did Ellie. But – a naughty thought occurred to her – Ellie could escape if Pat stayed to field queries from the Party Planner.

'Dear Pat,' said Ellie. 'I have to deliver a cheque to Diana's dressmaker this morning because if the woman doesn't get paid today, there'll be no wedding dress. So I'll have to go out for a while. Can you hold the fort for me? Oh, and can you order us a minicab to take us to the church this evening in time for the rehearsal; that's for Rose, Mia and me. As for the rest, forget the routine. Smile at Mr Balls and make endless cups of tea, but go light on the biscuits because there aren't many left.'

Ellie scribbled out a cheque for the dress, wincing, and made a couple of phone calls. There was no point visiting someone if they were going to be out.

Denis's wife Valerie lived in a three-storey brick house near Scotch Common. It was one of the few remaining Victorian houses in that part of Ealing, and one of the most expensive. Ellie recognized the battered red car as she turned into the driveway. It hadn't taken her long to walk there, and the fresh air had done her good, helped her to think clearly.

Valerie opened the door to reveal a wide hall littered with abandoned shoes, bicycle helmets, and a deflated football. A number of children's and adults coats hung on a rack, but perhaps not as many as Ellie might have expected. There was also a lack of child noise. Somewhere in the depths of the house Radio Three was playing a waltz by Strauss.

'Mrs Quicke? I recognize you from your picture in the local paper. That was a nasty accident, wasn't it? Are you all right now?'

'More or less. Do call me Ellie.'

'That's not your daughter in the picture though, is it? Or do you have two?'

'No, Mia's just a friend staying with me till after the weekend. The children are out?'

Ellie followed her hostess down the hall to a large kitchen at the back. Here was more evidence of children's activities:

workbooks and comics on the table, one grey sock in the middle of the floor, a muddle of newly washed and dried clothes waiting to be ironed. The fitments were all in the fashion of five years back. Someone had spent money on the house, but not recently.

Valerie said, 'My mother and father came to collect them first thing this morning, taking them over to France on the ferry. They'll be out of touch for a while.'

'How wise.' Ellie suspected a lie told in a good cause. The children were probably on their way to Scotland, perhaps to an activity camp somewhere.

'They told me what happened yesterday and how kind you were to them. They also told me what their father wanted them to say. I wasn't going to have them questioned by the police. Coffee?'

'Please.'

As Valerie turned to the coffee machine, Ellie saw that one side of her face was yellow. From a bruise? Ah, so Denis hit his wife as well as his children? Valerie was not quite what Ellie had expected. Denis's wife had a worn, lined face, but her clothes sense was impeccable, even if neither jeans nor cotton T-shirt were this year's fashion. Her hair had been brushed into a smooth blonde mop showing grey at the parting. Her speech was pure Roedean, an exclusive girls' boarding school. Add grandparents who could take the boys off somewhere at the drop of a hat and a new picture of Denis's marriage emerged.

The coffee was good, strong and black. Ellie added sugar and milk. Valerie didn't. Valerie was very thin. Anorexic? No. Racehorse slender. Good bones, well educated. Moneyed background?

Valerie said, 'You wanted to see me about . . .?'

'The abuse that you and the children have suffered.'

Valerie looked out of the window at a garden which accommodated climbing frames and football nets. 'I don't know anything about that.'

'Why doesn't he hit the middle two?'

Valerie continued to look out of the window. 'Is it any business of yours?'

'I'm just wondering what will happen when he starts on my daughter. Diana's not like you. I don't think she'll take it.'

'I didn't, either. At first. But after a while . . .' She shrugged.
'Once you've been properly done over a couple of times and
haven't the strength to fight back, you tend to cringe the
moment someone raises his hand.'

'You admit he beats you?'

Another shrug.

'And the children?'

'They didn't adapt well to their new school. The fees are
an arm and a leg. He was furious when their school reports
were so poor.'

'In this recession . . . wouldn't it be best to return them to
their state school?'

A voice devoid of emotion. 'He wanted it.'

'I can see that it would involve a loss of face if he took
them away now, but lots of people have to downsize nowadays. Or did he hope your parents would subsidize the fees?'
A guess, but a lucky one.

Valerie shook her head from side to side, over and over.
She grabbed her mug of coffee and downed it in one. 'They've
decided it's time he stood on his own two feet. I agree.'

'Ah. They'd been subsidizing you for some time?'

Valeria relaxed. She pulled out cigarettes, a disposable
lighter, and found an ashtray. She lit up, coughed, and began
to talk. 'You must think me a fool to have put up with it for
so long. Pride, you know? I didn't want to admit anything
was wrong for, oh, years. He didn't hit me at first, not when
things were going well. He was proud of me and the boys,
and of this house; his position in society. My father was in
the construction business, did well, sold out at the right time,
has a good pension. Nothing was too good for my brother
and me when we were growing up: ponies in the paddock,
private schooling, holidays abroad.

'Denis took to the lifestyle like a pro, although I found out
later – much later – that in fact he was a grammar school boy
who'd flannelled his way up from nothing, a terraced house
in a poor suburb of Coventry. His father worked in the motor
industry on a production line . . . but we don't mention that,
of course. In fact, it took me a while to discover he hadn't
been educated at Harrow.

'Can you believe how naïve I was? I was never a Brain of
Britain, nor a beauty. I was working in a travel agency – a

job my father found for me – when in walked Denis and took
me away from All That. His words. "I'm taking you away
from all that." He was so powerful, so mesmerizing. I hadn't
a chance. He made sure I was pregnant before I took him
home to meet the parents. He'd done his homework, of course.
He knew exactly how much my father was worth before he
set eyes on me. That only came out later, too.'

'Your parents helped you buy this house?'

'They also helped him get started in the estate agency business. He was doing well enough, but not brilliantly, when he
met Diana and went into partnership with her. And finally
moved in with her.'

Ellie winced at an uncomfortable thought. Had Denis known
Diana was the daughter of a wealthy woman when he met
and wooed her? But surely even Denis wouldn't expect Ellie
to subsidize him? Would he?

Um. Possibly. Yes.

After Miss Quicke had died, Ellie had made a new will,
leaving the house to Thomas for his lifetime and everything
else to her charitable trust. Diana knew that, of course. But
did Denis?

Ellie probed a little more. 'So you're over him, looking
forward to being rid of him?'

A twist of the lip. 'Sure. I want out, and I don't want the
boys having any contact with him in future.'

'Then why not take their bruises to the police?'

Silence. Eyes down. A long pull on her cigarette. Valerie
waved the smoke away, looked out of the window.

'You want more than that,' said Ellie, guessing. 'You want
this house, or its equivalent. You want a fresh start, and you
want him off your back for good. Difficult to arrange, under
today's laws.'

'We'll manage.' She ground out the stub of her cigarette.
'If that's all . . .?'

Ellie played around with the suspicions in her mind. 'Why
haven't you divorced him?'

Valerie gave a little jump. She hadn't expected that question. She picked up their mugs and carried them to the sink.
'I have. Of course.' She ran the tap, and over the noise of the
water said, 'If you don't mind, I've a lot to do today.'

'Like going to the hairdresser? You didn't visit one

yesterday, did you? You haven't been to the hairdresser for weeks, judging by the amount of grey hair showing at your parting. So where were you yesterday?' Ellie made a further intuitive leap. 'You were at your solicitor's.'

Valerie turned off the tap and led the way to the hall. 'I don't have to answer your questions. Would you please go now?'

'Yes, of course,' said Ellie, deep in thought. 'I don't think you've even started divorce proceedings, have you? You could stop this wedding, but you don't want to do that. You want him to go through with it and then you'll have him for bigamy. After that, you can cut him out of your life without fear that he'll hit you again. It's neat, I must say. I could even find it in me to applaud, if it weren't my daughter who's involved.'

'Diana's tough. She can take it.'

'She's besotted with him.' Ellie spoke to the back of Valerie's head. 'If you let him go ahead and do it, you'll be an accessory to his crime.'

Valerie turned to face Ellie. 'I hear nothing, I see nothing, I say nothing. I haven't been invited to the wedding. For all I know, this remarriage of his is a figment of your imagination, a rumour set about to upset me, his dutiful little wife.'

Ellie took in the firm set of Valerie's lips and the bruise on the side of her face. There were yellowing marks on her upper arms, too.

Ellie held out her hand. 'If I were in your shoes, I might well think the same. Do you have a good solicitor? Because if not I might be able to point you in the direction of one.'

'My brother has arranged all that for me.'

Ellie said, meaning it, 'I wish you the very best.'

Valerie laughed, short and sharp. She shook hands and opened the door to the outer world. 'I'm putting this house on the market and renting a house in a village near my parents. Don't tell him, will you? Hopefully I'll be gone before he finds out.'

Ellie consulted her shopping list. It wasn't far to the Avenue, to the fish shop. She might even catch up with Rose and Mia there. Perhaps they could make a fish pie and put it in the oven, ready to eat after the wedding rehearsal?

She bought some fish and took the next bus to the town

centre and another on to the North Circular. Dan Collins had promised to be free to talk to her at the Health Club from ten onwards, and it was nearly eleven now.

Prior Place – the building which had seen so much tragedy on New Year's Eve – had indeed been renamed. It looked sleek and prosperous. The Health Club on the lower ground floors seemed busy, and many of the flats above had already been let. Good. The more flats that were let, the better for the Health Club and the better for its manager.

Ellie had always felt sorry for young Dan, even if he had sided with his erstwhile Prior friends against Mia and Ursula. Well, he'd reaped his reward, hadn't he? Manager of a thriving Health Club. Ellie wondered if he still regretted losing Ursula.

The foyer was decorated in dark brown, but the furniture was all light coloured, clear-cut and modern. A striking-looking palm and some ferns added a stylish touch and made Ellie wonder how they were all getting on with the wedding preparations back at home.

Dan came forward to greet her. 'Mrs Quicke. How nice to see you again. I saw your picture in the paper this morning. That was a terrible accident, wasn't it?'

This was a more polished version of the student she remembered. He'd lost weight, which made him look older. He was wearing his usual T-shirt and jeans but this time they were designer wear. Yes, he'd definitely gone upmarket.

He took her into the Juice Bar and gave her a coffee she didn't want, helping himself to an espresso. It was good coffee. She'd have to be careful or she'd go hyper with so much caffeine.

'What can I do for you?' Very much at his ease.

'I have Mia staying with me this week.'

'Ah, yes. They got her name wrong in the paper, didn't they? How's she coming along?'

'Recovering.'

He crossed his legs. Uncrossed them and crossed them the other way. 'The accident . . . It must have made her feel, well, threatened.'

Now did he mean that Mia ought to be feeling threatened, or what? Ellie wasn't sure. 'She was very shaken and it set her back a bit. For a while she began to wonder if someone was trying to prevent her from giving evidence at the trial.'

'She's not becoming paranoid, is she?' A twist of eyebrow, a patronizing tone.

Ellie flushed. 'She's received various threatening communications which the police are taking seriously.' Cross your fingers, Ellie; you really ought to check on what the police are up to.

'I'm sorry to hear it.' Dan's eyes wandered to the bar and then beyond Ellie to the foyer. Keeping an eye on things as a good manager should?

Ellie persisted. 'I've been trying to find out if there's anyone around who might still think it a good idea to harm the girl.'

'Really? Mother said you were on that kick, but honestly, I can't think of anyone.'

'Ursula said a lad called Silly Billy might have noticed someone.'

Dan shook his head. 'He's mental. You know? Had a crush on Mia, used to follow her around. Bit of a nuisance. Can't think why she put up with him.'

'Can you remember his surname?'

A frown. 'Bright? No, that's not it. Wright. Maybe. I doubt if he'd have noticed anything.'

'I'm probably chasing hares, but someone is still trying to harm Mia. One thing puzzles me. If this Billy was so keen on Mia, why didn't he kick up a fuss when she disappeared?'

'I don't remember him being around then. Holidays, you know?' A grimace. 'Didn't someone say something about his having had a spell in the Funny Farm?'

'You mean, he was sectioned under the Mental Health Act?'

'It was just a rumour.'

'Do you know where I might find him?'

'At the uni, I suppose, or researching something in Central Library. He was always at a loss what to do with himself in the holidays.' He got to his feet in one lithe movement. 'Well, if that's all . . .? I make my rounds about this time of day.'

She got to her feet, too. 'I'm glad it's worked out so well for you, Dan. I really am.'

He opened the front door for her. 'It's no good looking back, is it?'

A figure appeared behind him in the shadows of the foyer. A slender woman with blonde hair, dressed in black. Thirtyish? Would this be the accountant put in place by the Priors to see that Dan ran the place properly? Keeping an eye on him when he talked to someone connected with his past love? Mm. Probably.

Ellie raised her hand in farewell and set about finding a taxi to take her home.

FRIDAY MORNING...

Why didn't the phone ring? She couldn't stay in for ever. She must leave the house sometime. Only then could he deal with her. The hours were slipping away, and so were his options. He'd rung the house but she'd gone out. Shopping, they said. Why hadn't he been told she was out? And where was she?

FIFTEEN

Friday morning late

She'd been lucky with the taxi, which had come along just as she was wondering how pedestrians were supposed to cross from one side of the busy North Circular road to the other. It was all very well to have a central reservation, but four lanes of traffic in either direction were a trifle intimidating to someone on foot.

A black cab had come along just at the right moment, peeled off into the back streets and delivered her to the end of the Avenue in next to no time. She asked the driver to stop outside the police station, and paid him in some of the cash which she'd drawn out of the bank to give to Ursula. It was lucky the girl had refused, or Ellie would have been running short.

The police station. Ellie refused to let herself be cowed.

When Ellie had rung the station earlier, she'd been told that DC Milburn was out but expected back soon. Let's hope half past eleven meant 'soon'. Detective Inspector Willis was away this week, so she wasn't available.

No, DC Milburn hadn't arrived yet. Would Ellie take a seat? She did so, sighing. How many hours had she spent waiting on this hard seat in order to see police who thought her a major time-waster, someone who dreamed up conspiracy stories just to annoy them? Yet more often than not she'd been proved right.

In Mia's case, was she really wasting their time? On the whole she thought not, though every now and then she wondered if she were really imagining things. But she hadn't imagined the sympathy card, the wreath, the packet of coconut ice. She began to make a list of everything odd that had happened, so that she could tell her story without getting in a muddle. After that she had nothing to do but stare into space.

Dear Lord, I seem to have missed out on talking to You recently. I've been busy, of course, but that's no excuse. Sorry and all that. You know the muddle I'm in. So much going wrong, and I do worry about Diana, though I'm sure she'd think I was being silly to do so. I know I ought to start talking to You by giving thanks, and I do. I really do. Mia is so much better. But You know all about that. And Ursula, such a lovely girl. Do look after her wedding day, won't You?

This business of Denis . . . Well, You know more about it than I do. Did he really kill that poor woman? Oh, surely I must be wrong about that. I know; leave it to the police.

Please take extra care of Valerie and the boys. I'm afraid she may be in danger if he realizes she wants to scupper his plans. Not, of course, that I know that's what she's doing.

So, what about this Silly Billy? I can't think there can be anything in it. Oh, here comes trouble . . .

'Mrs Quicke? What are you doing here? Did I ask you to come in to make a statement? Have you remembered that you saw the deceased yesterday? Is that it?'

A horsey neigh of laughter.

The 'Ears' inspector. Oh dear.

He leaned over her. 'This is none of your business. The Summers woman had lots of male visitors and we expect to make an arrest shortly. So keep out of it.'

She tried not to get flustered. He was standing far too close, trying to intimidate her. 'Did you check her bank account?'

'What, what?' Even his ears went red.

'You might something interesting, if you do.'

'It's an open and shut case and—'

'Denis was one of her male visitors. Did he tell you that?

No? Well, never mind. I didn't come in to see you about that. I came to see DC Milburn on another matter.'

'Another bee in your bonnet?' He stalked off, annoyance leaking from every line of him. She'd bet he wouldn't check Mrs Summers' bank account, either. Sigh . . .

'Mrs Quicke?' This time it was DC Milburn, stocky and single-minded as ever. 'You wanted to see me about something? We have checked, you know. All the people concerned in the Prior case are still in jail, except for Mrs Prior who has now left the area.'

'Yes, I know. But one or two other alarming incidents lead me to believe that someone – and no, I don't know who – may still be trying to harm, or perhaps just to intimidate, Mia. Can you spare a minute?'

Ellie was ushered into the usual grey interview room. She went through her tale, referring to her list of 'incidents' as she did so, aware that DC Milburn had begun to fidget.

Finally, the DC lost patience. 'Mrs Quicke, we have a great many important cases on our books at the moment and we're short-handed, holidays and so on. All this is rather trivial, isn't it? There's been no direct threat to Mia, has there?'

'I suppose not, except for the car which nearly ran us over on Monday.'

'An accident. A joyrider, probably someone under age who pinched the car for a laugh and then couldn't handle it. That Volvo was automatic, but the lad who took it was probably looking for the gear shift when it veered off the road and on to the pavement.'

'Killing a young mother and injuring her little boy.'

A grimace. 'Yes, I know. Terrible. But the only fingerprints we found in the car were those of its legitimate owner and her young family.'

'The steering wheel had been wiped clean?'

A nod. 'They know about that nowadays, these young tearaways. We are checking with all the known offenders in this area and hope to make an arrest soon.'

'If he's under age, he'll probably just get a slap on the wrist, even though he's killed someone.'

'By mistake. Yes. Probably. That'll be up to the courts to decide.'

Ellie shook her head. 'Will you at least send someone for

the package of coconut ice? It looks as if some rat poison has been mixed in with it.'

A smile. False? 'Of course. When we've time. It's probably just a spot of food colouring.' She stood up and held the door open. 'Do let me know if anything else happens, won't you?' She didn't mean it.

Ellie gathered herself together and left the police station, feeling frustrated and in need of sustenance. She remembered Thomas had said he'd grab a sandwich at lunchtime, and it was nearly one o'clock now. She had a quick tussle with her conscience. If she went back home, she could put the fish she'd bought into the fridge and relieve Pat from the duty of looking after the workmen. But, as Thomas had remarked, the house was no place for a sane person that day, and the fish wouldn't spoil if she took time out for lunch in the Avenue.

The Sunflower Café seemed a little too busy for comfort, so Ellie went on to Oscar's, where she ordered a panini and an Innocent drink, and went outside into the garden at the back for a bit of peace and quiet.

Her phone rang. It was Ursula. 'Mrs Quicke, I'm sorry to trouble you when I'm sure you've got a thousand and one things to do. I saw the *Gazette* this morning and, well, of course it's just a coincidence, isn't it? I just thought for a moment . . . but no one is really trying to kill Mia, are they?'

Ellie was silent for a long moment, thinking about this. She'd told herself it was an accident. Mia hadn't thought it was. Now Ursula – whose antenna were well attuned to what was going on around her – was raising the same question.

At last she said, 'I don't know. Coincidences do happen. I was nearly run over by a white van the other day when I visited Mia's mother, and it's a long shot to suppose someone mistook me for Mia. I don't know what I believe.'

'It set me thinking.' Ursula held the phone away from her to speak to someone else. 'Just a minute. I won't be a tic.' She came back to Ellie. 'The thing is, I've got to go out in a minute as we're trying to find a bridesmaid's dress for my little American sister, who's broken her arm and is trying not to show that it hurts, such a brave little girl. I told Mia about her, and Mia suggested Sandy might like to be a bridesmaid, too, and she's thrilled. Mia will look after her beautifully, won't she?'

'That's a lovely idea, but—'

'It's not going to be easy to find something for her to wear at such short notice, but I'm going to try. A simple white dress of some kind would do.'

'What about a bouquet? Can she carry one?'

'I thought perhaps she could carry a little basket of flowers, but I really haven't got time to pop into the florist's—'

'I'm in the Avenue now. Would you trust me to see to it? Mia's bouquet is being delivered to my place and, if I can find another, she can bring one for your sister along to the church tomorrow.'

'Oh, bless you. But, the real reason for this phone call is that I got to thinking about this so-called accident on Monday and I didn't like the sound of it, not one bit. So I've been ringing around a couple of my old friends from uni, asking after Billy. His name's Bright, by the way, and he lives some-where off Acton High Street.'

Ursula half covered the phone again to say to someone, 'Yes, yes. I'm coming.' And then back to Ellie. 'Through a friend of a friend, I reached a man called Ahmed who knows Billy, so I've given him your mobile phone number, if that's all right. I've got to go. See you this evening at church.'

Ellie left her phone switched on, reflecting that she wouldn't normally have had it on at all, if it hadn't been for the Party Planner insisting that she remained in touch throughout proceedings. She wondered how they were getting on back at home, and began to fret about it . . . until she decided that Mr Balls was being paid to smooth out any problems, and she really didn't need to concern herself with them. For the time being, anyway. She put the phone down on the table while she picked up her panini, which was dripping with cheese and looked luscious.

Her phone rang again. 'My name is Ahmed. Am I speaking to a Mrs Quicke?' A slightly nasal tone, a precise manner of speaking, a well-educated man possibly of Middle Eastern origin.

'Yes, indeed. Ursula asked you to ring me about Billy Bright?'

'I know nothing of any importance but Ursula insists that I ring you. I do not know her friend Mia to speak to, although I have seen her around. I am a Muslim, you understand, and she is Christian, so we do not socialize. She is not a girl to flirt or behave immodestly. Never. I was shocked when I heard.'

'You were not at the Prior's party that night?'

'No, no. I am not in that crowd, and I do not drink. In any case, I had gone back home for the holiday. Only, when I return at the start of the Spring term, I hear about it. A terrible thing.'

'She's been receiving threatening messages recently. We understand that Billy Bright was fond of her, and wondered if he might have seen something or know something, have some idea where to look for the man who is doing this. You know Billy?'

'I did. The poor lad was brilliant in his way, but not well able to understand the modern world. I respected his ability, which is possibly greater even than my own – I am going on to a PhD, you understand – but we do not socialize.'

'Because he was not a Muslim?'

'No, because he stinks. He has always been careless about personal hygiene, but after his mother dies, he wears the same clothes day after day, never cuts his hair . . . you understand?'

'Yes, indeed. I heard he was fixated on Mia and followed her around.'

'I know nothing of that. As I explained, we do not move in the same circles.'

'So what do you know, Mr Ahmed?'

Ahmed seemed to be weighing his words. 'I know that he does not resume his studies at the start of the Spring term. Our tutor says Billy has had a breakdown and is in hospital. It happens sometimes, with finely balanced minds.'

This was bad news. Ellie had hoped so much that Billy would have been able to give them a lead to Mia's persecutor. 'Was he in for long?'

'A couple of weeks, I suppose. After that we see him in the grounds and in the library, but he does not return to lectures. I speak to him once but he avoids my eye and walks off. We think perhaps he is on medication which makes him unable to concentrate.'

'Oh dear. Obviously he won't be able to help us. A pity. We can't think what to do next.'

'It is not my place to make suggestions—'

'All suggestions gratefully received.'

'It is not my field of expertise but it does occur to me, we have discussed among ourselves, that Billy's breakdown may be a consequence of the terrible thing that is done to Mia. Amateur psychology is worth nothing, but it is known that he is devoted to his mother, who died . . . after which he transfers his devotion to Mia, who is always kind when other girls laugh at him. You understand?'

'Yes, I do. You believe that when he heard about it—'

'It turns him into a "gibbering wreck". Is that the correct idiom? One of my friends uses those words about Billy when he comes across him in the Ealing Broadway Centre, talking to himself. My friend is shocked because Billy is cursing Mia.'

'This was before he was sectioned, I suppose?'

'It is last week.'

'What?'

'My friend says Billy is clutching his mobile phone, talking to it or to himself.'

A nasty thought wormed its way into the back of Ellie's mind. 'What time and what day was this?'

'I have no idea. I ask my friend on Monday if it is important. He is away this weekend.'

'Was the mobile phone also a camera, capable of receiving pictures?'

'Aren't they all?'

No. Ellie's wasn't. No, wait a minute; she'd been given her current mobile by a friend and it might well have a camera included in its innards, though Ellie hadn't the slightest idea how to operate it. 'Might it have been last Monday?'

'I suppose. Yes, it is possible.'

'Mia and I were nearly run down by a car when we were in Ealing Broadway on Monday last.'

Ahmed laughed. 'That is not Billy. He is not able to drive.'

'No, of course not. A terrible thing; a young woman killed and her two children left motherless, though their family has taken them in, thank God. A number of people rushed up to see what was happening. Some tried to help, but others just stood around gaping. Two or three of them took photographs on their mobiles. I don't know if you've seen the local paper today—'

'No.'

'Well, there was a photograph of the aftermath of the

accident on the front page and it could only have been taken
then and there. No official photographer was around at the
time. I'm just wondering if a picture of the tragedy was sent
to Billy's phone by a well-wisher. You can see Mia's face
quite clearly. Also, when the police came up, I had to give
my name and address and say that Mia was staying with
me. Anyone in the watching crowd could have heard me
and sent the information to Billy.'

'Ah. Someone at uni is talking about an accident and says
Mia is involved. Some of the students put these things on
Facebook.'

'Bear with me. What I'm wondering, you see, is if Billy
had thought her so perfect before, if he'd put her in his
mother's place in his mind, and then learned she'd been
abused by her family and their friends . . . Might this not
have tipped him over into hating her? Perhaps he convinced
himself that she'd really been a wanton creature all along?
Then, perhaps, he might wish to punish her for wrecking
his illusions?'

'You are the amateur psychologist now?'

'It might have happened that way though, mightn't it? His
behaviour is disconcerting, you must agree.'

'Yes, it is.'

'It was good of you to ring me. Thank you. If you hear
anything more—'

'I will ring you, yes. If you are correct in what you think,
he should be sectioned again, for his own safety.'

'And hers.'

'Yes. And hers.'

Ellie put the phone down and concentrated on her panini,
which was now cold but still delicious, though inclined to
deposit dripping cheese everywhere. The more she thought
about Billy and his breakdown, the more convinced she was
that that poor deluded creature was responsible for the recent
persecution of Mia. It hadn't been the Prior family or their
friends; they'd all been duly accounted for, anyway. It hadn't
been her mother, who'd move on to fry other fish.

Now, if Billy Bright was at the bottom of the threatening
messages Mia had been getting, was it right to dismiss his
attempts as trivial? No, because he'd progressed from sending
lilies to a sympathy card to rat poison. That is, if it really

were poison in the coconut ice. Ellie would take a bet on its
being lethal.

Which left her with a dilemma. If she was right, then Billy
Bright had committed a criminal act, although he was probably not altogether responsible for his actions. Should Ellie
inform the police of her theory . . . which was only a theory
based on hearsay?

She rather thought she should. However much they might
laugh at her, the police needed to know about Billy, and if
he so much as put a foot wrong in future, they'd be able to
cope. To section him. And, if he was on medication as Ahmed
had surmised, then it should be adjusted immediately, if not
sooner.

She picked up her phone, and put it down again. She could
just imagine how 'Ears' would greet her suspicions. Would
DC Milburn think the same? Probably.

Ellie set her teeth. She would get herself a cappuccino, put
in lots of sugar, and then see if she had the nerve to report
the man.

She had some coffee, and although it didn't seem to give
her the necessary Dutch courage, she got through to the
police station. DC Milburn was out. Of course. Would she
like to leave a message? Ellie envisaged the message being
taken down and left on DC Milburn's desk. She could
imagine the policewoman reading it, and laughing. She
would say, 'Whatever nonsense will Mrs Quicke think up
next?'

Well, tough. Ellie dictated the message slowly and clearly.
'Please tell WDC Milburn that I believe a student by the
name of William Bright, who lives somewhere off Acton
High Street, has been responsible for the threatening
messages that Mia Prior has been receiving . . . How do you
spell Mia? Yes, that's right. And William Bright is known
as Billy. Shall I spell that for you? No. I'm told he lives off
. . . Oh, you got that, did you? I am told he experienced a
breakdown after Mia's problem became known, was
sectioned for a while, and hasn't been the same since. Yes,
sectioned. As in Mental Health. And yes, I am very worried
about what he might do next.'

Ellie listened while the message was read back to her. 'DC
Milburn will get this when she returns to the station.'

Good. Ellie put her phone down again. She had done all she could, hadn't she?

Well, no. She had a nagging feeling that she hadn't.

Her other big worry surfaced to give her violent indigestion. What was she supposed to do about Denis, the likelihood that he had murdered Mrs Summers, and his possibly bigamous intentions? What could she do? And Midge . . . Had he returned or was he lost to them for ever?

Ellie scolded herself back to the present. She had more practical tasks on hand than she could manage in the time at her disposal. She must get something light to eat for tomorrow night after the weddings, and buy a joint for Sunday. Also she must call in at the flower shop and arrange for another bridesmaid's bouquet for Ursula's little half-sister. What was her name? Sandy. Short for Alexandra?

How like Ursula to include a little girl with an arm in plaster in her celebrations. Most brides only thought of the look of the thing. Diana, for instance . . . No, don't think about Diana, who wouldn't have wanted a bridesmaid who might outshine her.

Oh, Diana. I fear you are riding for such a nasty fall.

Ellie grabbed her bags and set out for the butcher's.

Friday afternoon

He felt feverish. He couldn't understand why she hadn't been taken out in an ambulance – or a hearse. He'd have preferred the hearse. His mother had been taken away in an ambulance, although they'd said there wasn't much hope of saving her. She'd taken too many pills, they said. He'd howled like a crazy dog when he found her lying there. Why did she have to go and leave him like that? She'd said the pain was too much to bear, that the cancer was eating her up, but she could have borne it for his sake, couldn't she?

Mia had been so kind to him, afterwards. He had had no idea what she was really like, then. She'd had designs on him, that was it. She'd pretended to be a good girl while in reality she was nothing but a slut. A used-up prostitute.

He couldn't understand how she could live with herself. She ought to have done the right thing and committed suicide. Hadn't he given her enough hints? Last night he'd scrambled over the side door into the back garden, hoping to find a way into the house, into her room. But there was a great big tent in the way.

This morning he'd strolled past the house and seen vans and cars coming and going. The front door was propped open as people took things in and brought things out.

An elderly man was making heavy weather of taking some boxes into the house from a florist's van, so it was only right to lend a hand. At last he was in the house. Delivery boys never get asked for their credentials, do they? She wasn't there, though. He wandered all over the ground floor till some cleaning woman stopped him and asked if he was looking for the toilet.

He took the hint and went back to helping the delivery man to take some candelabra out of the boxes and leave them in the dining room. The candelabra were twined round with ivy. The man said his daughter would be adding flowers to them later, but that she was round at the church at the moment doing the flowers that had to be finished before the wedding rehearsal this evening. He said what church it was, too.

Six thirty this evening. He would get her this time.

SIXTEEN

Friday afternoon

Ellie went from the butcher's to the greengrocer, because Mia was getting through bananas and oranges even quicker than Thomas. As an afterthought, she bought some cold meats from the deli for anyone who might want a sandwich over the weekend and hadn't time to cook a meal.

Then she went to see the florist in the Avenue. The owner was nowhere to be seen and unfortunately her assistant turned out to be a ditherer. Ellie said, 'Look, all I need is an extra bridesmaid's bouquet. Can't you do one for me?'

'The boss is out and I can't . . . She's at the church now, doing the flowers. The bouquets and buttonholes for both weddings are already on the van together with the rest of the table decorations, so that all she has to do is give them their final touches on site tomorrow morning.'

Exercising patience and flashing her credit card, Ellie persuaded the girl to find a basket suitable for a child to carry – even one with an arm in plaster – and to fill it with white, yellow and lilac flowers, firmly set in a block of wet Oasis. The only problem then was that Ellie would have to add the basket to what she was already carrying. Should she get a taxi? No, it was probably quicker to walk. Tiring, but quicker.

She arrived home feeling hot and tired . . . only to wish she'd stayed out longer. As Thomas had said, the house was no place for a sensible person that day.

In the hall the Party Planner was mopping his brow thoroughly enough to shift his toupee to one side, while the cleaning team dodged around him and electricians shouted incomprehensible reports of this and that. Someone had moved the bridal arch so it stood by the stairs; probably to make it easier to take tables and chairs through to the dining room.

'There's no need to panic, dear lady. You may trust me to see everything will be absolutely tickety-boo.'

'Of course.' Ellie gave him a grim smile. 'What else do I pay you for?'

His chest swelled, but his voice trembled as he patted his cheeks dry. 'We cannot always trust others to be as professional as one would wish. The decorator – a fine woman normally, but in some distress – a daughter's illness, a husband gone astray – but what is that when one is supposed to remember the chair covers as well as the tablecloths? One despairs, one really does.'

Ellie edged around him, aiming for the kitchen. 'I rely on you to get it sorted.'

In the kitchen Rose was dispensing mugs of tea to members of the workforce, while Mia tied yards of a prettily figured lavender organza ribbon around tiny containers of bubbles, each one in the shape of a wedding cake. Three large men were making the most of their tea break, but when Ellie's hard eye was turned upon them, they beat a retreat.

Ellie looked a question at Rose.

Rose shook her head. 'No sign of Midge yet.'

Ellie unpacked fruit, fish, joint and cold meats, and held

up the flower-filled basket. 'Will this do for Ursula's little sister, do you think?'

Rose exclaimed with pleasure. 'Now there's a pretty thing.'

Mia said, 'I could put some of this lavender ribbon round it so she could string it round her neck when she needs both hands free.'

Pat bustled in, grimly pleased to see Ellie returned. 'Thomas rang; he said he'd tried to get you on your mobile, but you were engaged. He said he'd no luck at the registry office. They wouldn't tell him anything.'

Ellie nodded.

'Stewart rang to say little Frank's still refusing to dress up for the wedding and be a ring boy, and he – that is, Stewart – has been ringing Diana to see if he could get Frank off the hook, but she insists he go through with it and is dropping his outfit over there this afternoon. Stewart says he's made some sort of bargain with his son; Stewart will bring him to the party and take him away as soon as the vows have been exchanged and the lad's done his bit. Then they'll all go off on their holidays as planned.'

Ellie nodded. Perhaps that was the best that could be hoped for.

Pat shuffled bits of paper. 'Mrs Belton rang. Ursula's mother. She wants to come round to inspect everything, which I suppose is understandable but not helpful at the moment. She's on about a wedding cake, but we haven't had a wedding cake delivered for Ursula, have we?'

Rose stowed Ellie's purchases in the fridge. 'I'll cook the fish when we come back from the rehearsal. As for wedding cakes, there's one come for Diana. Five tiers with bride and bridegroom figures on the top. What you'd expect.'

Mia held up the basket by its new ribbon loop. 'Is this long enough, do you think? Ursula said she didn't want a cake. I'd have ordered one for her if I'd thought about it early enough.'

Ellie switched on the kettle. 'Thanks, Pat. I appreciate your standing in for me. Do you want to go off early? I don't think we'll be getting any work done today. Time for a cuppa, everyone?'

'Yoo-hoo!' A hard, clear voice. Diana!

Everyone froze.

Rose dropped her voice to a whisper. 'What does *she* want?'

'To sleep here overnight,' said Pat. 'Didn't I say? She rang earlier to make sure the guest room would be free.'

Rose muttered, 'That's supposed to be Mia's room.'

Mia shrugged. 'Well, I'm not using it, so of course she can have it. I like sleeping above Rose's room.'

Rose pulled a face. 'Well, I've no time to go round changing sheets, so she'll have to lump it.'

Ellie made herself a cup of strong tea in a mug, added milk and – at the last minute – some sugar. She also took the last biscuit from the tin, thinking that she was going to need all the carbohydrates she could lay her hands on. 'I'll deal with her.'

As she passed through the door into the hall, stepping sideways to avoid Mr Balls, something gauzy and light came floating down from the landing above, followed by a high-heeled sandal. Mia's bridesmaid's outfit? Ellie looked up to see Diana on the landing throwing the second shoe down.

Mr Balls took the phone away from his ear and stared as the fabric slowly settled on the floor. A cleaning woman carrying a box of polishing materials looked up and exclaimed in horror. The second shoe caught on the bridal arch and hung there, swinging to and fro.

Diana brushed one hand against the other. 'I don't know what that's doing in my wardrobe. I need the space, so you can find somewhere else to put it.' She vanished down the corridor.

Ellie picked up Mia's dress, rescued the sandals and mounted the stairs. She took the outfit into Mia's bedroom above the kitchen, carefully hung up the dress and placed the shoes below it. No great damage done, except to her temper.

She found Diana in the pretty guest room overlooking the garden, unpacking her wedding gown, shedding layers of tissue paper around . . . which someone else would have to pick up.

Ellie threw up the bottom half of the sash window. No Midge. She sent up an arrow prayer. *Dear Lord, can You keep Midge safe for us, please? Of course I realize he's a street-wise cat and is probably staying away to show his disgust at this disturbance in his routine. But there are fast cars zipping up and down the road and . . . Enough!*

You know what I'm really asking You for now.

Patience. Wisdom. In spades.

And if You can spare a thought for my poor daughter, because my throat aches to think of what she's heading into . . .?

Well, that's about it. Oh, I forgot. Please. And amen.

'Cat got your tongue?' Diana at her most acid. 'Cross because I've turfed the orphan child out into the storm?'

Ellie shook her head.

Diana hung her dress up, admiring it as she did so. She had brought a large suitcase with her, plus the box which had contained her dress, plus an enormous handbag. Once the dress was in the otherwise empty wardrobe, she began unloading toiletries from her bag on to the dressing table. She twitched a look at her mother. 'Why the long face?'

'I paid a visit to Valerie this morning. She's recovering well from the last beating he gave her.'

Diana's busy hands stilled for a moment, and she met her mother's eyes in the mirror. 'She irritates the life out of him.'

'She's sent the children away. Two of them show signs of abuse. Apparently they didn't get good enough school reports to satisfy him.'

A shrug. 'No skin off my nose.'

'Oh, he doesn't go for the face, usually. He hits the boys around the buttocks and legs. Valerie must have been specially "irritating" to get it in the face. How long do you think it will be before he starts on you?'

'He won't. Believe me, if he raised his hand to me he'd rue the day.'

'Tough talking, but once you've been worked over once or twice, you won't dare cross him. That's what Valerie says, anyway.'

Another shrug. 'Valerie is history.'

'Not exactly. She's still his wife. She hasn't divorced him yet. She's waiting for him to commit bigamy, and then she'll call the cops, her solicitor and the tabloids. If you let her.'

'What!'

Silence. Ellie let her words sink in.

Diana produced a light laugh. 'You're joking, of course.'

'You didn't know? You signed papers to say you were divorced—'

'He did too.'

'Only, he isn't. He's taking you for a ride. What I can't make out is why. Why go through all the rigmarole of a false registry office wedding? Why the charade of the big reception—'

'He *loves* me.'

'—Unless perhaps he means to cancel the registry office booking at the last minute, saying the paperwork hasn't come through in time? Then, with all the preparations for the reception so well advanced, he'll persuade you to go through with the rest of it, make vows before everyone, get you to commit yourself to him publicly.'

Diana picked up her mobile phone, considered it, and laid it back down again. 'Even if there's been some sort of mistake and he's trying to cover up the fact that the divorce papers haven't come through yet, we can always get married later.'

'You admit the possibility of error on his part?'

A shrug. 'I know he's so keen to marry that he'd do anything to . . . Not that I mean *anything*, precisely.'

'Ring him and see if he's still on track for the registry office.'

She lifted her phone, and put it down again. 'It would mean I didn't trust him.'

'Do you?'

'Yes, of course I do.' Now Diana was getting angry. She started to rub cream on her face to remove her make-up. 'Admit it; you've never liked him. You've never understood him – or me.'

'No, I don't understand him. For instance; why did he kill Mrs Summers?'

'What?' The jar of cream dropped from her hand, bounced off the dressing table and landed up on the floor. Another mess for someone to clean up. 'How dare you! What makes you say that? Ridiculous!'

'He had motive. It was she who tried to rent a big house for you, giving false references and a cheque that bounced. He can't have been pleased when she was found out. She might well have found herself arrested for fraud, if she hadn't so conveniently died, because she wouldn't have taken the blame, would she? She'd have told the police who'd put her up to it, and then he'd have been arrested, too.'

Best not say anything about emptying her bank account because that was just surmise and might be proved wrong.

A light laugh from Diana. 'He told me all about that. It was supposed to be a surprise wedding present for me, but it all went wrong. If only he'd left it to me, I could have got you to let me have the house and there'd be none of this bother. Because of course you will let me have it.'

Ellie wondered if Diana were right. Might not Ellie have given in eventually and parted with the house? She said, 'He's clever, I'll grant you that. He knows how to manipulate you. But why go to so much trouble? Granted, he needs money to support his lifestyle. Valerie's parents have stopped supporting them, and I don't think she has any money of her own to judge by the parlous state of the car she runs around in. Getting rid of Valerie must make sense.'

'He loves me, now.'

'You have some bits and pieces of property, but he's been living with you and off you for six months now and knows exactly how much you're worth. He knows that he can easily get you to part with what's yours. But it's not enough, surely, to commit murder for?'

'Murder?' Diana half rose from her seat and then sat down with a bump. 'You're trying to frighten me. He wouldn't harm a hair of my head—'

'No, he harms Valerie instead. And his sons.'

'That's different. That's all in the past. I'm his future. Together we'll conquer the world!'

Ellie sighed. 'Sounds good. Feels rotten. Will you cancel the wedding until you can work out why he's lying about everything?'

'He's not lying, and I'm not about to give up my dream wedding—'

'So long as it's not your deathbed.'

Diana finished removing her make-up and smoothed foundation on to her face, looking at Ellie in the mirror. 'You are a spiteful, malicious old woman. I see how it is; you're jealous of my good looks and good fortune. You've never loved me as a mother should!'

Ellie returned her daughter's scornful eye with a steady look of her own. There was colour in Diana's cheeks. Perhaps she really did feel that she was unloved? Was there a hint of self-knowledge there? Did she know she was unlovable?

Ellie didn't reply at once. The answer that rose easily to

her lips was that of course she loved her daughter. She'd told herself so many times over the years. Sometimes she'd qualified it – especially of late – by admitting to herself that although she loved her daughter, she didn't like her very much.

Was even that true? As of now, this minute, did she feel love for her daughter?

Well, what was love? Not that warm fuzzy feeling that you have for animals. For Midge, say. Where was Midge? Oh, Midge; do come back soon!

Love could be caring for a good friend. It could go very deep. Ellie's love for Rose and Rose's for Ellie was deep. Unspoken, but manifesting itself in dozens of little ways, day in and day out.

Ellie also cared deeply for a number of other people, some of whom were family and some just friends. Some of these reciprocated with warmth, some less so, but there was a pretty wide circle of people whom Ellie could honestly say that she loved.

Lust had nothing to do with it. Lust was what Diana felt for Denis, and she probably mistook it for love, though it was nothing like it.

Lust was only a very small part of what Ellie felt for Thomas, and he for her. Oh yes, rumpy pumpy was very nice indeed, to be looked forward to and enjoyed and smiled about afterwards.

Love was something else. When she thought of Thomas she felt . . . connected. Was that the right word? Yes, connected to him. Loving thoughts passed through her mind about Thomas. The feeling she had for him was deeper and far warmer than lust.

Although she knew in theory that love doesn't demand a return on its investment, love was also Thomas making time in his busy schedule to check out the registry office for her. Love was her worrying about his weight. It was deeper than friendship, warmer than even those much-valued friendships where the to and fro is equally balanced.

Love is patient, love is kind. That was a quote from somewhere. The bible, probably. She'd never been much good at remembering chapter and verse. Thomas would know.

'Love,' she said to her daughter, 'can be eroded by neglect and abuse. Valerie has stopped loving Denis because he beats her and the children. Mia stopped loving her mother because it was made clear to her that she was nothing but a nuisance in that family. I'm not sure that Ursula loves her mother, because Mrs Belton is a self-centred woman who never thinks of what might be best for her daughter, but only of how everything might look to the rest of the world.

'It seems to me there can be something beyond love between mother and child. Valerie is taking a risk, defying her husband to give her children a life free from fear. Ursula has never by word or deed allowed a criticism of her mother to cross her lips. Mia knows and understands her mother, but is more sad than angry about what has happened. Love may have died, but there is still a strong tie between mother and child.

'Perhaps some people would still call that bond love. I'm not sure that I can. But I do acknowledge that the tie is still there. I suppose I would die to save you if you were in danger, and it hurts me to think what misery you're letting yourself in for, by hitching yourself to Denis. But I am no longer prepared to go on pretending that I love you indulgently, and unconditionally.

'Yes, I will pay the bills for this charade of yours tomorrow, and I suppose I will try to pick up the pieces when Denis strips you of everything and leaves you without a penny. But don't take me for granted in future.'

Diana stared at Ellie, their eyes meeting in the mirror. 'You don't love me?' Perhaps for the first time Diana faced the truth. She repeated the words on a rising inflection. 'You really don't love me any more?'

'Do you love me? I think you love little Frank after a fashion, but you don't love him enough to let him off making a spectacle of himself at the reception. And yes, I do think he'd be better off seeing less of you, if you continue to chop and change, wanting him with you one minute and forgetting all about him the next. Have you bothered to talk to him about his spending his holidays with you in future? Frank is only a little boy, remember, and he's terrified of Denis. What will happen when Denis decides he'd not pleased with Frank for some reason and starts to beat him?'

Diana put a hand that trembled over her mouth. 'No, no. That would never—'

'I expect Valerie thought that too, once. Take a good look

at the road you're taking, Diana. Back out of this sham marriage before it's too late.'

Diana resumed work on her foundation with a hand that trembled. 'You're trying to frighten me, and you're not succeeding. I'm marrying a man I love with all my heart. Won't we have a laugh when I tell him what incredible stories you've been making up about him?' She set to work with the blusher on her cheekbones. 'I'll be out tonight, of course, having a rave-up with some girlfriends. Leave the front door on the latch, will you? Or better still, let me have a key.'

Ellie walked out of the room, feeling her age. Where was Thomas? She needed him. Ah, he'd said he'd meet them at the church for the rehearsal, didn't he? Was she dressed suitably? She looked down at herself.

No, she wasn't. She was wearing one of her oldest summer dresses, the one she used for shopping or around the house in the mornings. Not exactly millionairess quality.

She wouldn't think about Diana any more. It hurt too much.

There was a stir in the hall and Pat called her name. 'Ellie! Are you there? Mrs Belton's arrived to inspect the arrangements.'

Ellie produced a smile that wavered and went downstairs to greet yet another uninvited guest.

FRIDAY EARLY EVENING...

So she'd ordered a cab, had she? From home to church only. Time; half past five. Arrival at church five to ten minutes later, depending on traffic. Excellent. He knew the church well, because he'd sold various houses around there when times had been good in the past. The church was a heavy-set affair with a garden of sorts around two sides of it. Shrubs overhung the path. Plenty of space for parking.

He could take the van and position it at the cross roads, just beyond the church, and wait for them to come out. They'd probably be walking back home. It wasn't far.

His phone rang, and he answered it. Diana, in something of a state.

He ground his teeth, fought back the words that he wanted to say. Be still, my heart. It won't be long now . . .

SEVENTEEN

Friday early evening

To judge by her flushed face, Mrs Belton had come straight from the hairdresser where her brutally cut short hair had been permed into a poodle style. A perm as strong as that would probably last for months, but did nothing for the health of the hair, nor did it soften her heavy features.

'I thought you could save me the cost of a taxi by giving me a lift to the church because it's too far for me to walk in this heat. Ursula ought to have picked somewhere closer. Not that she listens to a word I say, out and about with her father and his second family, wining and dining and taking them to the Tower of London and shopping, if you please, instead of making sure everything is all right for tomorrow.'

'Um,' said Ellie, counting on her fingers how many people would have to fit into her minicab.

Mrs Belton looked around her and sniffed. 'I don't understand why Ursula wanted to have her wedding reception here. Such a hole-in-the-corner effort for the most important day in her life.'

She sailed into the dining room, where the buffet table had been sited at the far end and a batch of tables and chairs had been stacked to one side. There were no tablecloths on the tables, nor cutlery, nor glasses. The candelabra – ivy entwined – were on the buffet table.

Mrs Belton recoiled, raising both hands in the air. 'Is this where you plan to have my daughter's reception?'

Ellie said, 'The caterers and the florist will be in tomorrow morning to set up.'

Mrs Belton stalked back to the hall to stare at the bridal arch, which was now at the foot of the stairs. 'And what may that be?' The arch was indeed looking rather the worse for wear, with a scatter of jasmine flowers marking each of its previous positions in the hall.

Ellie looked at her watch. She really needed to change before they set out for the church? Would the minicab take all of them in comfort? Possibly not, but . . .

Mrs Belton moved into the sitting room at the back of the house. More small tables and chairs had been moved in here. The television set had disappeared, and the settee had been pushed up against the fireplace. They would probably have to have the lights on for the reception, as the marquee came within a yard of the French windows, shutting off much of the daylight.

Mrs Belton had caught sight of the marquee. 'What on earth is that!'

Ellie found herself wringing her hands. She told herself to stand up to the woman. 'It's a marquee for a reception later in the day. Ursula will have the use of these two rooms and the hall. The other party will go straight through the hall to the marquee and not come into these rooms at all.'

'What? You are telling me that . . . Words fail me!' Words didn't fail her, of course. She marched back through the hall, entered the conservatory, paused for a second as the scent of the gardenias hit her, and then tramped on into the marquee.

Here the walls had been hung with golden drapery, while tables and chairs had been roughly grouped around two sides of the tent. A long table at the back had been dressed with cloths and more golden drapery. Fairy lights had been strung here and there. Gold ribbon twined round the posts which held up the roof, and boxes had been stacked up on the long table . . . including cutlery and glasses? Where was Diana's wedding cake? In one of the boxes?

Mr Balls looked up from some paperwork as they entered. His slaves hovered, one on her mobile and the other adjusting the placing of a dais near the exit to the kitchen.

'Now this is more like it!' said Mrs Belton. 'We shall have the reception in here, where everyone has plenty of room to move about. The photographs will be taken in the conservatory. I'll see if I can get one of my contacts to provide some music for later on. I wonder you hadn't thought of it before.'

'I'm sorry,' said Ellie, glancing at her watch again. 'That's out of the question. This marquee is for a reception later in the day.'

'But—'

'The original arrangements stand.' Ellie's temper was beginning to rise.

'What? But that's . . . If I'd known, I'd have . . . Anyway, what are you doing about the cake?'

Ellie set her teeth. 'Ursula doesn't want a wedding cake. Her friend Mia is providing some canapés over and above the food ordered from the caterer. Mia has also bought some favours for the guests. Now if you don't mind, I need to change before we leave.'

'Oh, that's all right. I expect Thomas is giving you a lift. He'll not go without you.'

'He's going direct, but I have a cab ordered, and I expect we can squeeze you in.' The woman would probably want to sit in front with the driver, anyway. 'Well, if you could wait down here for me . . .?'

The front door was thrown wide and in rushed Marge, Mrs Summers' next-door neighbour, her jacket flying open. 'Ellie, you've got to help me! They've arrested my son!'

Mrs Belton bridled. 'Who, may I ask, are you? Don't you realize you are intruding on a most important occasion?'

Ellie put her arm round Marge, who looked as if she were about to collapse, and steered her to a seat. 'Come on, sit down. Take your time.'

Mrs Belton looked at her watch. 'We'll be late for the rehearsal.'

'Just a minute,' said Ellie. And to Marge, 'It's all right. Put your head down between your knees . . .'

Rose popped her head around the door, opened her mouth to speak, but on seeing Mrs Belton and Marge she withdrew again.

Ellie said, 'Hold tight. I'll get you a drink of water.' A gin would probably be more to Marge's taste, but Ellie didn't have any. She rushed into the kitchen and ran the cold tap.

Rose said, 'What does she want?'

'She's a neighbour of Mrs Summers . . . The childminder who was found dead, remember?'

'She's not staying, is she? The cab will be here in a minute. Do I need to wear a hat?' Rose patted her hair.

Mia was rushing scrubbed new potatoes into a pot of cold water on the stove. 'There, everything's ready to cook when we get back.'

Ellie filled a glass with cold water, looked at the clock and winced. She picked up the flower basket. 'I'd better take this along to give to Ursula's little sister. Is the back door locked?'

Mia said, 'Mr Balls is still here. I'll ask him to make sure everything's locked up, shall I?'

'Thanks, Mia.' Ellie darted back to the hall, dropped the flower basket on the hall table, checked the grandfather clock – were they going to be late? – and helped Marge to sip some water.

'We must be off!' announced Mrs Belton. 'We don't want to be late.'

'Late for what?' demanded Diana, descending the stairs. 'What's all the fuss about? This place is bedlam.' A car horn sounded in the driveway. 'Ah, is that my cab? I'm taking cabs tonight so I can drink and not drive.'

'No, it's not yours,' said Ellie. 'You'll have to ring for one if you want one. Oh, and if you're going to be that late . . . Here, take my key, but leave it on the hall table when you get back in, as I'll need it tomorrow.'

Mia rushed back from the conservatory. 'Mr Balls says he'll see everything's locked up, but he would like a word with you, Ellie.'

'Sorry. No can do. Marge, we're due at the church in less than ten minutes. Can you wait here till we get back? We'll only be about an hour.'

Marge grabbed Ellie's arm. 'They've arrested Duncan. Can't you tell them it wasn't him?'

'Why have they . . .?'

'Because he helped her out with odd jobs, the fence that fell down, her doorbell, a tap that dripped. They think he was one of her regulars, but he wasn't, honest he wasn't, at least not like that, if you see what I mean. Of course he popped in to see her just as he does to see me, but they think he did it because the neighbours have seen him going in and out, though I told them there were other men doing the same thing and they weren't *all* being helpful, or rather, they were helping themselves, if you know what I mean.'

'Yes, I know what you mean.'

Diana wandered out into the driveway, talking into her mobile.

Rose came out of the kitchen. 'The cab's here.'

Mia picked up the flower basket. 'Can we all get in?'

'What?' Mrs Belton was offended. 'I don't see why everyone needs to come.'

Ellie said, 'Rose, you go ahead with Mia and Mrs Belton.'

'You're just as important as I am,' said Mia.

'Don't leave me!' gasped Marge. 'You've got to tell them it wasn't Duncan!'

Rose dithered. 'I could stay behind, if you like.'

'Certainly not! Mia needs you,' said Ellie. 'Let's all squash in, right? Mrs Belton can go in the front, and the rest of us will manage somehow.'

Mrs Belton stalked out of the house, outrage in every line of her body.

Rose looked out. 'It's one of the bigger models. I think we can probably all squeeze in. I really wouldn't want to miss it.'

'Nor shall you,' said Ellie. 'Come along, Marge. I haven't got anything special to do when we get to the church, so we'll sit in the back and you can tell me all about it while the others have their rehearsal.'

It was a tight squeeze to get everyone into the back of the car, but no one complained and the driver – who was one of those Ellie often used – put his foot down to get them to the church on time.

Getting out, Ellie said, 'You've got our booking for tomorrow morning, haven't you? Three people to be collected from my house about eleven twenty, to get us to the church in good time for the wedding at twelve.'

'Will do.'

Ellie noticed a large white van parked a little way down the road. She shivered. Then she told herself she was getting paranoid, seeing white vans everywhere, even though they were a common enough sight on the roads. This one, she told herself, had nothing to do with her previous near-miss from being run over.

Ursula was already there, with a group containing two children: a toddler in a youngish woman's arms, and a plain little girl with an arm in a plaster cast. The other bridesmaid, what was her name? Sandy.

Hawkface – Sam – was there of course, chatting to an older man who must be Ursula's father, and a couple of younger men, one of whom must be Sam's best man.

As they greeted everyone, Thomas – still in civvies – came
out of the church, smiling, laughing, looking at his watch.
'We're on time. Good. You've brought the printed Order of
Service with you? Splendid. Put the packet on the table at the
back, just inside the door, will you?'

One of the men peeled off from the group to take a package
inside the church. The best man? An usher? A roly-poly, good-
natured looking man.

Ursula hugged and kissed Mia and introduced her to little
Sandy, who was both shy and plain. Mia held out the basket
of flowers. 'This is for you, poppet. You can hang it round
your neck or carry it in your hand. What do you think?'

'It's lovely. Thank you.' An American accent, a shy smile
revealing braces on her teeth. Today Sandy was wearing a
brightly coloured T-shirt and floppy shorts. She was the sort
of child who would get left out when her mates picked sides
for a game.

Mrs Belton ignored her ex-husband and his family to stalk
into the church. 'Let me make it clear that I do not intend to
share the front pew with anyone else.'

The best man raised his eyebrows, but everyone else
accepted that this was what Mrs Belton was like, and that
they might as well put up with it.

Ellie liked the look of Ursula's father, a big, strongly built
man with a lively eye. His second wife was not as young as
she'd looked from a distance, but also seemed intelligent and
kindly.

Marge clung to Ellie's arm till she suggested that Rose
take her into the back of the church. 'I'll join you in a
minute.'

Thomas urged a early start, and the party began to dribble
through into the church. Mia got down to the level of the little
bridesmaid, to explain to her how they were to walk together
behind the bride.

Ursula reached out to take Ellie's arm and said in her
ear, 'Did Ahmed ring you? Ever since I talked to him, I've
been thinking about Billy. Do you think he's gone off his
rocker?'

'Sounds like it.'

Mr Belton offered his arm to Ursula. 'Come along, my dear.
I've been looking forward to this.'

Ursula gave him a brilliant smile, but whispered – quickly, urgently – to Ellie, 'I thought I saw Billy on the other side of the road just now. Can you keep an eye out for him?' She took her father's arm, collected her bridesmaids, and led the way into the church.

Ellie cast a wild glance around and spotted a couple of bystanders gawping on the other side of the road. There was no sign of a scruffy young man, which is how Billy had been described to her. Perhaps he'd smartened himself up and was the man walking a dog along the opposite pavement? No. Man and dog turned off into a side road. Besides, nobody had mentioned that Billy had a dog, had they? She wished she knew what he looked like.

She could hear Thomas talking inside the church and went in herself, leaving the doors open behind her. The church was large and shadowy, with a polished tiled floor. A huge stand of white flowers had been arranged by the font just inside the door, and another, even larger, up by the altar. The florist had done a good job.

This church was a lot later in date than the one in which Ellie used to worship. This one had chairs rather than pews, and a grand piano as well as a big organ. One or two people wandered around, fitting new candles into brass candlesticks, polishing the brass lectern.

Thomas talked to the bridal party up by the altar, showing them where to stand and what to do. Ursula and Sam were holding hands. Nice.

Marge caught hold of Ellie's arm. 'Can't you do something? He didn't do it, I tell you!'

'Come outside where we can talk.'

Thomas's laugh rang out through the church, followed by a ripple of amusement from the rest of the party.

Ellie led Marge out to the porch. 'Now, calm down and tell me exactly what's happened.'

'That policeman yesterday, the one with the red ears, he wouldn't listen when I tried to tell him that her next door had lots of visitors, and that Denis was there every week. Denis kept contradicting me, saying his were purely pastoral visits, and that I was always half cut by six in the evening and didn't know what day of the week it was. He's scary, isn't he?'

There were tears in her ears which she wiped away. 'I tried to keep calm, I really did, but I could see the policeman was taking Denis's side, and in the end I told him that it was Denis's boys who'd trashed the place, and Denis said that was slander, and he'd be writing to his solicitors to sue me if I repeated it.'

Ellie put a comforting arm around Marge. 'He is scary. I agree.'

'The policeman said they'd ask the neighbours about people calling next door and Denis said he'd be off, and he went out of the door talking to the policeman, and they were laughing, and I got myself another little drink because it was all just too awful, wasn't it? Then Duncan came, and I'd forgotten he was coming and hadn't anything to give him for supper, and he was upset because he'd liked Mrs Summers and been in and out of her house for years, helping with this and that. He's a good boy, you know, never given me a minute's trouble. He said he'd seen other men going in and out over the past year or so since her husband died, and we talked a bit about them, trying to work out how many there were and what they looked like.

'Then he went off to get some fish and chips in his van—'

'His van?'

Marge stared. 'Yes, of course. His van. He's a carpet fitter, delivers and fits carpets all over this side of West London, works for a firm out at Uxbridge. Been doing it for years.'

'A white van?'

'Yes. Not one of the largest or the newest, but yes; a white van. Why?'

Ellie thought, No. This can't be the same van. Can it? 'No reason. Carry on.'

'When he came back the police were waiting for him, because the neighbours had said they'd seen him around a lot in his van, going in and out of Mrs Summers' house, and the police wanted to know what he'd been doing last night and he, well, he lost his temper a bit because he's always had a short fuse, and I must admit we'd both had a little drink before he went out for the food. So there was an argument, and it got a bit heated, and I'm not sure who pushed who first, but they breathalysed him, arrested him, and took him away, and now I don't know what to do because he didn't kill her but they think he did!'

'I understand,' said Ellie, thinking about the hazards of drinking, driving, and having a short temper. 'From the police point of view, you must admit—'

'It was only a small glass he had. Well, maybe two.'

'What about the list you were making of her other visitors?'

'I took it out to the police while they were arguing with Duncan and tried to give it to them, but they were shouting and laughing, pleased with themselves, didn't want to know what I had to say . . .' Tears began to streak her cheeks. 'They said I was drunk, which I wasn't. I hardly touch alcohol nowadays.'

'Of course.' Ellie gave Marge a hug. 'Well, what I suggest is that we get my solicitor on the job. As soon as we've finished here, you must come back with us and I'll ring him. It's a Friday night, but he ought to be able to get someone working on it. They'll listen to him, even if they won't to us.'

Marge sought for a hankie in her handbag, sniffing, still crying. 'I can't afford—'

'I can, and if I can do anything to upset Denis, I'd be only too happy to do so.'

Marge blew her nose, sniffed, tried to smile. 'He's a bully, isn't he?'

'First class.'

There was a stir in church, and down the aisle came Ursula on Sam's arm, followed by her bridesmaids and the rest of the wedding party, all laughing and chatting except for Mrs Belton, who almost trod on Mia's heels in her anxiety not to brush against her ex-husband. Tomorrow, of course, the bridegroom's parents would be there as well, and Mrs B would be able to make her exit on the arm of the groom's father.

'Everyone happy?' said Thomas, following them all out. 'Any questions? The organist has your choice of hymns and so on?'

'I can hardly wait,' said Sam, putting his arm around Ursula.

'Me neither,' said Ursula, smiling a promise at him.

'Well, now. Who's needing a lift?'

'My car's just around the corner—'

Ursula picked up her little sister. 'Isn't this going to be fun? Mia, would you like to come back with us? We're having a family "do" at the Thai restaurant in the Avenue.'

Mia shook her head. 'I'm helping Rose cook for our lot tonight.'

'Count me out,' said Mrs Belton, 'but I could do with a lift back to the Avenue if anyone's going my way.' It was an order, not a request. The roly-poly usher nodded her towards his car, and she made a stately exit.

The party began to thin out, some going round the corner, some walking the other way. Thomas led the way to his car, followed by Rose and Marge, while Ellie waited for Mia to have a last word with Ursula.

And then . . .

Woosh!

A roar from a powerful engine, a squeal from mistreated tyres. A woman's scream. A man's hoarse shout.

'Mia!'

Someone ran across the road, right across the traffic, aiming for Mia with arm upraised, straight into the path of the white van.

There was a dull thud.

A limp figure was tossed up into the air and fell to the pavement. A heavy walking stick fell from his hand.

A woman screamed.

The van accelerated and drove off, turning left into the traffic on the main road ahead.

Ellie clutched Mia. Or Mia clutched her.

'Mia! Are you all right?'

Mia nodded, unable to speak, eyes on the life-sized rag doll at their feet.

Ursula had seen what had happened, was running back.

Sam had his mobile out, summoning help.

Ellie was trembling. She told herself she was all right.

Thomas caught hold of her. 'You're not hurt?'

She nodded.

Someone was still screaming. Well, it wasn't her, and no, it wasn't Mia.

Rose was on her knees by the rag doll lying on the pavement. There was some blood, not much. Thomas knelt, too.

Marge pulled on Sam's sleeve. 'I think I got the number.'

He passed his phone to her, and she gave the number to the police.

Mia said, 'Oh, no! It's Billy! He's not badly hurt, is he?'

Thomas said, 'Don't try to move him.'

Mia knelt on the pavement. 'Poor Billy. He saw me and ran right across the road in front of the van. Oh, this is dreadful! Is he very badly hurt?'

Rose took Mia's arm and tried to pull her away. Mia resisted. 'I'm not leaving him. He's not dead, is he?'

'No,' said Thomas. 'He's coming round, I think. But don't try to move him.'

Mia stroked his hand. 'Don't give up, Billy. I'm here. Just hang on. The ambulance will be here in a minute.'

Billy opened his eyes and tried to speak, but failed. He seemed to recognize her . . .

I didn't really want you to die, Mia. That was a mistake. I love you . . .

Blood trickled out of the corner of his mouth. His eyes went dull and dark, but remained open.

'Oh, no!' Mia wept.

Ellie looked at Ursula, and the girl looked back at her. Steadily. With meaning.

Should they say anything about Billy's mental health problems? Or about the heavy walking stick which he'd been holding, raised in the air, ready to hit Mia as soon as he got close enough? If he'd been responsible for the recent threats to Mia, then there would be no more of them in future. Did Mia need to know what they suspected?

Ellie helped Mia to stand and turned her away from the body on the pavement. 'Come and sit down.'

Thomas was praying in a low voice.

Rose took charge. 'We'll have to wait for the police and the ambulance people, but there's no need for us all to stand around, is there? Why doesn't everyone go back into the church and sit down till they arrive?'

EIGHTEEN

Friday evening

I t was after eight before Thomas managed to cram everyone into his car and drive home. Luckily no one needed to be checked out in hospital this time.

Rose got out first, yawning and stretching.

Mia followed her, sighing. 'Poor Billy. He was so very alone in the world.'

Rose got out her key. 'Supper. How soon do you think we can get it on the table?' She opened the door into the house.

Ellie helped Marge out of the car. 'We'll ring my solicitor now. You'll come in, won't you?'

Marge grimaced. 'I could murder a glass of wine.'

Thomas locked up the car, and Ellie glanced around. Nobody was creeping through the bushes tonight. No other cars were there, so the Party Planner and his cohorts must have departed for the day. Presumably Diana wouldn't return till much later.

Once inside, Ellie showed Marge where to wash and brush up. Thomas put his arms around Ellie and held her close. She did the same to him, resting her head on his shoulder. Such a comforting embrace. No need for words.

Ellie released herself at last. 'I'll go and change upstairs.'

'I'll see if Midge is back.'

Friday night

A trying evening, full of tiredness and failed attempts to be bright.

Supper was absent-mindedly eaten in the kitchen. Marge was connected with Ellie's solicitor, who discovered that the police had only charged Marge's son with being drunk in charge of a vehicle, and not with murder. He was to be released next day on bail, pending further enquiries – by which, presumably, they meant the murder. Marge cried a lot and drank half a bottle of wine before being soothed to bed in the room little Frank used when he stayed over.

Mia seemed none the worse for her outing, though she did wipe her eyes now and then and say she must remember to pray for Billy. Rose annoyed everyone by saying there was nothing like a spot of bother to make you grateful to be alive.

Ellie told herself that all their worries were over. Weren't they? Well, except for the Denis and Diana problem.

After supper Thomas avoided their usually comfortable sitting room, as it had been denuded of everything that made it homely but went up to spend time in his quiet room.

Ellie didn't join him upstairs, being too agitated to sit still. Under normal circumstances she would have calmed herself down by doing some gardening; dead-heading and weeding were therapeutic. But today she couldn't even get at the garden properly. Instead she paced the marquee for an hour. She told herself there was nothing more she could do. The police were trying to track down the white van at that very minute. She told herself to stop worrying and leave everything to them.

She tried ringing Denis. He wasn't in the flat he'd been sharing with Diana, nor with his wife, Valerie. Or ex-wife. Whichever. Would he turn up at the registry office tomorrow? What could Ellie do to stop Diana committing herself to him?

Answer: nothing.

Diana didn't return home. She'd probably be out till the small hours.

'Come up to bed,' said Thomas, holding out his hand to her. 'You must be worn out.'

'Yes. No.' She climbed the stairs beside him. Their bedroom had been cleaned and polished to within an inch of its life. This was where Ursula and Sam would change into their honeymoon kit on the morrow.

Thomas said, watching her, 'I'll be glad when it's all over.'

'Yes, the disruption is tiresome.'

'I did try to get some information at the registry office, but the top bod was off and no one seemed able to tell me anything. Perhaps I should have tried harder.'

'I don't think it would have made any difference. She's set on having him.' Her voice tailed away as she got ready for bed. She showered, brushed her teeth, got into bed. Her eyes were wide open.

Thomas got in beside her and turned out the centre light.

'Thomas; both times when I was with Mia, she was on the inside and I was walking next to the kerb.'

'I was afraid of that.'

She tried to make it clearer. 'I was the target, not her.'

He nodded. 'It's giving me the heebie-jeebies. Do you know why? Or who?'

'It wasn't Billy, that's for sure. I don't think he even saw the van coming at us this evening. He only had eyes for Mia. He was coming at her with that stick in his hand. I suppose he meant to attack her only the van got to him first. So who was driving the van?'

'I was talking to Ursula when I heard it start up and looked around . . . Did you see who was driving the white van when you called on Mia's mother?'

'It was behind me at first, and when I looked up I couldn't see inside. The window was tinted. Then I jumped into the bushes. The minicab driver didn't see, either, although I suppose the police will ask him about it now.'

'Was it the same white van?'

'I don't know. It was past me and gone in a flash. No markings, but a lot of them don't have markings on, do they? Rented, I suppose.'

'They'll find him now they've got the licence number. Thanks to Marge. Her liver may be in a bad state, but her mind's sharp enough.'

Silence.

She said, 'I can't see Denis driving a white van at me.'

'You mustn't jump to—'

'I know, I know. There is absolutely no reason to suppose that he should want to kill me, but I can't think of anyone else who—'

'Why should he want to kill you?'

'I don't know.' She slid down the pillows. 'I'm being unreasonable, aren't I?'

He turned out the bedside lights. 'I'm going to stick to you like glue tomorrow. Not a hair of your head shall be harmed.'

'Nonsense.' She began to giggle. 'You've got to officiate most splendidly at the wedding and do a hundred other things out of my sight.'

'I'll just have to catch up on my praying, then. You are one very special person, Ellie Quicke. You do an immense amount of good in the world without ever asking for thanks or even acknowledgment, and I'm asking God to keep His eye on you.'

He put his arm around her, and soon she could tell by the rhythm of his breathing that he'd fallen asleep. She lay awake, eyes wide, wondering how a white-van man had known where and when to find her on at least two occasions.

Saturday morning

Ellie hadn't thought she would sleep at all, but in the event she managed a good six hours' of unconsciousness and woke to find a pearly sky brightening to gold. It was going to be another hot, airless day. Thomas's side of the bed was empty. He'd be up and in his quiet room already.

She threw back the curtains and looked out over the marquee to what she could still see of the garden below, which wasn't much. She spotted Mia, hanging up fat balls for the birds. Mia looked like a child, in sandals and a cotton nightie. Mia was smiling.

Well, at least the threats to Mia should stop now. Thank the Lord.

Ellie knew she ought to be thanking the Lord for a lot of other things, too, but there were so many problems buzzing around in her mind that she had to take a deep breath, and tell herself: Stop! Concentrate! Do one thing at a time!

Is someone really trying to kill me?

No reply.

'*Well, dear Lord. You know how I'm fixed today, all the things I'm worrying about. Not just about the silly little tragedies that will no doubt occur such as the caterers forget-ting to bring a knife to cut Diana's wedding cake, but the big things such as . . . such as please will You bless Ursula and Sam in their marriage? Now that is important.*

Breakfast was important, too. She got herself dressed and

went along the corridor to see if Diana wanted any on this
her second wedding day. Diana's door was firmly shut but
Ellie eased it open long enough to see that her daughter was
asleep in the spare-room bed.

Marge was stirring in little Frank's room and said she never
ate breakfast normally, but would make an exception today.

Down in the hall, Ellie found the keys which Diana had
borrowed on the hall table. Good.

Thomas and Rose made a substantial breakfast for them
all: fresh orange juice, scrambled eggs and bacon, toast, tea
and coffee. Mia jumped up and down from the table to collect
things, eyes bright, full of excitement. Rose was quieter,
smiling fondly at the transformation in the girl.

Thomas advised them to eat something to still the wedding
nerves, and all but Marge – bleary-eyed – agreed with him.
Marge moaned, driving everyone mad. Finally Thomas said
he'd drop her at the police station so she could bail her son
out. With luck. She brightened up at that and went off with
him happily enough.

Diana didn't appear.

Ellie rather hoped Diana wouldn't be too demanding that
day, but ... Suppose it had been Denis who'd tried to run
Ellie down? No, no. In the cold light of day, she really couldn't
see him driving a white van. Or stealing a Volvo.

The Party Planner arrived, followed closely by the first
of the workmen. The front door was propped open, and
people began to traipse through the hall and back again.
There was an argument between the cleaners, who wanted
to polish the floor, and the florist, who wanted to finish the
decorations. One lot of tablecloths had still not arrived. The
man who was to run the disco rang to say he was going to
be late.

Mia flitted about, colour in her cheeks and light in her eyes.
'Isn't this exciting?'

Yes, it was, in a way.

The phone rang. It was Ellie's grandson, little Frank. 'Do
I really have to dress up and be a ring-bearer?'

'I'm afraid you do, my poppet. Think about the lovely
holiday you're all going to have straight afterwards.'

A stifled sob. Oh dear.

Stewart came on the line. 'Never again, Ellie.'

'Agreed. If I don't see you before you take off, have a wonderful time away.'

'Yes. That Summers woman. Her death was on the local news this morning. Was it a random thing, or is there a connection?'

'No proof yet. Forget about it. Have a good holiday.'

There were raised voices in the hall. The first set of caterers were bound to clash with Diana's lot. Oh well. That was for Mr Balls to sort out.

Normally the bridesmaids would foregather at the bride's home to help her to get ready, but Mrs Belton – true to herself in this as in all other matters – had decreed that she would not have extra people cluttering up her flat that morning, that she herself would deliver her daughter to the church, and that the bridesmaids should meet the bride there.

Possibly this was to avoid her ex-husband setting foot in her flat? Seeing that there was no help for it, Ursula had meekly agreed, while assuring Mia that they would make up for it with lots of visits as soon as the honeymoon was over.

While Rose cleared away the breakfast table and checked that there were enough cold meats to make sandwiches for lunch – always providing anyone was hungry enough – Ellie went upstairs to tidy up their bedroom and bathroom and then to see if Diana was awake. Which she was.

'Would you like some breakfast?'

Diana laid down the mobile phone she'd been using. 'I brought a flask of tea with me so I won't need anything till later. Bring me some freshly roasted coffee at noon. Denis says there's been a hitch and we can't have the registry office wedding this afternoon.'

Ellie carefully said nothing at all, but waited for Diana's reaction.

A shrug. 'Oh, well, we'll go ahead with everything here. All our friends have been told to expect an exchange of vows and a good party, and that's what they're going to get.'

Ellie nodded. She wondered what friends the couple had. People like themselves, out for what they could get? Friends in the trade?

Diana yawned. 'After all, I can always change my name to his by deed poll.'

Ellie nodded again. She went to draw back the curtains, till

Diana winced and said to leave them. Ellie said, 'We'll be off to church soon for Ursula's wedding. How will you amuse yourself till it's time for your "do" this afternoon?'

Diana threw herself back on the bed. 'Is it too much to hope that I can be left in peace for a few hours? I've a cracking headache.'

'I'll bring you some aspirin.'

'I've got some. Just tell everyone to be quiet downstairs, will you?'

Ellie thought, Oh yes? I don't think so. But said nothing, and left.

The chaos downstairs gradually sorted itself out. The caterers arrived and polished their cutlery and glasses till the designer brought the tablecloths. The florist helped the designer to dress the chairs, since she'd finished her own work and everything else was behindhand. The cleaners buffed the hall floor to a mirror finish and glared at anyone who dared to cross it after that. The electricians said they'd finally got the mike working, while Rose and Mia provided cuppas and cleaned up after everyone else.

The caterers were still laying tables when Ellie coaxed Mia and Rose to leave the kitchen in order to get dressed.

Thomas returned from taking Marge to the police station – from which she'd been able to retrieve her son – and checked over what he'd got to take with him to the church. 'You've ordered a cab to take you there?'

'No, but I will,' said Ellie, suddenly understanding how it might have been possible for white-van man to know where and when she was going to be. 'Thomas, suppose—'

A quick kiss, an anxious look, an extra-tight hug. 'I must be off. Don't be late. You're responsible for getting Mia there on time, remember.'

Ellie nodded, thinking rapidly. Once he'd gone, she rang the police station and asked if DI Willis happened to be back from leave yet. She wasn't. 'DC Milburn, then?'

'Not available.'

'"Ears"?'

'WHO?'

'Oh. Sorry. Will you give him a message for me? I think the missing link is the cab company. When I ring for a cab, they know where I'm going and roughly how long I'll be.

I think that someone who books the cars in and out may be giving my movements to the man who drives the white van. Would you look into it, please?'

Heavy breathing at the other end. Her message was repeated without comment. She shut up her phone and went to change into her wedding outfit, remembering that the master bedroom was going to be used later that day as a changing room, so she'd better not leave it or the en suite untidy.

Before she'd finished, Mia came dancing into the room, carrying her bouquet of lavender dianthus and white roses, livened with puffs of gold ribbon. 'Aren't I looking pretty?'

'You are indeed!' Ellie snatched up her hat and crammed it on. 'How long have we got, and where are my shoes?'

Mia found them for her. 'This is all due to you, all this. I do love you, you know.'

Ellie laughed. 'You love everyone today.'

'That's true. I am so fortunate.' She sobered. 'When I think back . . . but I'm not going to think back any more, or at least, not intentionally.' Her smile lit up the room. 'I'm going to be positive and helpful and loving and kind, and not get annoyed by Mrs Belton, and pray that Ursula has the loveliest possible wedding today because she deserves it.'

'She does, indeed.'

Someone rapped on the bedroom door, which was ajar. Diana, in a negligee, holding a cup of coffee in her hand. Diana looked drawn and irritable. 'Do you think you could be a little quieter, please?' She returned to the spare room.

Ellie and Mia giggled to one another, like chidden children. Ellie snatched up her gloves and handbag, and they went downstairs to find Rose waiting for them in the hall. Rose was togged up in a bright pink costume with a pink rose – a large, home-made boutonnière – in her button-hole.

'I love you too, Rose!' said Mia, embracing her friend.

Rose laughed. 'Mind my hat, you silly thing! The cab's waiting for us.'

Ellie took one last look around. The caterers were laying tables. Mr Balls and his slaves were ticking boxes on lists.

Ellie warned Mr Balls, 'You have one hour max.' She stepped into the cab, wondering what awaited her at the end of the journey. Another attempt on her life, or a simple church service?

SATURDAY MORNING . . .

He cursed his luck. He couldn't understand how she'd escaped death so many times. A cat had nine lives, but she . . . she had to die! There was no other way.

He'd tried to sleep, but couldn't. Craig had rung him almost every hour, wanting the rest of his money. He'd trusted Craig, given him a solid down payment, and the stupid git had let him down in spades. Craig had ditched the van as soon as he'd got it back; maybe the police wouldn't find it straight away, but maybe they would. Now Craig had no wheels, only half the money he'd been promised, and the job still hadn't been done.

As the hours wore on, Denis changed his mind. Craig was ceasing to be a tool and becoming a threat. The police were going to catch up with Craig sooner or later, and do him for dangerous driving at the very least. With any luck, they'd also work out he'd been a frequent visit to the Summers woman, which was how Denis had come across him in the first place.

So – a brilliant idea! He'd get Craig to meet him at the wedding reception in one of the unused downstairs rooms. If Ellie wouldn't come out of the house, he could go in. He'd kill her and blame it on Craig. He'd have to kill Craig, too, of course. Two birds with one stone. He wouldn't use a stone. A hammer, perhaps? A mallet? He had one in the car. A tyre lever, maybe. No, a knife. A long, sharp knife. Quick in and out and no blood spatter to betray him.

He must tell Craig to meet him at the house, tell anyone who asked that he had an urgent message for Denis, and then . . . somehow or other Denis would get Ellie to go with him to meet Craig and with a couple of thrusts to the heart he'd do away with the pair of them.

Wonderful! Surely the police must by now suspect that it was Craig who'd driven the van which had tried to run Ellie down, so they would assume he'd finally got to her. Denis would be the hero of the hour. He'd say he'd seen Craig attack his future mother-in-law . . . He'd tried to intervene but been too late . . . There'd followed a struggle for the knife, and in that struggle, Craig had been killed. By mistake, of course. Perfect. The police would go for it. Diana would go for it, and she'd fall into his arms in gratitude — and lust. Never forget lust when dealing with Diana.

Soon he'd be able to persuade Valerie to divorce him. He'd only have to threaten to hit the boys again, and she'd be putty in his hands. As always.

So, on with the wedding. It was entirely necessary that he bind Diana to him with hoops of steel. He'd have liked someone a trifle younger, but there was no doubting her abilities in bed. That made up for a lot. That and the money she was going to inherit.

He made a phone call to Craig, shaved with care, and put on his wedding finery. There was everything to play for, today.

NINETEEN

The cab driver dropped them outside the church, smiling to see the excited crowd arriving there. 'You want I wait for you today?' he said.

It would be convenient if he did, but . . . 'No, thanks,' said Ellie, 'not today.'

Mia jumped out to run to Ursula's little American sister, spotlessly clean in a new white frock, braces on her teeth glinting in the sunshine. 'Well, just look at you!'

The roly-poly usher handed Ellie a boutonnière of a white rose, which she pinned to her lapel.

She tried to remember exactly what instructions she'd given to the cab firm when she took Mia to the solicitor's at the beginning of the week. She'd told him she didn't need a cab for the return journey, as they were planning to have lunch out in the Broadway. Had the Volvo been part of the plot to kill her, too?

Someone had a masterful touch on the organ inside the church. She looked around for a white van. Or another Volvo. None in sight. Anyway, there were too many people hanging around for a car to target one particular woman among the throng at the church gates.

But he knows where to find me, all the time!

Mia was laughing, happy, carefree for once. Rose caught Ellie's arm. 'Isn't it a beautiful day for it?'

Yes, it was. An usher held out an Order of Service to Ellie, and she took it. She and Rose would sit at the back since they planned to rush back home while photographs were being taken of the wedding party after the ceremony. Pray heaven the caterers would be ready in time.

The Volvo might have been a joyriding accident. Yes, it might.

The white vans . . . no. Was it the same van which had tried to run her down outside the Priors' place, as the one last night outside the church? Difficult to say. Neither had any logos on their sides. The most she could say was that they were the same size, plain, white, clean. Newly rented?

The church was filling up with happy people. There were a respectable number of people on Sam's side of the church, and yes, he was already there, chatting over his shoulder, smiling. His best man at his side.

They were both wearing tailcoats. Goodness gracious! How often did that happen nowadays? Rented? Ah, of course. It showed a nice feeling that they'd bothered. He would never look handsome, but he looked distinguished, would improve with age . . . Yes, that must be his brother acting as best man, and his father was in the row behind him, and also, possibly, an uncle; they all looked very much alike. Medical men? Foreign office? Highly placed civil servants? She'd known, once. Not that it mattered.

What about their womenfolk? All large, capable-looking women, with four − no, five − children in tow. Yes, Ursula would feel at home in that family.

He knows where to find me . . .

The music changed. Was Ursula going to be late? It wouldn't be like her.

Thomas walked down the aisle in his robes, smiling, chatting to this person and that. Was there to be a choir? No?

Rose nudged Ellie. 'Mrs Belton's hat!'

Mrs Belton's hat was indeed a wonder to behold. Ellie stifled a laugh. An unfortunate choice, the wrong shape and colour. Cerise pink was not easy to wear even if you had a wonderful complexion or good make-up, and the poor woman had neither. No one would giggle to her face, would they?

Thomas greeted the bride's mother and led her to the front row, where she sat in solitary state. Ursula's stepmother and the toddler sidled in behind her.

Thomas reached Ellie's row and leaned in to say, 'Remember?' They both smiled, as it had been in this very church that they'd exchanged their own vows, some months ago.

Ellie opened her Order of Service – well designed, nicely printed, undoubtedly something Ursula had organized – and resolved to put white vans and Volvos out of her mind.

There was a stir in the porch, and the organist broke into a well-known wedding march. Ellie felt tears stand out in her eyes, as Ursula – big-boned, positive, strong-minded, clear-thinking, warm-hearted and radiantly beautiful – made her way down the aisle on her father's arm, with her little sister holding Mia's hand and following close behind.

Ursula was wearing a white brocade coat dress, screamingly simple, with long sleeves and the merest hint of a train. No exposed shoulders for her. Her hair hung, honey-blonde, down over her shoulders, topped by a crown of tiny white flowers – orchids? – from which fell a short gauzy veil. Her bouquet was all white. She was all white, except for the colour in her cheeks and lips, which looked natural and probably was. Her eyes were brilliant, fixed on the man who was waiting for her at the altar.

The little girl tripped and nearly fell half way down the aisle, and everyone went 'Oh!'

Ursula and Mia were equal to the occasion. They picked the child up and, seeing that she was ready to cry, her father hoisted her up on to his free arm.

Laughing, throwing back the veil which had fallen over her face, Ursula continued down the aisle to where Sam was waiting for her. Light glinted on tears on Mia's cheeks, but she smiled as she took Ursula's bouquet from her and stood aside for Mr Belton to give his daughter away.

Rose sniffed. Ellie reached for her hankie.

Thomas's voice filled the church with the age-old words of welcome.

As the bride and groom withdrew to sign the register, Ellie whispered to Rose, 'Let's get out of here, shall we?'

They left the church and stood outside in the sun.

'That was beautiful,' sobbed Rose. 'So . . . so family! Ursula didn't think of herself at all and how it might look. Did you see the look on her man's face as he took her hand at the altar steps?'

A limousine was at the kerb, waiting to take the bride and groom on to the reception. A second hired car waited behind it to transport her relatives and the bridesmaids. From the cab firm Ellie used?

He always knows where to find me.

Ellie considered walking back home. Yes, but would Rose make it? She didn't walk much anywhere nowadays. Some late arrivals drew up in a black taxi, exclaiming that their train had been late. They hurried into the church, so Ellie and Rose took the taxi on home.

No minicab drivers hovered. No white vans, either.

Is he waiting for me back at the house? WHAT DOES HE WANT?

She went over it again in her mind. Forget the Volvo. Perhaps that really had been an accident. On two other occasions a white van had tried to run her down. Why?

She paid off the taxi outside her house, and hurried indoors. People were criss-crossing the hall, all was bustle, the kitchen had been taken over by the caterers, Mr Balls and his minions were orchestrating the event. Neither Ellie nor Rose was needed.

Rose took off her hat and fluffed up her hair. 'I could do with a cuppa before the hordes descend. How about you? We could have it in my sitting room, where it's nice and quiet.'

'A good idea. I'll just see how Diana's getting on first. Perhaps she'd like her mother to dress her for this wedding, since she has no bridesmaids.'

'Humph!' said Rose.

Ellie mounted the stairs and checked that her bedroom and bathroom were neat and clean, ready for use by Ursula and her groom in a while. Someone – one of the ushers? – had brought up two suitcases and left them beside the bed.

Was Sam himself going to drive them away to their future, or was someone else taking them to the airport? Would two

more suitcases now be safely hidden in a friend's car, with air
tickets, passports and travellers' cheques?

The florist had been thoughtful and had set a vase with
some white roses in it on the dressing table. Ellie took off
her hat and put it away. No need for formality now.

Or was there? Would Diana expect formality that afternoon?

She went along the corridor and tapped on the spare
room door. Diana opened it, wearing a kimono and looking
disgruntled. 'I thought I asked you to keep everyone quiet
downstairs.'

'They'll be back from church soon. Is your headache better?
Can I get you anything?'

Diana went to look out of the window at the marquee below.
'Are you asking me what I'd like as a wedding present? You
haven't given me anything yet.'

'You haven't got married yet.'

'Well, you know what I want. Make over that nice big house
of yours to me.'

'In the first place, it's not *my* house. It belongs to the Trust,
which was set up to provide housing for people who can't
otherwise afford it. I can't just take a house off the list for
myself. You know that really, don't you?'

A shrug. 'If push came to shove, you'd do it, wouldn't you?
The other people on the Trust think you're next door to a
saint, so they'd play ball if you asked nicely.'

Somewhat to her surprise, Ellie now realized that she wasn't
going to give in on this matter. 'I'm not even going to try it.
Tell me, Diana; why is Denis trying to kill me?'

'What!' Diana swung round, open-mouthed.

Ellie sank on to the chaise longue at the bottom of the bed.
'Twice now a large white van has driven straight at me and
would have mown me down if I hadn't been saved, first by
jumping into a hedge and then by a man throwing himself
into its path.'

'What?' Diana seemed genuinely bewildered. 'But . . . but
Denis can't drive a van. You need an HGV licence for that,
don't you?'

'I didn't say he was driving. I don't know that he was. What
I think is that he might have arranged it. Yesterday someone
managed to take the licence number of the van, so it's now
being sought by the police.'

'But that's got nothing to do with—'

'I can't think of anyone else who—'

'Denis wouldn't do a thing like that!'

'Or get someone else to do it?'

'But . . . No, why on earth should he?'

'That's what I've been trying to work out. You know that Denis used to visit Mrs Summers every week for a session in her bedroom?'

Diana snorted. 'Don't be absurd.'

'It seems your idea of him and mine are far apart. I think he killed Mrs Summers, and I think he's behind the attempts to kill me, too.'

Diana's face suffused with red, proving she wasn't wearing any make-up yet. 'You mean to sit there and accuse Denis of being a mass murderer without the shadow of any evidence to . . . No, Mother, not even you could be so—'

'If I died—'

'You've got a good few years in you yet.'

'Yes, but if I did . . . How would that benefit him?'

'Well, it wouldn't. How could it? If you hadn't made that absurd will, leaving everything to the Trust and cutting me off with a pittance, then I suppose . . . No. Ridiculous! Are you trying to make out he's a fortune-hunter?'

'Valerie tells me he did well out of his previous in-laws until they stopped funding him. Perhaps he's looking elsewhere for an income.'

'Yes, but . . .' A frown, a shrug. 'He must know that . . .' Her voice trailed away.

'You never told him that I'd written you out of my will?'

'The subject never came up. I mean, he had plenty, I had the flat and then our old house, so . . . no. We were doing all right till the recession came—'

'And Valerie's parents stopped supporting them.'

Diana seated herself at the dressing table and met Ellie's eyes in the mirror. 'I don't believe it.'

'I know you don't want to believe it. In a way, I don't want to believe it either, because what he's doing scares me witless. All right –' she held up her hand – 'what I *think* he's trying to do to me. I admit I may be wrong. Why don't you ring him up, ask him if he loves you enough to marry you as you are, without any inheritance? See if that makes a difference?'

'That would be to doubt him. I don't doubt him. Not one little bit. I love him. He loves me. End of story.' She picked up a brush and began to whack at her hair.

Ellie, defeated, got to her feet. 'I expect you'd like something to eat at lunchtime. Ursula's reception should be starting off soon, but I'll ask Rose to make you a sandwich and bring it up here for you. Is there anything else you'd like?'

'Some peace and quiet.'

Ellie left. She looked at the closed door of Thomas's quiet room and wished she could go in there, lock the door, and not come out till the day was over. But she couldn't do that because she was, in a way, acting hostess.

Well, Mrs Belton was officially the hostess. Of sorts. Heaven defend the guests if Mrs Belton was allowed to address them all in her usual hectoring tones.

She could hear lots of squeaks and bumps coming from down below. She looked at her watch. Any minute now the wedding party was due to arrive. She went to stand on the landing, looking over into the hall. The grandfather clock chimed twelve, but alas, no ginger cat decorated it.

There was silence down below.

Mr Balls gyrated in the centre of the floor. He had changed into a black tail coat with a red waistcoat, had fluffed up his yellow wig and held a silver-topped cane in his right hand.

Caterers and waitresses were lined up before him.

The bridal arch had been moved yet again, this time nearer the front door.

He inspected each of his staff in turn. 'By special request from the bride and groom we are not to hold up proceedings for photographs, except for one single one of the reception line at the beginning. Is that understood? We are on a tight schedule and cannot afford to lose a minute.'

One of the catering staff sent him a black look – perhaps the photographer was a relation of hers? – which he fielded and returned. 'The reception line will be here, with bride and groom beneath the arch. The guests will move on to the drawing room for drinks and canapés. Two drinks for every person and no more. Hot canapés. At one precisely we will move to the buffet in the dining room, where there will be more wine and the buffet will be served. At that point the drawing room will be cleared of glasses and plates, and the door shut. Understood?

'Meanwhile, the buffet will progress. At two we will start clearing plates and serve champagne for the short speeches and the toasts. At half past two, the married couple will retire upstairs to change. They will leave at three, if not before. We then have half an hour to clear and close down the front room in preparation for the second reception . . .'

Ellie lost what he said next, as Diana had come to stand beside her. Diana was still wearing her kimono and hadn't yet put on her make-up. She had a pleasant expression on her face. What did she want now?

Diana tipped her head towards Mr Balls, still holding forth below. 'He's good, isn't he?'

'Excellent. I'll get you some food as soon as I can, but it's difficult with the caterers in the kitchen.'

'I expect you can manage something. You are going to let me have that house, aren't you?'

Ellie shook her head.

Diana persisted. 'It will make all the difference to the start of our new life together.'

'Even if I could, I wouldn't. I'm not doing anything to help you tie yourself down to Denis. I presume he's been on the phone to you, asking you to get the house for him?'

'Of course. It's the only thing that makes sense.'

Ellie shook her head again. 'Be satisfied with this party I'm giving you, and with the public relations boost it will give the 2Ds.'

There was a stir at the front door as Mr Balls threw it wide open to admit the newly-weds, smiling into one another's eyes, their arms closely entwined.

'Welcome!' boomed Mr Balls.

Ursula pirouetted, arms outstretched. 'Oh, but this is beautiful. Where is Mrs Quicke?'

'Here I am,' said Ellie, descending the staircase to be enveloped in a hug from Ursula, and to receive a double kiss from Sam.

A rush of family members, a babel of voices, children running around, Mia starry-eyed and pink-cheeked . . . Mrs Belton looking as if she could smell something rancid . . . Mr Balls creating a line-up with the newly-weds under the bridal

arch . . . A photographer fussing around . . . and being moved
on by the Party Planner as the first of the guests arrived to
be passed on down the line and into the drawing room.

Ellie escaped into the kitchen quarters, where the catering
staff were taking trays of Mia's canapés out of the oven and
filling glasses of wine to be carried on trays through to the
guests.

Ellie found Rose in her own room, brewing up tea and
building sandwiches.

'May I have some for the afternoon bride?' Ellie asked.

'Cuckoo in the nest, more like,' said Rose, handing over a
tray. 'But I suppose we must do good to those who despite-
fully use us, as the bible says. Though *spite* is definitely one
of the words I'd use for her.'

'Dear Rose.' Ellie kissed her old friend's cheek. 'I'll take
it up to her straight away.'

'No, you won't. You'll sit down and have something for
yourself first. What's more, over there is a plate of Mia's
canapés, hot from the oven. They're really good. You'll have
to taste some, or she'll be disappointed. How is the tragedy
queen, anyway?'

'Needy. Whatever I give her, she wants more, and I suspect
Denis is twice as greedy as her. He gives me the shivers.' She
took a canapé, said, 'Mm,' and took two more. Then another.
And a ham sandwich. Plus a mug of tea. 'Ah, that's better.
I'll take Diana her tray up now.'

She opened the door to the kitchen warily to avoid crashing
into the caterers, dodged around two of them and managed to
get herself out into the hall without spilling anything . . . only
to come face to face with Denis, dressed to kill in full wedding
fig, with a tote bag slung over one shoulder. How did he get
in? Ah, the front door was open for all comers, wasn't it?

*He's here, in my house. But surely he can't harm me here?
Can he?*

She couldn't think of anything to say, except, 'You're early.'

He smiled. 'I can't wait to see my bride.' He noticed the
tray. 'Is that for her? Where is she? I'll take it up to her.'

'I must ask her first.'

Diana's head appeared over the banister. 'Come on up,
Denis.'

He took the tray up the stairs.

TWENTY

Saturday afternoon

Ellie was nearly knocked over by a small boy running out of the sitting room, giggling. He was followed by his elder sister, her white skirts flying and her flower basket slung behind her. Mr Balls appeared, leading a surge of people through the hall and into the dining room to attack the buffet.

Ursula and Sam didn't notice Ellie, but Thomas – following close behind them – did. He gave her his own glass of white wine and put his arm around her. 'Cheer up. It's all going beautifully. Your organization is a marvel.'

'Not mine. Mr Balls.' She raised the glass to her lips and took a sip. 'Denis is here. He's gone up to see Diana.'

'What?' Where could they go to talk quietly? Waitresses began to ply to and fro, kitchen to dining room, while others cleared used glasses from the room at the back. The guests spilled over into the hall, talking and laughing, everyone merry. Some children took the opportunity to run and slide on the parquet floor of the hall and were told not to do so by the grown-ups. An elderly lady limped by on two sticks, with an attentive son in attendance. Mrs Belton swam through, apologizing in a loud voice for the guests having to move from one room to another.

Thomas urged Ellie across the hall and into the drawing room, which was now empty of guests. 'What did Denis say?'

Ellie threw open the French windows. Someone had been smoking in there, and the room needed airing. 'He said he couldn't wait to see his bride.'

'Was that a euphemism?'

'Probably. Sex seems to be the main attraction. The registry office appointment didn't come off, by the way, so he's no legal right to call her his wife. She wants me to give her that big house he's been after. Under the terms of the trust I can't, and out of principle I won't even ask if they can have it.'

'Let's get out of here.' Thomas drew her out into the only

patch of garden not occupied by the marquee. The sun was bright, the air was warm. Bees clustered on lavender bushes which ought to have been cut back before now. The hollyhocks were almost over. Some roses were having a second blooming.

Ellie relaxed a trifle and then looked up, for a murmur of voices was coming from the window of the spare bedroom upstairs. Diana and Denis were arguing.

Was that a slap? Ellie jerked to attention, and so did Thomas. Silence. Then came the sound of laughter.

Ellie drained the rest of her glass of wine. 'I needed that. Thomas, will you stick close to my back while he's in the house?'

'What can he do here, with everyone around you?'

She tried to smile. Of course Thomas was right, and there was nothing to be afraid of, today. Perhaps it would be a different story tomorrow . . . but then, tomorrow never comes, does it?

'Let's mingle, see that everything runs smoothly.'

There was a clash of cymbals close by and a drum roll.

They both jumped. Ellie put her hand to her heart. 'The DJ must have arrived and is setting up in the marquee for Diana's party. Rose got me a sandwich earlier. You must grab something to eat yourself, or you'll never last the course.'

They left the French windows ajar to air the room and went back through the hall to the dining room, to catch Mr Balls thumping the floor with his cane to attract everyone's attention. The speeches were about to begin.

Thomas had a word with a waitress who was clearing dirty plates and glasses away, and a couple of plates piled high with delicious cold meats and salads wafted their way, while glasses of champagne appeared on a nearby table, just for them.

As promised, the speeches were not long, and before Ellie had finished her plateful she had the pleasure of hearing Ursula thank her and Thomas for lending them her beautiful house for the day.

The photographer snapped away, the children issued everyone with bags of bubbles, and as glasses of champagne were raised for the final toast, so the pearly bubbles floated out and around the room, almost hiding Ursula and Sam as they laughed and kissed. *Flash, flash, flash!* went everyone's cameras, amid cheers and more laughter.

Mia jumped up on a chair and stammered out, through tears and smiles, what a wonderful friend Ursula had been to her, and was helped down by the roly-poly usher, who seemed to think that Mia was the fairy off the Christmas tree.

Mrs Belton remarked loudly that she only wished she could have provided the newly-weds with a better send-off, which cooled the temperature so much that Sam looked at his watch and said that they ought to change their clothes as they had a plane to catch.

Ellie led the couple upstairs and into the master bedroom. She wondered how long they'd take to change or whether they would take advantage of the bed to . . . No, they would want to take their time over that later, wouldn't they?

She went downstairs to check that a notice had been attached to the drawing room door reading 'Private'. Good.

Mr Balls led everyone out into the hall to witness Ursula and Sam, dressed in casual clothes, descend the stairs. Ursula threw her bouquet right up into the air – Ellie feared it might get caught on the chandelier, but it didn't. Ursula's plain little younger sister caught it and danced around, holding it up high in the air. Ellie had rather hoped that Mia would catch it, but the girl didn't even try. Well, never mind.

The roly-poly usher brought the two suitcases downstairs and stowed them in a suitably expensive-looking car outside. Ursula kissed everyone, including Ellie and Thomas. Sam kissed some people and shook hands with others.

Confetti and rose petals whirled around. Ellie panicked. This was all going to take a bit of clearing up, wasn't it?

They were off. Guests streamed out into the drive to wave them goodbye, and then began to leave themselves.

Caterers and waitresses scurried about. Someone swept the floor of the hall.

Peace and quiet.

The clock struck a quarter to four.

Mr Balls appeared from the kitchen quarters to hurry one set of caterers away.

'I'm exhausted just looking at you, Mr Balls,' said Ellie.

'Dear lady, you are magnificent. Remember, this is my job. Now, why don't you find yourself somewhere to sit down out of the way and have a sherry to keep you going?'

'My study,' said Thomas, leading the way. 'At least we've got a couple of chairs free there.'

Ellie looked back at the clock. How soon would the next set of guests arrive? Someone bustled back into the hall. One of Ursula's guests, who'd left a coat behind. The coat was retrieved, but before Ellie could sit down and take off her shoes, the doorbell rang again.

The first of Diana's guests had arrived.

'Do we have to form a reception committee?' asked Thomas.

'I don't think so. Let's lurk at the back of the hall until we know if we're needed or not.'

The bridal arch had been moved to stand over the doorway into the conservatory. The guests flooded in. A very different lot of guests: high-maintenance business women, ditto men. Sharp, discontented faces. Abrasive voices talking of break-fast appointments, air travel, favourable deals. Botox, face lifts, invasive perfumes and aftershave lotions.

In the middle of all this Diana's first husband, Stewart, showed up with little Frank in tow. The boy had been got up in a gold page-boy's suit and looked as if he'd been crying.

Frank sniffed. 'The shoes are too big. They'll fall off me.'

Ellie gave him a hug. 'You'll manage. I'm really proud of you, darling.'

Thomas shook Stewart's hand. 'It's very good of you to delay your holiday like this.'

'I've promised Frank, ten minutes is all it will take. He will wait with me at the back till the vows are exchanged, take the ring up to Diana in this gold box – the one I'm hanging on to till the last possible minute so he doesn't lose it – and then he comes away with me. We're all packed up ready to go, so we'll zip back home, pile everyone into the car while Frank changes out of his glad rags, and then we're off. Right, Frank?'

'If I must.' He gave Ellie a moist kiss and got a hug from Thomas.

Stewart said, 'We'll find a couple of seats at the back till we're needed.' They passed on into the conservatory, as another pair of high-stepping, expensive-looking executive types arrived.

'Smile on,' said Thomas. 'It'll soon be over.'

An immaculately-clad figure in a grey morning suit passed

down the stairs, strode across the hall into the conservatory, and thence into the marquee. Denis had no best man, apparently.

He can't hurt me here. Can he?

Rose and Mia, still in their wedding finery, came to join Ellie and Thomas at the back of the hall. 'No reception line,' said Ellie. 'Well, that's a relief.'

The flood of guests abated. The clock struck the half hour, and Diana glided down the stairs in her superb dress, carrying a bouquet of gold flowers. Another expensive package, scented and beautifully made up.

She spoke to Ellie without looking at her. 'Is Frank here? Is he properly dressed?'

'He is. Stewart is looking after him and will take him away immediately after.'

Diana relaxed a trifle. Then firmed her jaw. She nodded to Mr Balls and went to stand at the door to the conservatory, waiting for a signal to enter. Mr Balls preceded her through the conservatory and gave the signal for the man running the disco to play something slow and churchy – possibly by Handel? – so that Diana could make her grand entrance. Alone. Superbly herself.

No need for a man to walk her to her fate. No need for bridesmaids. No need for love or friendship.

Ellie and Thomas followed at a suitable distance with Rose and Mia, and stood at the back beside Stewart and little Frank. The boy bit his lip, his eyelids fluttering. He looked as if he'd rather like to make a dash for the exit.

Denis waited for his bride in front of the high table.

Ellie had to admit that they made a handsome pair: he being so tall and well-built, fair-haired and well groomed; she being elegance itself, even though, as Rose had once remarked, she could have done with more meat on her bones.

Someone rang the front doorbell. Ellie ignored it. Some latecomer? Footsteps passed across the hall behind them, hesitated, and then went into the drawing room. Oh, really? Wasn't that out of bounds?

She couldn't spare the time to investigate, as the Party Planner thumped with his staff on the floor and asked everyone to please be upstanding for Diana and Denis to make their vows to one another before their friends.

Diana laid her bouquet down on the high table and turned to Denis, who took both her hands in his, looking down into her eyes. To Ellie's amazement they launched into the age-old church vows. 'To have and to hold, for richer for poorer . . .'

Ellie rolled her eyes at Thomas, who shook his head and sighed. Stewart had his hands firmly on little Frank's shoulders. Frank wriggled, hating every minute of this.

Denis said, 'Amen,' loudly. Both he and Diana turned to look down the marquee, waiting for little Frank to do his bit. Stewart placed a gold box in his son's hands and gave him a little push. Frank lost one of his shoes on his way up the tent and, oh dear, the box flew out of his hand and fell open on the floor. A gold ring rolled out and came to rest at his mother's feet. He went on his knees to collect it, but Denis, temper only just controlled, leant over and hauled the boy to his feet by one arm.

Frank went red, his arm held up at an angle. Stewart started forward, but Diana saved the situation. She bent down to pick up the ring and smiled at Frank. 'Well done, you!'

Rigid with fury, Denis let the boy go. Frank staggered and would have fallen, but that a bystander caught him up and set him on his feet again. There was a murmur of indulgent laughter, mixed with some condemnation of Denis's rough handling. Frank, disorientated, plunged for the nearest exit – which happened to be beyond the dais where the disco had been set up.

Someone started to clap. Diana held up the ring, smiling and frowning at once, lightly passing the incident off. 'Boys will be boys!' She handed the ring to Denis, who pressed it on her finger, smiling ferociously.

Ellie and Thomas slid back into the hall with Stewart. 'Frank'll have gone out to the kitchens. That's the only way—'

'He might go right round the marquee—'

'I'll go this way, if you go that—'

Ellie said, 'I think someone's in the drawing room. I can get out into the garden that way, and we can meet in the middle.'

The notice saying 'Private' was still on the door, but when she went in it was to find herself confronted by a big man in casual clothes. Definitely not a wedding guest.

He took a step back. 'You! What are you doing here?'

'This is my house.'

'But –' he looked at the door behind her – 'he didn't say—'

'Say what? Who didn't say?' She went to pass before him to the windows, but he caught her arm. He was strong. She could feel nervous energy pulsing up and down.

'Let go of me. I have to—'

He swung her to a chair. 'You sit there, while I have a think.'

'But I'm supposed to be—'

'I said, let me think!'

She could hear music striking up in the marquee outside and, more faintly, Thomas and Stewart calling Frank's name. She sat still, watching the newcomer, who was studying her. Then came the clash of plates as the caterers began to serve the sit-down meal for the party guests.

The man was tall, well-built and fair-haired. The description rang a bell for Ellie. This was the sort of man Mrs Summers had liked to entertain. Did he own a white van? Was it he who had tried to kill her at least twice this last week? And – crowning question – what was he doing here?

She said, 'Denis asked you to come here. Why?' And then, realizing part of the truth, 'He said he'd pay you off for what you've been doing for him. Is that right?'

'Yes. Shut up. Let me think!' He was no brain of Britain, though he was no fool, either. Had he driven the van in the attempts to kill her? If he had, then why wasn't he trying to kill her now? Answer: either he hadn't been paid for what he'd done earlier, or he wasn't the one who'd actually driven the van.

So was he the killer, or an accessory?

Denis was next door, on the spot. Denis had brought this man here. WHY? To make sure she died this time? But getting the deed done in her own house . . . How on earth could he expect to get away with that? Perhaps if she could work that one out, she'd know what to do next: scream, or offer him a drink?

She said, 'Were you there when he killed Mrs Summers?'

'What?' He changed colour, clenched his fists. 'No, I – what do you mean? He didn't. I mean, it was some passing maniac.'

'He got her to undress, knocked her out, tipped her into the bath and turned on the tap. Did he tell you why?'

He was shocked. 'No, that's . . . She was a bit of all right. I can't believe—'

'Why did he have to kill her?'

'I don't know. I don't know that he did.'

'But you know he's been trying to kill me all week.'

A frown. 'Not to kill you. To frighten you. Yes. I know that. Why do you think I let him borrow the van?'

'The Volvo wasn't anything to do with you, then?'

His eyes slid away. 'He was thinking of buying one. I know how to hot-wire cars, so he asked me to get one for him to try out for an hour. He offered me plenty for doing it, and I'd had a bit to drink, like, and agreed. Stupid, really. He could have got a test drive in one from any dealership, and I don't want to get done for stealing cars, do I?'

She swallowed. So the Volvo had been intended to kill her, too. 'Were you in the car with him when he drove it at me?'

'He was laughing, said he'd got the accelerator and brake mixed up. I sweated blue murder over that, I can tell you. Couldn't get away fast enough. Talk about reckless.'

'It was your van he used to "frighten" me with when I visited Mrs Prior?'

'He got me to put that tinted stuff on the windows so that no one couldn't see in, but I didn't know what he wanted to borrow it for, did I?'

'You let him borrow it, all the same. You were in the van with him on Wednesday in the driveway to the Prior's house?'

He worked his jaw. 'No. I let him hire it off me for a coupla days, but I said I wanted no part of whatever it was he was planning. When he got it back to me last night with the dent in the front where he'd been in a hit and run that was it for me, I can tell you.'

'The man he hit last night died.'

'He said the man came from nowhere, right across him, couldn't avoid hitting him.'

'True. But he could have stopped, after.'

The visitor rolled his shoulders. 'I think he's mad.'

'I think so, too. Do you know why he wants to kill – er, to frighten me?'

A shrug. 'Something to do with getting a lot of money? He promised me plenty helping to give you a fright.'

'He frightened me, all right.'

Her visitor was calming down, even as Ellie's nerves tightened up.

She coughed, to relax her throat. 'What's your name? You know mine, I suppose? Ellie Quicke. He wants to marry my daughter, Diana. That's a party for them that you can hear out in the marquee.'

The noise of the party was growing. Faintly, she thought she could still hear the men calling for Frank. Where could the little boy have got to? Was he hiding somewhere because he'd made a mess of handing over the ring? Why didn't one of the men come looking for him in here?

'My name's Craig,' he said. He sat down opposite her. 'Look, finding him a Volvo to test drive and lending him my van is one thing, and so is giving someone a fright, but losing my van's another. That's my livelihood, window cleaning, and I need a van for it. How I got into this beats me, but I've had enough. I'll borrow some wheels and get back up north where I come from. I'm sorry you got a fright, but you know what he's like, don't you? He's not easy to say "no" to. So as soon as he pays me I'll be gone, right?'

'I don't think he's going to let you get away with it as easily as that,' said Ellie, understanding how they'd both been set up. 'I think he intends to give you and me a final pay-off here and now. He'll say that you killed me, and he killed you. That way he provides the police with a dead murderer and a dead mother-in-law. And he'd get away with it, wouldn't he?'

The door opened behind her, and in came Denis, breathing lightly, his eyes twitching from one to the other, one hand behind his back.

Craig said, 'Is what she says true?' He started towards Denis.

Denis brought his hand from behind his back. He was holding a long, shiny knife.

He swung the knife into Craig's stomach, driving it in with an upward movement. And withdrew it.

Craig's face contorted. His hands clutched at his middle, and he folded down on to the floor.

TWENTY-ONE

Ellie started up from her chair with a scream in her throat.

'Now, Mother-in-law, it's your turn.' He swung the bloodied knife at her in the same underarm gesture that he'd used to stab Craig. She jumped back, but caught her heel in her chair and slipped to the floor just as little Frank popped in through the French windows, grinning and shouting, 'Boo!'

Denis turned on the boy, his lips drawn back from his teeth.

The door into the hall shot open and in rushed Stewart, saying, 'I can't find—'

Everyone froze.

Frank aghast.

Ellie on the floor.

Stewart, wide-eyed.

Denis half turned to see who had entered. His knife dripped blood on to the floor.

Stewart moved first. He hit Denis. His fist started somewhere down by his knees and travelled straight up to connect with Denis's chin.

Ellie heard Denis's neck snap. His eyelids closed and he stretched his length out on the floor, next to Craig. The bloodied knife fell to the floor beside him.

Frank screamed.

Ellie scrambled away from Denis, using the chair to help herself up. She was trembling. 'It's all right, Frank. All over. Stewart; get an ambulance. Is Craig dead? We need something to tie Denis up.'

Stewart nursed his hand, wincing. Then he held out his arms for Frank, who rushed into them, sobbing. The little boy had lost both shoes by now, and he looked as if he'd been crawling through the undergrowth.

Thomas arrived, took one look, and went into action. His mobile came out to summon police and ambulance. He checked that Denis was not dead, removed his tie, turned him over, and tied his wrists together. By that time Craig was groaning, trying to lift his head from the floor, hands still clutching at his stomach.

Thomas gently pushed Craig back on to the floor. 'Keep still. Don't try to move. The ambulance is on its way.'

Stewart turned Frank's head away from the bodies on the floor. Ellie tried to stand unaided and found she could make it.

Diana appeared in the doorway. 'What the . . .? Is that Denis on . . .? Who is that other man? Why have you tied Denis up? Set him free, instantly.'

'We'll let the police decide,' said Ellie. 'He and his accomplice have a few questions to answer. It's Denis who's been trying to kill me, all along.'

Diana stared. 'Why should he do that?'

'He made a mistake. You didn't tell him that I'd made a will leaving everything to the Trust, did you? I suppose you thought being an heiress would make him even more keen to marry you. That's what all this has been about. My money.'

'You mean, he was only after me for my money?'

'Sex as well, I suppose. You were well matched there, I take it.'

'Yes, but . . . He wouldn't, he couldn't go so far as to . . . I mean, he hasn't killed you, has he?'

'He got this man Craig to "borrow" the Volvo on Monday and drove it at me. He missed me because a passer-by pushed me out of the way, but he killed a young woman and put her toddler in hospital. It may not count as murder, but it's certainly manslaughter in my book. Then he rented Craig's van and drove it at me twice more. To kill. It was only by the grace of God that he failed to do so.'

'That's nonsense. You make it sound as if he's been following you around for days, but he's been at work all week.'

'He only caught up with me when I took a minicab. I think he's been paying the controller at the minicab firm to let him know where I'm going to be. That's how he knew I'd be with Mia walking along from the solicitor's office to the restaurant, because I'd told the cab driver that was what we were going to do. The controller also knew when I paid a visit to Mia's mother and when I'd be at the church last night. I'm sure he killed Mrs Summers, too. I'm sorry, Diana, but he's a bad one, through and through.'

It was Diana's turn to freeze. She didn't change colour because her make-up was too good. But her eyes fastened on Denis's unconscious form, and after a long minute, she recoiled.

They all heard a cheer from the marquee, as the disco began to play something loud and tuneless. Diana said, 'We're supposed to be cutting the cake now. Denis said the knife wasn't sharp enough, and he came out to . . .' She sank on to the nearest chair. 'What am I going to do?'

Thomas said, 'Leave it to Mr Balls.'

Ellie nodded. 'We'll tell the guests that Denis has been taken ill, and that you're so sorry, but when they've eaten would they please go home as there'll be no disco-dancing tonight.'

Diana gave a sharp nod. 'I'll be upstairs if you need me.' She turned and left the room, the train of her beautiful dress swaying along behind her.

Someone leaned on the doorbell. This time it was the police, closely followed by an ambulance.

Saturday evening

The house was quiet at last. The ambulance had taken Craig – cursing the day he'd ever met Denis – off to hospital. He'd lost a lot of blood and the cleaners were not going to be pleased about that, were they? Did blood ever come out of wooden floors? Well, never mind, the carpet would cover the stains when the room was put back to rights.

The police listened to what Ellie and Stewart had to say and formally arrested Denis, who was sitting up and looking around him by that time. He said nothing except to ask for a solicitor before he was removed by the police.

Mr Balls suggested that the caterers continued to serve the rest of the meal to the guests, and that they should then be asked to depart, as there would be no disco that evening. Ellie recalled, with deep thankfulness, that the event had been fully insured.

The caterers cleared their equipment away and departed. The cleaners descended to stack chairs and tables into the hall and to give everything a quick wipe over.

Finally Mr Balls himself departed, leaving one of his

minions outside to explain to late-arriving guests that the disco
had been cancelled.

Getting the house back to normal was going to take for
ever, but they would start on it on the morrow. Also on the
morrow, she would find time to check up on Leon, who had
saved her life at the beginning of this affair.

But for now, Ellie went up to see if Diana wanted anything.
She got a resounding 'no', so went away again.

Stewart took little Frank home, arranging to start their
holiday proper on the following day.

Thomas and Ellie changed into casual clothes and gravi-
tated to the kitchen. Rose, also back in everyday clothes, said,
'Does anyone fancy anything to eat?'

Incredibly, Thomas said he might.

'Not caterers' food,' said Ellie. 'I couldn't bear it.'

Mia, still wearing her pretty bridesmaid's dress, said, 'Ta-
da!' and produced a dish of lasagne from the oven, while Rose
prepared a salad to go with it.

Thomas said, 'Mia, you are worth your weight in gold.'

Mia went pink. 'That's what Jim said. He's one of the
ushers. The one who's carrying a bit too much weight, though
I must say he's got a lovely smile. He was talking about business, of course. He's in an old-fashioned publishing firm and
thinks we might discuss their using the printing firm which
I've inherited. He loves good food. I told him about the recipes
my cousin had given me, and about doing the canapés for
Ursula, and he ate six on the trot and wanted to know if I'd
thought of writing a cookery book. My firm could print it,
and his firm could publish it. He's nice.'

Thomas, Ellie and Rose all nodded. Perhaps something
might work out there for Mia. Perhaps not. Give it time.

After they'd eaten, Ellie drifted around the house, which
looked as if it could do with a good spring clean. She
thought she heard an echo of her aunt's voice saying, 'I
told you to take out insurance. It's a good thing you listen
to me occasionally.'

She stood in the entrance to the marquee. Fairy lights
twinkled, golden draperies swung, expensive flowers scented
the air. The DJ had removed his equipment, but the tent seemed
to echo and re-echo with the noise of the party that had
ended so abruptly.

Something brushed against her legs. Midge had returned, looking none the worse for his absence. Ellie picked him up and huffed into his fur, which he permitted for all of five seconds. Then he jumped down and, tail waving, made off to the kitchen for sustenance.

From somewhere came the sound of music; not the raucous noise the DJ had produced, but a gentle quickstep, thirties style. Thomas had unearthed and reinstalled his stereo equipment from where he'd put it in his study. An old-fashioned dance tune filled the air, seductively.

He joined her in the marquee, holding out his arms. 'Shall we?'

'I didn't know you could dance.'

'You never asked. I was ballroom champion of my old school. My foxtrot has to be seen to be believed.'

She tried to smile. Not a good effort. 'Prove it.'

He proved it.

She produced a better smile. 'You've convinced me.'

'Dance, dance, little lady,' he said.

So they did, driving the dismals away.